A HOUSE AT WAR

ELIZABETH O'LEARY

A HOUSE at WAR

St. Martin's Press
New York

Library of Congress Cataloging-in-Publication Data

O'Leary, Elizabeth.
A house at war : the continuing story of the
House of Eliott / Elizabeth O'Leary.
p.   cm.
Sequel to: The House of Eliott, by Jean Marsh.
ISBN 0-312-13513-0 (hardcover)
1. Costume design—England—London—History—20th
century—Fiction.   2. Clothing trade—England—
London—History—20th century—Fiction.   3. Sisters—
England—London—Fiction.   4. Women—England—
London—Fiction.   5. London (England)—Fiction.
6. World War, 1939–1945—Fiction.   I. Marsh, Jean.
House of Eliott.   II. Title.
PR6065.L44H68   1995
823'.914—dc20   95-21657   CIP

First published in Great Britain by Macmillan London

First U.S. Edition: September 1995
10 9 8 7 6 5 4 3 2 1

A HOUSE AT WAR

CHAPTER ONE

The silk slipped and slithered between his fingers. 'It's almost dirty. Why do English – British – women so seldom see beauty in clarity of line and colour?' Cyril pulled his most arch and petulant face and angrily scrunched a representative's sample swatch of discarded taffeta. 'They're calling it Marina blue, you know. Ghastly, isn't it? A dull blue for a dull woman, whatever they may have you believe. She's positively swarthy, with a big nose and hippo hips. If she's a fairytale princess I'm the Queen of Sheba.' He paused to light a cigarette. 'I simply can't understand what went wrong.'

Beatrice smiled. 'Cyril, darling, you don't have to be angry for me. I don't care any more. Neither does Evie. I agree that the colour's awful but if we'd made her dress and all the rest of the wedding and trousseau things we'd probably have been asked to make countless hideous copies for all the other women who shouldn't even think of wearing that drab blue. Besides, I think perhaps that you're being a little unfair to the Duchess of Kent. She may not conform to your notion of the beau ideal but lots of people do happen to think that she's immensely chic.'

Privately Beatrice believed that one or two of Cyril's most mischievous public remarks about the Duchess of York's own 'powdered, porky milkmaid's look', given that he was known to be such a friend of the Eliott sisters, hadn't helped, any more than his coy observation that the marriage of the Duke of Kent had been a great loss to mankind. The Duchess of York, apparently, had advised Marina, her distant Greek cousin by marriage, to go to Captain Molyneux. But Beatrice truly didn't mind. She took Cyril's hand. 'Besides, you old curmudgeon, that was well over a year ago. I adore your loyalty, but don't you ever forget a grudge?'

Cyril Hunter pulled another face. It made him look like a cross Pagliacci. 'You know me, Beatrice. I can have old scores to settle after knowing someone for less than twenty minutes.' He grimaced again. 'It simply wasn't fair.'

'Since when has life been fair?' Beatrice looked rueful and then glanced at her watch. 'Pour yourself another drink while I dress. We should really have been there half an hour ago. Don't mind missing the standing-around preliminaries, though.'

'Jack joining us tonight?'

'Hope so but doubt it.' Beatrice frowned again. 'He said there was an off-chance that he'd get there by ten, but you know how it is with him these days.'

Cyril raised both palms. 'Evie?'

'Shouldn't think so.' Beatrice paused at the door of the drawing room at the house in Upper Brook Street. 'She's at the theatre tonight. Her new friend Viola wanted to introduce her to a young actor after the show. It's the first night of her new play. Everyone says Viola's bound to be marvellous. Anyway, I expect they'll all go out to supper afterwards.' Beatrice pushed back her fringe. 'Give me fifteen minutes. Must do something about this face.' Cyril smiled to himself as he waited. Beatrice's foxy auburn beauty had deepened, if anything, as she grew older, hollows in her cheeks becoming more lovely. As a young woman her high brows and pointed nose, the flinty look about the eyes and the long upper lip had been considered far from conventionally attractive but, Cyril had noted a few months earlier when she turned forty, her brows framed her features magnificently and good bones only got better. He poured himself a generous gin-and-It. He knew very well that Beatrice's fifteen minutes would stretch to thirty and that only ten of them would be spent on her face. She wanted to sit for a while by each of her three children.

They sat in the cab on the way to Le Coq d'Or, fingers companionably laced. 'I still don't understand why you don't feel cross about that wedding business, Bea. Why do I have to be furious for you?'

'I really don't know, my love. Traffic gets worse and worse, doesn't it?' Beatrice said as she squeezed Cyril's hand in the darkness, which hid her exasperation. 'I really, really don't mind so why don't you stop worrying away at it? Why should I care? I have my lovely daughter and my two boys. And Jack, of course. I have all the things that matter – in spades, as Jack would say if only he were here. I suppose I wish that Evie could be happier and more settled, but I guess she's contented too, in her own way.' Beatrice sighed then bristled a little. 'That, of course, is something quite different.' She smiled and released Cyril's hand. She didn't really like to discuss her sister with other people, even intimates such as Cyril. 'What's another wedding dress? I've done dozens – Evie and I have, I mean.'

The vehemence of Cyril's response startled her. 'Because you would have dressed her better. Because the women of

Britain would not have been demanding that ugly muddy blue ever since and because I wouldn't have had to work so hard to make her look like the "great beauty" when I photographed her. I suppose she's passable compared to most other princesses in recent British history but truthfully she looks like Suzanne Lenglen, without the grace, like a horse or a Greek sailor. No, that's unfair to the sailor boys.' He giggled. 'She's slightly better-looking than her sister-in-law . . . but the retouching, my dear. I always felt that I should bring along a bag of McDougall's self-raising flour for each of them to tip across their faces before I focused.' Cyril laughed and so did Beatrice. He continued, 'I suppose we all need our fairy tales and that's how I earn my crust but Jack would know how hard I had to work if he saw the plates. And you should hear what they say about—' Cyril waved his hand about.

Beatrice grasped it again. 'That's enough. I don't want to hear what they say about anything. Cyril, the past is past and we're still in business. Doing well, in fact. If some of our dowagers want things made up in her famous cloudy-dowdy blue, so be it. Makes it possible to make nicer things in nicer colours for nicer people. Business is business. You must understand.'

Cyril lit a cigarette, a black Russian taken from a heavy silver case. 'Of course I do. I wouldn't be here tonight, living as I do, unless I'd forced myself to ravish her in her wedding dress. Photographically, of course', he added as he met Beatrice's startled glance. 'Would just have preferred to advance your business. You helped me on my way ten years ago, after all.'

Beatrice braced herself for the familiar reminiscence about the shoot that launched Cyril's career, an accident deriving from one of Jack's composed skivvy sessions for an illustrated news magazine and one which had led to Cyril taking a series of pictures that paired hollow-cheeked débutantes with hollow-eyed shop assistants and nippies. Cyril could be maudlin at times: it was the price one paid for the waspish insouciance he displayed more often. Her unease was almost palpable and her relief at seeing her sister as the cab drew up in front of the restaurant was as great as her surprise. 'Evie. I didn't expect to see you tonight. Are you all right?'

'All right. *All right?* Bea, I can barely speak. I have such marvellous news. Can we go somewhere to talk?'

Beatrice let go of Cyril's hand. 'You go in, my dear. See you in a few minutes.' Then she turned to her sister. Evangeline was incandescent in a Chinese yellow silk cloak, lined and trimmed with a smoky fox fur that almost exactly matched her eyes. She scratched the back of one calf with a grey suede shoe that had three buttoned straps and a curved Louis heel. The long bias-cut panels of her buttermilk satin dress fluttered in the night breeze and their folds created rippling shadows in the warm golden light shed by Coq d'Or's doorway lamps. She looked sensational but Beatrice forbore to comment. 'Evie. I can't talk now, don't you see? Jack might arrive at any moment. Unlikely, but I'd hate not to be here to meet him since I had to conscript him into coming in the first place.' She ran bony white fingers through her sister's marcelled waves, too stiff and corrugated for Beatrice's taste. 'Don't you remember? We tossed for the pleasure of attending. It's Priscilla Dawlish's bash to celebrate, of all things, her wretched magazine's eighth birthday. Can't this wait until tomorrow?'

Evie shrugged. 'If it must then I suppose it must. Sorry, Bea, you did draw the short straw, didn't you?' She grinned.

'Still, one of us had to see the play, see Viola, tonight. I'm glad it was me.' Her contrition was short-lived and distracted. 'But it mustn't wait very long.' Her eyes shone again in a way that Beatrice had almost forgotten. Evangeline did a little dance on the pavement and motioned to her cab driver that she would be returning to him soon. 'This plan of mine, Bea, this idea. It's so exciting, I just couldn't wait to talk to you about it. Trust me.'

Despite herself Beatrice laughed. 'Give me one clue, Evie. One word. We'll talk tomorrow but give me an inkling, please.'

Evangeline called her reply as her cab drew away. 'Not one clue, Bea, but three. Costume, stage, Hollywood.'

Beatrice didn't catch the last word as Evie's cab turned into Mayfair Street. She hesitated before entering the restaurant, hoping that Jack would be there. She saw as soon as she caught Cyril's wave and noted the empty chairs at their table that he wasn't one of a group at the far end which, tonight, occupied the whole of the short stroke of the L-shaped restaurant. She handed her little beaver cape to a girl in a corner kiosk, straightened her shoulders and wove down the room towards Cyril, pleasurably aware of the swish and rustle of her skirt as she did so. The noise of fabric, the slap of satin and the tiny, barely audible friction of lace could be the making of a garment just as cleverly as the touch of velvet or silk. Little filmy pennants of russet chiffon drifted from her shoulders and across her back as she stepped towards Cyril.

'I've ordered some Bolly,' he said. 'Don't worry. He'll probably be here in a minute.' They were silent for a few moments as the waiter uncorked and poured for them.

Beatrice remained quiet and thoughtful but gulped her champagne rather fast.

'What's wrong, Bea? You don't normally hose it down like that.' Cyril touched her wrist. 'You told me yourself that you were only half expecting Jack and it's early yet.'

She looked up. 'I'm not worried about Jack. As you kindly pointed out, I'm used to my husband having "better things to do in the evening than attend dinners in expensive restaurants which climax with trite speeches from shallow people about trivial matters".' Beatrice swallowed. 'I'm worried about Evie. Since she came back from Paris there's been one crazy scheme after another. She really hasn't settled down properly. Her work, her ideas, are still fabulous but she's like a magpie, always flying away towards the next thing that glints. Seems to have forgotten all she ever knew about constancy, practicalities, the boring bits, the elbow grease. Just now she skittered in with another of her glittering, impossible ideas.' Beatrice sighed heavily and drained her glass.

'You have your own children to worry about now, Bea. You've mothered Evie quite long enough. Maybe she *is* a magpie – let her fly. Maybe she'll find whatever it is she's searching for.'

Beatrice gave Cyril a dark look from beneath her pale lids, marked only with a line along the lashes that might have been etched with a mapping pen.

He failed to see how her eyes had hardened and went on, 'You're too stern with her, too protective. You blame her, and her sadly rather too clever, too modern designs for your failure to get the commission for—'

Beatrice lifted her chin. 'Enough, Cyril. More than

7

enough. I blame Evie for nothing. Nothing.' She raised a hand and her face broke into a long, wide smile, reaching into the tiny creases about her eyes. They brightened and gleamed as he approached. 'Look. Here comes Jack.'

In the morning Evangeline was white and heavy-lidded, clearly tired but still enthused. Beatrice wanted to delay confronting the latest scheme and prolonged the preliminary chatter by encouraging Ethel to keep her sister's cup brimming with strong, dark arabica coffee. 'Did you and Cameron dine after the play?'

'Yes. We—'

'Where did you go? What did you eat?'

'We went to Luigi's. But, Bea—'

'Luigi's.' Beatrice paused. 'Jack and I used to go there often. Can't these days, of course. Children wouldn't hear of it.' She laughed, noticing Evangeline's impatience from the tail of her eye. 'Do they still do that divine chicken with olives and almonds?' She registered Evangeline's rising irritation but continued none the less. 'And how is Cameron's novel progressing? Is he going to put you in it?'

'I haven't the faintest idea and I'm not particularly interested.' The kick of the coffee and her sister's clear reluctance to address important matters had aroused Evangeline's temper. 'And, Bea, indeed they do still serve the chicken. I had it. So did Cameron. So did Viola, but most of the others, since you're so interested, had the trout with capers. We all thought that everything was too, too delicious. And we had a particularly fine Frascati.' Evangeline took a last gulp of coffee. 'And now, Bea, may we talk about something that's actually important? To both of us, all of us.'

Viola, Evangeline explained, had just been contracted to play the lead in Mr Korda's next film. Shooting would start at Elstree Studios in about two months. 'She's not looking forward to getting up at dawn and rushing back to the West End in the evenings but otherwise she's thrilled. She's wanted to act in films for ages.'

'Then I'm very pleased for her. But I don't yet see how this affects us.' Actually, Beatrice had a fairly shrewd idea, after last night's excitement, but she wanted Evangeline to spell things out, cook her own goose if she must. 'Mr Korda usually makes historical dramas, doesn't he? What is his new film to be about?'

'It's to be a biopic – I think that's what the film people call it – about the life of Nell Gwynne. And the thing is, Bea, Viola says she can stipulate that we make all her costumes.' Evangeline's eyes were almost dancing, her hands fluttering.

'Costumes, Evie? *Costume?* The reputation of the House of Eliott is based on innovation, on setting fashion, not upon replication, copies or looking backwards. I'm not at all sure that this is a good idea.'

'Oh, Bea, why do you have to be so dampening? For a start this will be the greatest fun. Secondly it's not going to be Viola's only film. She might easily go on to make modern pictures, in Hollywood, even, and think how wonderful it could be for us if we designed for her then. Think about all the marvellous publicity. For this film alone it will be pretty extensive. And besides, I've sort of promised.'

Beatrice was stung. She supposed she had scuppered an awful lot of Evangeline's ideas lately and even criticized some of them for being just too avant-garde. She could hardly blame her for taking inspiration from the past for once. She placed one hand over her sister's. 'Well, I'm not sure about the advantages of publicity. We'll have to control that sort of thing as our kind of client likes to think of us as personal property. But a promise is a promise. And you may be right. It could be fun.'

'I knew you'd come round to the idea.' Evangeline leaned on her elbows, palms cupping her jaw. 'Think of the velvets and brocades, the frills and the fichus, those wonderful hats. Think of the farthingales.' Evangeline laughed.

Think of the consequences, thought Beatrice. She rose. 'Right, then. But first we must get to work today. We have several appointments.'

'Slightly more than you think, Bea. Viola is coming in at eleven for a fitting.'

Her entry caused work at the House of Eliott to cease for several minutes. Viola Day had clearly instructed her manager to notify some of the newspapers and a cluster of photographers greeted her as she stepped from her cab. The women in the workroom crowded about the windows to catch a glimpse of the actress who was said to be one of London's greatest stage stars. She wore a long navy crêpe day dress with matching jacket, a trailing fox fur stole and a witty hat that Beatrice thought she recognized as a good department-store copy of one of Elsa Schiaparelli's. She extended her hand. 'How do you do, Miss Day? I'm Beatrice Eliott. Delighted to meet you. Some coffee?' The actress smiled assent. Beatrice took her elbow. 'Now, come with me.'

'She's tiny. Tiny,' gushed Beryl as she returned to the workroom, having left the tray in Beatrice's office. 'You could put your finger and thumb round her ankle and they'd touch. And she's got these amazing eyes. They're almost the colour of this.' Beryl reached for a swatch of gleaming amber silk.

'What was she like though? Was she nice?' One of the other girls had seen Viola in a matinée and was, of all of them, the most consumed with curiosity.

'Well, she called me "darling" when I put the tray down. Don't think Miss Bea liked that. In fact, I don't think Miss Bea liked Miss Day at all, for that matter.'

'How could you tell?'

'Oh, you know the way she double crosses her legs when she's narked, one foot hooked behind the other ankle as well as crossed at the knee.' Beryl sat down and gave a passable imitation of Beatrice in a bad mood and everyone in the workroom laughed.

They were silenced by the entry of Evangeline, who was looking for some sketches. As she left, she paused by the foot of the stairs, smiling broadly over her shoulder.

'You're all going to have to get used to this. Miss Day is to become a client. But remember that we have a number of others so may I suggest that you all resume your work now?'

'Viola's only contracted to a three-month run in the play so we'll have to start working on her film clothes at once. Incidentally, it's awfully good – you and Jack should try to see it. I'll baby-sit if it's Molly's night off or anything. You know, I rather like to have the children to myself sometimes.'

The sisters were picking at smoked salmon for their

lunch. Molly had been with the sisters – first as nursery maid, then as cook and all-purpose maid – for years. Now she was Beatrice's housekeeper. They laughed, fondly, for a minute or two about her most recent obsession – detective stories – but Beatrice could not resist airing her reservations for the second, and last, time. 'Evie, from what you tell me about this picture it's going to be all Gainsborough frills and Fragonard swings. All wimples and crinolines, whalebone and lacings, slashed sleeves, hose and doublet, mob caps and petticoats. I'm really not sure . . .'

'Quite apart from getting your history in a terrible muddle, Bea, I don't think you see the point. Well, maybe that's because you haven't given me a chance to make it properly yet. Viola is also up for a really important part in a film they're planning to make in colour in Hollywood. If she looks good in the Korda one we might be in with a chance to do the costumes for the Hollywood picture. It could be the making of us.'

Beatrice signalled for coffee as Ethel passed across the door. 'It's this business about it all being costume that still bothers me, I suppose. I'm still a bit alarmed, and surprised. I'm supposed to be the one who puts the brakes on in our partnership because you're sometimes too innovative. Why on earth do you want to look back? Our whole design philosophy has been based on the idea of clean lines and few, if any, frills. Why on earth are you urging us towards fantasy clothes, whether they're for Mr Korda's films or for some other picture made in California?' Ethel brought in the coffee and Beatrice motioned for her to close the door.

There was a long silence and Evangeline's breathing deepened. 'You'd better stand by for a bit of a speech, Bea.' She looked up and Beatrice could see that her sister's eyes were damp with tears. 'You never blamed me, not once, for Paris failing . . .'

'How could I? Why would I? You didn't cause the Wall Street crash.'

'Please let me finish, Bea. I know I wasn't personally responsible and I don't blame myself but I know how much money we lost with that so-called investment. And I stayed on in Paris with that sculptor wastrel for such a long time afterwards. I wonder now if I was really in love with him or simply using him as a reason for not coming home and facing reality again. No, Bea, don't interrupt.' Evangeline had seen Beatrice's impatiently clasped fists. 'And then, late and lazy, or at any rate thoughtless, I came back and worked on those Marina designs – all too modern, all too avant-garde and all against your better and wiser judgement.

'You always say that I'm the creator in the House and you're just the practical one. You underestimate yourself, Bea. You were so right then but you let me have my silly head. And I lost us the commission.'

'I'm not going to argue with you about that, Evie. It could have been something as ridiculous as the Princess not liking the width of the bridesmaids' sashes in your sketches. You can't blame yourself. I certainly don't.' Beatrice handed Evangeline a handkerchief.

'I do, though. And that, I suppose, is why I want to look back rather than forward just now, why period costume appeals to me so much at the moment. Panniers, reticules and garters . . . at least you know where you are with them.' A tiny smile tilted one corner of Evangeline's upper lip and she wiped away the last of her tears. 'There's money in it, Bea. Doesn't mean to say we don't do the modern things too. This is just an extra arm for us. Damage limitation.

Another string to our bow.' She appeared to be on the brink of tears again. Beatrice composed herself. Fortunately Ethel had left the coffee pot on the table by the door and would not have seen Evangeline's stricken face.

She tried, awkwardly, to lighten the conversation. 'Speaking of beaux, what does Cameron think of all this?'

Evangeline mumbled into the crushed elbow folds of her blouse. 'Cameron has been bafflingly indifferent to all my plans and ideas recently. He was horrible at dinner last night, just beastly. He spent the whole evening talking to Viola and afterwards he became positively shifty when I tried to talk to him about all this.' She looked up. 'Bea, why do I always choose these brutes? When am I going to be happy? Did I do something evil when I was a child, something I can't remember? Am I being punished?'

In the seconds that followed, as she watched her sister's head fall back into the cradle of her sleeves, Beatrice thought hard and fast. 'Of course you didn't and of course you're not. You have no need to redeem yourself. You blame yourself too quickly and easily, Evie.' She remembered Evangeline's radiant excitement the night before and compared it with the defeated child before her. Her reservations about going into theatre or film work were suspended. 'Evie, I agree with you. Let's get on with Viola's clothes. And who knows what next? But there is a condition.'

Evangeline lifted her head and raised an eyebrow.

'The deal is that you don't drop the new work for it. Remember we have several débutantes' dresses to make and a new collection to complete. A new collection. You know, modern.'

Evangeline wiped away the last of her tears. Mascara smudged her cheeks. 'Deal, Bea. Wonder if I'll be able to explain things better to Cameron next time. Tomorrow, actually.'

'Don't say anything, promise me. He isn't family. Not yet, anyway.' And from what you say, Beatrice thought darkly but not without a moment of relief, he never will be.

'I do wish my sister wanted to work in contemporary theatre or film if she had to make us take this step.'

'I understand why she couldn't,' said Jack Maddox much later that day as he peeled a pear.

CHAPTER TWO

Evangeline's preliminary sketches for some of Viola's costumes were exciting faintly alarmed curiosity in the workroom.

'Look at the skirt on that dress. Must need twelve yards, at least. We'll have to cut it out in the road. And how are we going to make it stick out like that?' Doris was ever the pessimist.

'The skirt will be cut in panels and we can do that on the big table. Don't forget we've dressed the Duchess of Bushey.' Everyone laughed. Beryl's was usually the most acerbic voice in the workroom.

Elsie looked over their shoulders. 'Miss Evie told me that one of her friends, someone arty, I suppose, is going to make what she called a farthingale out of strips of willow. They curve them, sort of.' The other two looked up blankly. 'It's a kind of hoop which Miss Day will have to wear under her petticoats. It'll make the whole thing stand out like . . .' She thought for a moment, 'like a cabbage cut in half. And she says she wants everything to be "in period", whatever that means. All I know is that she says we can't use zips or even buttons or hooks. The bodices will all have to be laced up, like a shoe. What a flaming nuisance. They'll take ages, what with all the facing and finishing for the lace holes.'

'Very instructive, Elsie, I'm sure. But may I remind you

ladies that it is gone two o'clock and you should all be at work. We have both Lady Pamela Inverness and the Honourable Miss Sealy-Lewis coming in this afternoon for their final fittings. Court Presentation is in less than a week.' Marjorie Palmer, new to the House of Eliott and workroom manageress since Tilly had been promoted upstairs where she was now *vendeuse*, took her duties seriously. 'Though why the Misses Eliott arranged for those two to be here on the same afternoon astonishes me. They can't abide each other and Miss Sealy-Lewis only has to be a few minutes late for them to overlap.'

'I'd say she was already more than a few minutes late, Mrs Palmer.' Beryl could not resist it. 'We've let out her seams twice as it is. Let's hope she'll land a laird or bag a baron early on in the season. Or, then again, maybe she's now what Miss Evie would call "in period" again.'

Marjorie stifled a laugh. 'That will do, Beryl. We have very little time. Is her gown ready?'

'As good as. I finished the binding on the train this morning. We just have to see if it hangs correctly. Oh, and we need to make sure the headdress is right. Can't for the life of me see why they want to stick those feathers in their hair. Makes them look like little white squaws if you ask me.'

'I didn't, Beryl. And you should realize that the white feathers are in acknowledgement of the heraldic emblem of a Prince of Wales, whose motto is *Ich dien* which translates from the German as "I serve". You would do well to follow that – and the example the King has always set.'

'Of course, Mrs Palmer, right away,' replied Beryl. She turned her head towards the others in the workroom, crossed her eyes and let her tongue loll out of the corner of her mouth. 'I hear the King's setting *quite* an interesting example these days, what with—'

Marjorie Palmer interrupted her, 'That will do, Beryl,' and turned to Doris. 'Is Lady Pamela's dress ready? Did you finish the beading?'

'Before lunch, Mrs Palmer. All I have to do now is to stitch in the bee.' For some years now every garment from the House of Eliott had been signed, usually at the nape, with a tiny embroidered bee, or the lining silk had been watered or woven with the device. Inevitably the seam-stresses often referred to their workroom as the bee-hive. The stylized insect was a visual pun on the first letters of Beatrice and Evangeline's names. So beautiful were the linings and finish of some coats and jackets that certain daring débutantes had taken to wearing them inside out. 'I do wish she'd taken Miss Evie's advice about the dress. It's so . . . so busy. Makes sense of the bee, I suppose.'

'It is not your place to opine upon the clothes you help to make, Doris.' Marjorie Palmer would have continued, but Tilly stepped into the workroom. After her years as chief seamstress she had not yet lost the habit of regularly inspect-ing work in progress. It was a form of quality control and not resented, even though, these days, Tilly wore quiet but darkly elegant jersey suits instead of her overalls. She looked carefully at every detail of the two Court Presentation dresses, pursing her lips as she stood back from Lady Pamela's. There were organdie frills at the shoulders, a peplum at the waist, and heavy panels of seed-pearl embroid-ery had been set into the skirt as well as the bodice.

'Well,' she said resignedly, 'Lady Pamela did insist.' She turned round. 'Somehow I don't think this year's Presenta-

tion is going to be our finest hour, girls. Thank God we've
got other things on the go.' She pinched up a drift of silk
from Caroline Sealy-Lewis's dress. 'This would have been
superb but it was designed and cut for someone willowy. It
should have stood straight and still as a Grecian pillar and
then billowed out when she moved or danced.' She frowned,
half at the absurdity of hearing herself air newly learned and
understood words and half, ruefully, at the dress. 'Not your
fault, girls, but now that it's had to be let out so much it's
more moulding, somehow, less fluid. Dress like this doesn't
suit a curvy shape so well.' She stepped back again and
smiled. 'Still, it looks lovely on the dummy.'

'That's something, then, because on the other dummy
it'll look—' Beryl was silenced by a glare from Marjorie.
Upstairs the doorbell rang, and Tilly quickly patted her hair
and straightened her skirt before hurrying up to greet the
Honourable Caroline, calling to Elsie as she left to have the
gown brought up to the fitting room.

While she was out of the workroom Beryl and Doris
muttered together in a deliciously confidential way. The two
women had little in common but once they began discussing
the morals of the upper classes they found they could
exchange views happily for hours. Doris's opinions sprang
from her staunchly Welsh Methodist background and her
tendency to disapprove of any kind of levity, Beryl's from an
envy that bordered upon spite. She was apt to pronounce
that it was 'the rich wot got the gravy' as if she had coined
the popular maxim herself. For different reasons the two
women drew similar conclusions.

'It's a disgrace,' said Doris through a mouthful of pins.

'Miss Sealy-Lewis being knocked-up, or what?'

'Beryl, really.' Doris seldom used such vulgar expressions but could hardly pretend not to understand them. 'I mean the way our so-called betters fail to set any sort of example.'

'And still get away with it. I know what you mean, Doris. There's the Honourable Caroline in a spot of bother. She won't have to resort to a gin bath or some horrible seedy old woman with a knitting needle in a back-street, will she? She'll go off and spend a month in the country and the laird will never know. And as for the Prince of Wales and his Yankee trollop—'

'That's *enough*, Beryl. I won't hear a word against him. He's being very sensible, waiting for the right young woman. She's just keeping him company in the meantime. I hate to hear you gossiping like that about him. It's these posh harlots,' Doris remembered her Old Testament, 'Jezebels, which get my goat. We're practically expected to curtsy to them and yet they're no better than strumpets.' Her bosom heaved in outrage and she almost stitched her own sleeve into the cloth she was trimming.

Beryl was about to launch into one of her other favourite litanies, the one about Judy O'Grady and the colonel's lady, when Elsie walked back into the workroom.

Lady Pamela was delighted. The heavy satin fell in deep, gleaming folds and the masses of tiny pearls felt deliciously, lustrously smooth yet simultaneously tactile to her fingertips. Behind her back, as she twirled before the long cheval mirror, Evangeline caught Beatrice's eye, raised a hand and briefly pointed two fingers at her ear. She swiftly transformed the gesture of mock-suicide into a thoughtful pat of her hair as Lady Pamela turned again. 'It's just as I hoped it would be.

Absolutely perfect. A complete duck of a dress.' A complete
dog's dinner, thought Evangeline, smiling sweetly. 'I simply
must thank your workers personally. May I?'

Evangeline shrugged. She had mixed feelings about the
gown but knew it was always a fillip for the women if a
client troubled to express her appreciation. 'Certainly.
They'll be delighted.' She led Lady Pamela downstairs.

'I just want', began Lady Pamela in the doorway before
her smile froze, 'to know who that dress is for.' Her glance
had lighted upon the plain, frail, bias-cut ivory silk of
Caroline Sealy-Lewis's dress, draped on a dummy.

'It's for another débutante, Lady Pamela.' Evangeline's
reply was quick and cautious.

'Well, why can't mine be more like that? It's much too
fussy, can't you see? I want you to take away that overskirt
thing at the back. Peplum, did you call it?'

'We can do that if you wish, Lady Pamela, although you
were, I think, quite insistent about it when we first went over
the sketches. And it will upset the balance of the dress if we
do so.' Evangeline hoped the irritation she felt was not
evident in her voice.

'And you haven't told me whose dress it is.'

Evangeline sighed. Lady Pamela would learn all too soon
anyway so there was little point in dissembling. 'It's for Miss
Sealy-Lewis.'

To her surprise Lady Pamela's face broke into a wide
smile, which baffled the women in the workroom. 'Well,
that's all right, then. She's getting to be rather like a fat
white seal herself these days so that dress will be wasted on
her. They'd never allow her on the *Hindenberg*. Not unless
they made three other passengers bail out over the high seas.'
She laughed loudly and turned to Evangeline. 'It's a dreadful

shame that they've had to make such an exquisite frock for someone who'll soon barely be able to get through the door.' She fingered the cloth. 'Can we think about a dinner dress for me, cut a little bit like this? In plum-coloured silk velvet, perhaps, for the autumn, with long sleeves?'

'Of course.' Evangeline's relief was expressed in a chatty enthusiasm. 'We could finish the wrists with little Anne Boleyn points if you like.' She laid a hand on Lady Pamela's arm. 'Let's have some tea and consider other details.' At least for the next commission she might now be able to steer Pamela Inverness away from the ruffles, bows and ruching which she had favoured in the past.

There was silence in the workroom until they heard the soft click of Evangeline's door closing. 'Manners. I thought ladies were supposed to have manners. Still, I suppose cows can be posh as well as common. Cats, too. Mind you, I'd never swap our family's moggy for one of those thin yellow ones with the black ears which are supposed to be so superior.' Heads nodded in agreement after Beryl spoke. As soon as Marjorie Palmer left the room, with a thunderous look, to attend to other matters, the conversation continued. Nimble embroidering, the whirring of machines and the threading of piping cord through tiny, slippery tubes of satin did not hinder it.

Doris was deftly arranging white feathers in a paste copy of the base of the parure that was to be Caroline Sealy-Lewis's headdress. 'Don't know about manners. I thought Mr Manners was someone you left a little bit of food for on your plate. I do know that I'd get a clip round the ear if I didn't behave myself.'

'Is manners the same as good behaviour, then?' someone asked.

'Manners is keeping your trap shut when you're cross.'

'No, I think it's to do with showing consideration.'

'Is manners something that we can have as well as the toffs?'

'Course. Think of the Prince of Wales.' Beryl pointedly laid down the fabric she was trimming, reached for Doris's last, unfastened feather and stuck it in her bun. 'He don't show much consideration, does he? Not to his parents, not to anyone. No respect. From what I read in *Reynolds News* he seems to spend all his time in nightclubs and them cocktail lounges. That's not how a Prince of Wales should behave.'

'I won't hear a word against him. He's lovely. So handsome,' repeated Doris. 'It's not for the likes of us to pass judgement.'

One of the other girls, Coral, was seldom given to debate. She had a stammer and a brother who had been injured in a mining accident the year before. 'I'm surprised at you, Doris, what with your family coming from the valleys, just like mine. My mother always says that fine words don't b-b-b-butter no p-p-p-parsnips. I never knew what she was getting at until His Nibs came to Cardiff. "Something must be done," he says. If you ask me, something must be done – about him. All m-m-m-mouth and trousers. All show, no real c-c-c-care or k-k-k-kindness.' It was the longest speech any of them had heard her make. 'Manners isn't all to do with raising your hat to a l-l-lady. Doris, you're wrong to think so highly of that Prince of Wales. He's a horrible little man, in my opinion. He made us all in Wales – not just me da and me brothers – think we'd be rescued. And what's he done? Damn bloody all.' Coral flushed and picked up her needle again. Then she raised it sharply. 'I can tell you all where I'd like to stick this.'

Amid laughter in the workroom, Marjorie Palmer returned. 'What's all this? For heaven's sake, get weaving. The next client will be here any moment and everything had better be ready when she arrives. Miss Bea and Miss Evie are so relieved that Lady Pamela has left that I don't want them flung into a bad mood now.' She picked a stray thread of silk from the dummy that bore another débutante's gown. 'Someone stand by to take this upstairs the moment it's called for, please.'

'We were just talking about the Prince of Wales. Wondering about that American ladyfriend of his, you know.' Beryl gave an arch smile as she picked up one of the unfinished headdresses. 'Is it true, Mrs Palmer, that he's going to present her at Court this year? Said so in the Court Circular in *The Times* the other day. Will she curtsy in front of the Queen like Lady Pamela and Miss Caroline? People say she's old enough to be his mother.'

Even Marjorie knew of Beryl's addiction to following 'her' ladies' social lives through reading the society pages of whatever day-old newspaper she could persuade out of her newsagent friend when she collected her copy of *Reynolds News* or *Film Fun*. She was a particularly avid student of the Court Circular. She pursed her lips. 'I couldn't possibly comment. And nor should you.' The doorbell rang and Marjorie had to run upstairs yet again. At the landing she remembered to call down. 'If you really must let out Miss Caroline's seams again, please say that it's the latest fashion, or your mistake. Anything. Don't say a word to make her think that we . . . well, you know.'

It was a few minutes before the dress on the dummy was requested. Fingers flew and the treadles of Singer machines whirred until Beryl stopped pedalling the metal plate at her feet and tore the gold thread with her teeth. She had clearly been seething and stewing. 'What I want to know is this.' The workroom fell silent. 'Just why is it that when Caroline flamin' Sealy-Lewis gets knocked up, put in the family way or whatever, she still gets to be presented to the Prince of Wales? And when my sister fell for a baby she got her cards from Woolworth's. It's just not fair.'

Marjorie heard Beryl's outburst as she descended the stairs and went to finger the Honourable Caroline's dress draped on its dummy. She handed it to Beryl and she echoed, unconsciously, Beatrice's remark to Cyril. 'Life isn't fair. It never was and never will be. Now, let out those seams again, Beryl, if there's any more selvage.' She held out the lovely plain white silk. 'I'm afraid that Miss Caroline does seem to have put on a little more weight in the bosom and tummy departments. We must do our best.'

Beatrice raked long, bony fingers through her hair. Her nose was reddened at the tip. If Jack hadn't known better he would have imagined she was coming down with a touch of flu. She had pushed first the casseroled pork and then the rice pudding around her plate, eating almost nothing. 'Did Ned seem any better? I worry so much about him, poor little chap.'

'What do you think is wrong, Bea? You fret so much about him and yet we've seen it all before with Clare and Tom.' He paused. 'All children get measles, chickenpox and mumps. The other two survived – they pulled round within two weeks. Don't you remember how I taught Tom his letters, and then showed him how to hold his knife and fork while he was sitting up in bed? It's not something to get into a tizz about, these childhood illnesses.' Jack hesitated. He knew how precious Edmund was to Beatrice, but hated that preference. Tom and Clare were to be equally cherished, he was determined. But he also knew that his wife, above all, was to be prized. He kissed the long, sharp nose. 'You could open tin cans with that, darling.'

Beatrice was to be neither distracted nor mollified. 'These modern inoculations for some of those illnesses are marvellous, I agree, but, Jack . . .' Her love, concern and panic for little Edmund, the afterthought baby who had surprised them both, seemed almost to obsess her, as if she was attempting to pay old dues to Clare and Tom for whom she had been prepared to give less time and display fewer obvious evidences of love.

Jack drew breath. 'Is there anything I can do to help?

'How on earth *could* you help with something like a fever in the nursery? You're not here half the time, anyway.'

The cross, sulky way in which Beatrice usually denied the existence of any problem made Jack absolutely certain that this time there really was something the matter. 'Try to tell me, Bea. Better out than in.' He poured each of them another glass of claret.

'Nothing you can do. Wish you could. Sorry, Jack. It's been a bad day at work and I feel desperately guilty about not seeing the children before they went to bed. Did they miss me? Did they ask for me?' Beatrice reached for the linen handkerchief tucked into her cuff. Jack knew that she was close to tears but also that he must wait until she was ready to elaborate.

'Yes, they did. But they're old enough to know now – or at any rate Clare and Tom are – that you can't always be with them at bedtime. I dried all three of them after their baths and read them a story.' Jack winced, hesitated, lit a cigarette and tried to engage Beatrice's eyes. 'It was perfectly fine, Bea, but they do need to see more of you.' He waited for a moment. 'I'm a bit worried about Tom.'

Beatrice seemed to slip out of a coma. She placed her glass on the table. Concentration and clarity returned to her eyes. The green cleared, Jack thought. It was no longer a cloudy, muddy-pond green but a green with a fierce protective light. 'What do you mean?'

'I noticed, when I dried him today, how all his grazes and scratches and bruises are down his left side. We know his eyesight isn't too good. That's why we had Dr Gordon make those spectacles for him. But, Bea, I think we may have to take him back. He falls over all the time. Molly says he knocks into furniture and sometimes doesn't even seem to have seen the things he trips over. I've begun to notice in the garden when we play together that Ned, who's still only a baby, really, has better ball control than Tom when we three are playing rugger for Saracens.' Jack passed a hand across his wife's knitted brow. 'I worry that our poor little Tom needs more help. Look at his scabs and bruises next time you bath him.' Jack took his wife's hand. Her tears were plopping fast and heavily upon his knuckles.

'I will.' She looked up. 'We must.' She picked up her handkerchief again. 'Nothing else matters.'

Later, sipping brandy with their coffee by the fireside of their small private sitting room – a place where guests were seldom entertained – Jack had soothed Beatrice enough to talk a little of his own work. Having made plans to take Tom to another specialist and apparently less frantic about

Ned's quickly passing fever, Bea seemed ready to listen to him at last. It was late spring but this was a winter room, suited to darkness and shadows, and curtains with deep, heavy folds; crimson and russet tints in the Persian rugs tuned in with the the deep, flat yellow of the walls and the dark terracotta paintwork above the cornice and on the ceiling. A single lamp gleamed in one corner and the fire flickering in the small hearth – even on late summer evenings Jack and Beatrice loved to watch the flames – cast a glow that reminded Jack of some of the evenings they had spent there before Clare was born and many, he remembered, afterwards. He took his wife's hand. 'Bea darling, you remember that film I made for the British Institute? The one about the building of County Hall?'

'Yes, of course. Even I thought it was a triumph, more exciting than I could have imagined when you first told me about it.'

'County Hall was here, in London, at home. But now the Institute want me to make another news documentary and this one would have a much broader sweep.' He picked up his glass and poured a splash more brandy. 'It's over five years now since the General Strike. The Ministry of Information has asked me to make a much longer film for the cinema about the reverberations – what's improved, what's got worse, what we've learned, what can't seem to be unlearned . . .' He continued to elaborate. The film would follow the newsreel and preface the main feature in cinemas nationwide. It would be an entertainment of sorts, of course, but also subtly instructive rather as Basil Wright's film *Nightmail* – about the workings of the Post Office – had been.

'But Jack, that's marvellous. Why are you worried?'

'I was coming to that. Don't you see, Bea? I'll need to be away from home an awful lot. Newcastle, Manchester, Birmingham, Wales, Glasgow, Bristol and a dozen other places. I'll need to visit all the main industrial centres. How do you feel about that? It'll take months.'

Beatrice thought for a moment. 'Obviously I want you here with us, but you'd only be away for a few days at a time, wouldn't you? Not weeks on end.' Jack nodded. 'It's what you want to do, isn't it?' He nodded again. 'Then I think you must definitely agree. We'll manage, and Cyril can always be my escort if I need one while you're away.'

Jack could not prevent a brief look of contempt from glancing across his face. 'Cyril, bloody, bloodless Cyril. Well, I suppose you'll be in safe hands there. No need to worry about my wife's virtue while he's around.'

'Jack, please, don't be unfair.'

'Oh, don't mistake me, Bea. I rather like the man. He can be very amusing. I just don't understand how, in this day and age, a man can content himself by taking photographs of frocks, flattering vain actresses and society hags with his retouch jobs.'

Beatrice bridled. 'That's almost exactly how you plied your trade when I first met you, Jack Maddox, or had you forgotten? And why, pray, is it demeaning for a man to take the photographs but acceptable for women to make the clothes? Or perhaps it isn't.'

'I didn't mean it like that, Bea. God, I'm sorry.'

But Beatrice was determined to continue her defence of Cyril. 'Besides, Cyril's not as shallow as you think he is. You might realize that one day. He's one of those men who isn't really at ease talking to other men. He confides to his women friends and we see a much more serious side. At least, I do.'

'Give me an example.'

'Well,' Beatrice began, '*Mode* is featuring our next collection over several pages in its September issue and Cyril's taking the pictures. It was his idea to take the photographs on a series of factory floors, with a sort of "after the ball was over" theme – you know, the party or the Season's over.'

'I don't understand. What's the point? Anyway, sounds to me very much like a rehash of those skivvy pictures I took years ago. Cyril copied that idea then and now it sounds as if he's planning to plagiarize himself as well as me.' He saw Beatrice frown. 'I didn't mind, Bea. You know I positively encouraged the fellow. It pleased me to see the ideas behind my photographs spread as widely as possible. Go on.' He stroked her hand, trying to be patient and to control his irritation. The last thing he wanted to do was to spoil a warm evening of tensions defused. 'Anyway, as all of us know, there's an element of derivation in all creative work.'

'Well, there'll be the very best of our new designs worn by rather wasted model girls with backdrops of machinery and these pinched, apparently frail factory girls. His idea is to plant the idea that there can be strength in seeming fragility and to show that under the skin all the girls are—'

Jack snorted. 'That's Cyril's idea of social realism, is it? Using factory workers as props? Your clothes simply taunting and tantalizing them? I'm surprised and disappointed that you can't see that.' He drained his glass. 'I thought we were getting somewhere, Bea. Getting nearer to sharing ideas and ideals as well as a house and a family and . . .' He hesitated. 'Perhaps it's just as well that I'm making this film for the Ministry. Think I'll turn in now.'

Beatrice sat alone for several minutes, watching the last

low flickers in the grate. There had been a short period of grace tonight but now all her worries and unease returned. She walked upstairs and quietly pushed open the nursery door. A line of light had gleamed below Molly's as she passed earlier. Molly had indeed graduated from romantic fiction and must now, Beatrice thought, be in the grip of one of her rather ghoulish crime novels. Each of her children was sleeping peacefully and by the glimmer of the night-light she could see that Edmund's face was less flushed. His breathing seemed steadier. She kissed the top of each of their heads. Clare's dark auburn curls were soft and springy while Tom's thick fringe was as dark as Jack's had once been. Finally she lifted some damp fair strands from Edmund's forehead and thought her heart would burst.

Jack stirred when Beatrice climbed in next to him and put an arm around her. She rested her head on his chest. 'It'll be all right, Bea darling, won't it?'

She was pleased that in the darkness he could not see how close to tears she was.

CHAPTER THREE

L unch was at Quaglino's. Priscilla Dawlish's favourite table at the St James's restaurant, which had remained fashionable for years now, was strategically placed in one corner and offered both a modicum of privacy and a first-rate view of the other diners. The place was large enough to accommodate a dance and yet so beautifully lit and designed that it managed to retain frissons of mystery, promise and glamour. The one better table, in her view, could seat only three – and that at a push – and during a very intimate meal, Priscilla declared, one would not give a monkey's toss about who else was in the restaurant.

'What's a monkey's toss?' enquired Beatrice. Evangeline stifled a giggle.

'A monkey's toss, my dear girl, is . . .'

Priscilla laid a restraining hand on Cyril's wrist. 'Cyril, please. That will do. If I had wanted educational vulgarity today I would have suggested we lunched at the Pig and Whistle.' She raised a steeply plucked and carefully pencilled black eyebrow. 'And speaking of vulgarity, look over there. Isn't that Syrie? She, of all people, should know better than to wear that colour.' She squinted towards a table at the back of the room where a middle-aged woman, somewhat resembling, it might have been said, Priscilla herself, was being seated. Her companion was a rather studious-looking young man, his hair unfashionably brilliantined and tidy, his glasses wire-framed and round and his suit clearly borrowed or off the peg. It didn't fit him at all well.

'Who is he?' asked Evangeline. 'He looks rather interesting.'

'I should say so, Evie. Name of Guy Birdsey. He's Syrie's new protégé. They say he's quite brilliant.' Cyril leaned forward.

'They say all sorts of things,' said Priscilla darkly. She turned to the sisters. 'Syrie obviously thought she needed a little new blood for her interiors business. Apparently she virtually picked that boy off the streets. They also say', she frowned, 'that what Guy Birdsey can't do with a swag or a flounce you could write on a sixpence.'

'Mmmm. I'd heard that too. I'd love to see his flounces. And incidentally, Priscilla my darling, I've learned to distrust the veracity of any statement which begins with "apparently".'

'Cyril. I won't warn you again.' This time Priscilla tapped his wrist. 'Anyway, we didn't meet to talk about "they". We're here to talk about us.' She beamed. Priscilla Dawlish was editor of the British edition of *Mode*, one of the most influential fashion magazines. Many feared her tongue and her caprices and she was frequently mocked by both her rivals and her victims for her personal style, which was both severe and dramatic. Her clothes were always exquisite: dark, plain and beautifully cut, and because of her position Priscilla seldom had to pay for a single stitch. But there were those who maintained that they were wasted on a woman who could look like an unusually raddled fishwife, often swore like one and who had the unnerving habit of lossening the plackets she always asked to be concealed in her dresses after a particularly hearty meal. Some of her critics also said that her penchant for 'witty' jewellery – sparkling poodle brooches or starfish necklaces made from pearl-studded coral – was a terrible waste of Schiaparelli's art. On Priscilla, some said, they might have dropped out of a Christmas cracker or have come from Woolworth's. That, Priscilla Dawlish would have replied, is exactly what Schiap had intended.

The first bottle of Chablis was almost finished and Priscilla beckoned for another. She had already waved away the waiter twice but now commanded Beatrice, Evangeline and Cyril to order their food. 'We might as well get this part over and done with and then we can get down to business. Not really hungry at all myself, so let's be quick about it.' She raised a finger to their waiter, indicating that her party was nearly ready. 'Evangeline, you go first.'

Evangeline had decided on consommé and sole Cubat, Beatrice on asparagus followed by an omelette Arnold Bennett, and Cyril chose quail's eggs with an anchovy dressing, and lamb cutlets. 'What a relief. Someone with a healthy appetite at last.' Priscilla laid down her menu and, after a last-minute deliberation, requested the *foie gras* and tournedos. 'And lots of potatoes. Lots. The dauphinoise, please.' By way of explanation she murmured about their high vitamin and thus energy quotient. 'I know now I'll never be in the front line of a League of Health and Beauty pageant – ridiculous bourgeois things they are, anyway, don't you think? But one must keep one's strength up. Most important.' Their first courses arrived, along with the second bottle of Chablis.

'How's Cameron? I thought he'd be with you at the Coopers' on Wednesday.' Cyril arched a brow towards

Evangeline as he smeared some bread with the last of his anchovy dressing.

'Cameron and I . . . Well, we . . .' Evangeline took a gulp of water, 'we seem to have had a little misunderstanding. Nothing to worry about,' she added hastily, dabbing her lips. 'You know how these things are.'

'I do, Evie, I do.' Cyril caught Priscilla's look – something between thunder and the lightning of intrigue. 'Couldn't possibly be anything to do with Viola, could it? One hears that they have something of a love-hate relationship, so of course your loyalties must be torn, yes?' He could sense Priscilla's shoulders leaning inwards, her fingers twisting her rings.

'I really don't want to discuss it just now. And, Cyril, you really are a bit of a brute to raise it.' Evangeline turned to Priscilla. 'It's just that Cameron doesn't always seem to like Viola very much, although at other times . . .' Evangeline's voice trailed off. 'And he thinks it's rather off that we're going to make her costumes for *Nell Gwynne*. I don't really understand his reasons, something about "prettifying a dirty piece of history", he said. We had a silly sort of fight, but it doesn't matter. We're not here to talk about my private life, are we?' She looked pointedly at Cyril and then at Beatrice for support, but her sister was preoccupied in studying the pattern on the damask tablecloth.

'But Cameron's new novel is said to be virtually encrusted with wicked weeny portraits of people like Viola. Like us, even.' Priscilla raised her wrist hopefully signalling for another bottle to be put on ice. She leaned even further forward. 'Can't you tell us just the teeniest bit about it? Is Elsie Mendl in there? Nancy Cunard? Mrs . . .?'

'No. Sorry, I can't. You'll have to ask Cameron himself.' Evangeline shot a stern look at Cyril as their main courses arrived.

Priscilla stroked her wrist. 'I understand, dear. All in good time. But do try to remember to tell me about it all when the dust has settled.'

Beatrice glanced at her watch: small as it was and set only with pavé diamonds it seemed to imprison her thin white wrist. 'I really think we must get down to business now. Evie can stay till tea-time, but I must be off by two. Clare has to have a fitting for new shoes, you see, and I promised to meet her and Molly at Harrods.' She was apologetic. 'These days every little girl seems to want to look like Princess Elizabeth and have strapped shoes just like hers. If I left her with Molly she'd come home with clogs or clumpy lace-ups and I promise you that my life wouldn't be worth living.' She laughed as she cut into her omelette, the creamy, fishy scent wafting over the table.

'Quite understand, my dear. So, to business.' Priscilla plunged her knife into a perfect steak. 'These pages. Tell me, you two, which gowns you most want featured and then I will explain my own preferences if they differ. Cyril will referee, won't you, my pet? After all, Cyril is an artist too and he is allowed to have some say . . .'

Beatrice had to leave before coffee but by then the general shape of the photographs and their factory locations had been agreed. There was little dispute about the clothes: the sisters conceded an evening gown to Priscilla and she agreed to trade a favourite afternoon dress for a battle-ship grey costume with trousers instead of a skirt. 'I think, Cyril, that we should alternate between group shots in which a number of dresses or outfits can be shown in one picture – the tea-dresses, for instance, or the ballgowns – because those are the situations where women are likely to be in groups or crowds, and other, differently styled ones. I'd like to see the unexpected garment given a page to itself. Lingerie or morning wear – because that is when a woman is most likely to be alone or, at least, not amid a hubbub. What do you think, Cyril?' Evangeline passed some preliminary sketches across the table.

He instantly revised his own plans. 'You're quite right, Evie. I hadn't thought of that but it's exactly how we'll do it. And with Priscilla's permission we can have some of the dresses in the group shots hand-tinted. Wouldn't that be splendid?'

Priscilla nodded. She loved the delicate tones that hand-colouring could bestow on black-and-white photography but the process was fiendishly expensive. However, she knew a young watercolourist who owed her a favour and it would be a travesty to waste the scoop of previewing the House of Eliott collection as beautifully as possible for the sake of a few pounds. Cyril was planning locations. His own studio would be perfect for the sculptured, almost theatrical group shots but the more intimate pictures might, he mused, be taken in people's homes. Certain society ladies would be delighted to lend them to *Mode* and Cyril was already wondering how he might be able to persuade Guy Birdsey to have a word with some of his clients.

'Splendid!' Priscilla clapped her hands. 'That all seems to be settled. Just make sure I have all the pictures within the next eight weeks. Pudding, anyone?' Beatrice smiled ruefully, shook her head and gathered her things. 'Lovely lunch, Priscilla, and thanks again, but I must dash now. Have fun, you three, and go easy on the character assassination.'

Evangeline watched her sister skitter deftly through the tables, hastening to collect her coat.

'Isn't this cosy?' asked Priscilla as the coffee arrived. 'That's sorted out, all bar the shouting. Now,' she settled back in her chair, 'we can, perhaps, talk a little more about Viola? Nothing that will compromise or upset you, Evie, of course.'

Cyril glanced downwards with a show of modesty and remorse. Evangeline looked pained and reached for her bag. 'Viola's my friend, Priscilla. And so is Cameron. Whatever he's writing about her or me or anyone else is his business. You might think it's yours as well and that's your business, literally, because you're a journalist. But I think I'd better leave you two now. I'd hate either of them to think I'd spoken about them without their permission.' She rose. 'Delicious lunch, Priscilla. And thanks so much for all the support.' She kissed her cheek. 'Thank you, too, Cyril, you wretch. See you on set if not before.' She kissed him affectionately too, picked up her handbag and walked to the door.

Both Priscilla's and Cyril's eyes followed her narrow back and slender ankles clipping across the marble of the floor. 'Lovely, those Eliott girls, both of them,' mused Cyril. 'Pity neither has a sense of humour.'

'So right, Cyril, so very true,' replied Priscilla. 'Will you have a brandy?'

'Why, yes. Thank you. No wonder Evie's a bit unnerved if Cameron plans to put her in his novel. I'd be tense about that. Cameron's always been able to charm the skeletons out of the cupboard.' He shivered theatrically. 'Anyway, I hope they make it up.' The brandy arrived.

'Evie's got nothing to worry about. Well, nothing much.

She's perhaps been a little too . . . shall we say, Bohemian, since she came back from Paris. Pity about all that but I suppose it did help her to get that other unfortunate *affaire* out of her mind . . . But Cameron likes a girl to be spirited. He wouldn't bother with her otherwise.'

'I think that Evie may want more from Cameron than you realize, Priscilla, I think she is cloaking some other desires, some other hopes, with her defence of Viola. I think she's tired of rocking boats. May be ready for a safe harbour – though, God knows, I wouldn't fancy Cameron as my skipper.'

'For heaven's sake, don't get all thoughtful and philosophical on me, Cyril darling. Evie's a dear and talented girl but life's too short to get immersed in other people's private little dramas, don't you think? The public ones – well, that's another thing. Let's have another brandy.'

'But, Jack, this is tremendous news. Well done, my boy.'

Without the least intention of attempting to insinuate himself into the English upper-middle classes, Jack Maddox's brother-in-law, Leonard Golder, had, by osmosis, absorbed some of their vernacular. 'I'm not at all surprised, however. The County Hall film was a triumph. As you know, all my friends at RIBA felt that it put the stamp of both artistic and social respectability on our profession. Architects were popularly regarded as little better than builders until a few years ago. That film of yours helped to change all that.'

'Nothing wrong with being a builder, Leonard. A very honourable trade. This rather fine house', Jack swept an arm around the dining room in Gower Street, 'was built by one.' He was lunching with his sister and her husband. Penelope had left the room briefly to mix the salad, always feeling that on days away from her East London mission one should at least share the chores at home.

'So, this new motion picture of yours, has the Ministry given you a budget?'

'Yes, quite a realistic one. There will be no expenses where locations are concerned and no greedy actors to pay, no costumes or sets to design. So all the money will go on the technicians – the very best – but I might still be able to do it for less than is expected. If I can, I'll use the rest of the money to commission an original music score. One from Mr Britten, perhaps. If not', Jack shrugged, 'I'll have to settle for something that already exists. Nothing too Blake or Elgar, though.'

'Nothing the matter with Jerusalem or Elgar,' announced Penelope as she brought the salad bowl into the room, followed by Min, the cook-general, who carried a dish of dressed crab then returned to the kitchen to fetch a bowl of buttered new potatoes scattered with chives. 'I'm with General Booth there. Remember he said, "Why should the Devil have all the best tunes?" Well, I say, "Why shouldn't the socialists and the Fabians be allowed to enjoy sublime music, even if it was created by the privileged?"'

'Not quite sure about Elgar, but Blake wasn't exactly a toff, Pen.' Jack enjoyed ribbing his sister gently. Her hair was getting quite grey now and drawn into a knot at the nape of her neck. But the approach of middle age rather suited Penelope, whose angular features and strong jaw had always contrasted uncomfortably with the dimpled, downy, rounded charms of her fellow débutantes. Probably led her towards the good works in her beloved East End mission, Jack reflected. She had been born just too late to have become a real suffragette and Jack suspected that she regretted this. Perhaps she was entering her prime, almost fashionable at last, without realizing it. It was even *de rigueur* now to sport a sun-tan: all those years of shunning cosmetics and spending hours out of doors had permanently weathered Penelope's complexion. He noted how well the plainly cut navy wool sat on her shoulders. Fair and square, he thought, that's my sister.

'Not the point, Jack, not the point. Listen to me for once. Blake's been claimed by the uppers but he wrote for the ordinary people. Jolly good thing if you remind everyone of the dark satanic mills in your film.'

'I want to avoid the obvious if I can, Pen.'

'Sometimes a cliché's just the thing, usually a bit of real truth there. Everyone will understand what you mean. Salad?' She handed him the bowl.

'I'll have mine later.' Jack balanced some crab on his fork. 'No, Pen, we may have to differ here. Mr Orwell says that easy phrases lead to lazy thinking and that leads to complacency. A comfortable acceptance of things. I want my work to provoke, to make people think, and think for themselves.' He chewed for a few seconds. 'Delicious. And that's quite enough about me. I came over to hear your news.'

'Tell him about your project, Leonard. Well, it's ours really, isn't it, darling?'

Her husband laid down his fork and took a sip of his wine. 'Your sister should take most if not all of the credit, Jack. Penelope', he beamed warmly across the table at her, 'kept telling me about how overcrowded the Shoreditch mission was becoming and how many of the new visitors were Jewish families from Austria, Poland and Germany.

Apparently many of them were far from penniless but simply had no friends or contacts in London. But despite being financially comfortable at home many have had to leave most of their assets behind and they aren't wealthy enough to set up camp in hotels. Besides, they want proper homes. So,' he took a breath, 'I have been engaged on a rather major housing project. With the financial help of the refugees – if I may so describe them – and other beneficiaries, I am engaged in the restoration and modernization of a number of apartment buildings in the Swiss Cottage and St John's Wood area. Hold your breath, but I might even be able to raise the finance to build one or two completely new ones near the park. I can guess what some people will say about the venality of my race. Perhaps they will be satisfied.' He laughed. 'The scion of one of your leading Jewish banking families has told me that he will do all he can to help.' Jack smiled as he listened to Leonard, concentrating hard but also remembering how Penelope had faced and weathered many raised eyebrows and dark mutterings when she had astonished her family and friends by announcing that she was to marry this charming, clever and cultured Jew. Some of their 'friends' had been baffled by their parents' warm embrace of Leonard and their pride in enclosing him within the family. Leonard and Penelope had met at a meeting of the Fabians. '*Coup de foudre*, Jack. That was that.' They had married within the month. He cracked a walnut, thought lovingly of his parents' decency and looked back to his brother-in-law.

'This is very exciting, Leonard. But surely you don't intend the refugees, as you term them, all to live together in a kind of civilized London ghetto.'

'Of course not. It will take tact and delicacy to achieve the correct balance. These people have come to us, to

England, and we want to ensure that they settle and integrate here. And yet they have a need to maintain links with their families and their own culture. You cannot really understand, I'm afraid.' Leonard frowned. His own family had left Austria over thirty years earlier and he remembered sharply his feelings as a twelve-year-old boy when he had arrived in London with his brave but bewildered stateless parents. He cleared his throat. 'No, all the housing projects will be carefully planned. Apartments will be available to anyone who can buy or any family in need. Now,' he waited until Min had cleared away their plates and had brought in a plate of cheese and set it beside the fruit bowl, 'we talk about families. Our family. Tell us about Beatrice. And how are the children?'

'Bea's fine. Busy, you know. The new collection is being finalized.'

'Do you ever find it a bit of a bore to go to all those parties and receptions with her, Jack? Come to that, won't she miss you dreadfully when you're away with all this filming you were telling us about?' Penelope and Beatrice were the greatest of friends but neither had ever quite understood the other's work.

Jack cut himself a wedge of Brie and took a Bath Oliver biscuit. 'I certainly hope so. I want her to miss me terribly, to beg me to come home or better still to cancel some of her wretched social engagements.' He heard how the inflection in his voice had altered and caught a glance exchanged between Penelope and Leonard. 'But no, everything's fine. I'll always be back at weekends, at the very least, and it's only going to be for a few months. Besides, Bea has a very accomplished companion always at hand when she needs to be squired.'

Penelope's left eyebrow lifted.

'Cyril Hunter. D'you know him? Photographer. Jolly good one, actually, wasted on fashion photography and theatre work if you ask me, but there you are. He's a decent sort and much better at those dos than I can ever learn to be. Suits Bea, suits him and suits me, in a funny way.'

'Don't you ever worry . . .?' Leonard's tone was hesitant.

'Worry about Cyril? Good God, man, no. Bea couldn't be in safer hands.' Jack grinned.

'And the children? It's awful, Jack, so long since we've seen you all together, what with one thing and another.' Penelope pulled a face. Min had cleared the fruit plates and had left coffee on the table.

Jack's face broke into a wide smile of paternal pride. 'The nippers? Yes, they're all fine. Clare is going to dancing classes now, with Madame Vacani, as well as riding. And she's so grown-up these days – insists on her clothes all being just so. Molly – you have to remember that after all these years Molly feels quite proprietorial about all the members of the family – doesn't get on too well with the governess but that's to be expected, I suppose. And Clare'll be going to school soon now. She insists!' Jack paused and his expression clouded for a moment. 'Looks so much like Bea sometimes, especially when she's cross, that it gives me quite a jolt.' He collected himself. 'Ned's a little tyrant, of course. I suppose you could almost call him precocious, he's so bright for his age. Last week he counted up to ten. Can you believe it? He's not yet two and he was as pleased as punch. He's a fine little chap. Sorry,' Jack looked sheepish, 'that's enough from the proud papa.'

'And Tom? How are his eyes?' Penelope saw a flicker of worry cross Jack's features.

'Tom's fine, Pen . . . Don't know if you can understand. They're all precious to me, but Tom . . .'

'His eyes, Jack? Did Dr Gordon help?'

'Well, he made him some spectacles, as you know, and they've certainly helped a bit although the poor little lad hates to wear them and the bridge has caused a sort of eczematic reaction on his nose. And that meant another doctor. Oh, he's strong and he eats well, and he's got the sunniest disposition. But I worry.'

'Why, exactly? Those glasses are corrective, Jack, like a brace on the teeth. In a couple of years his sight should catch up and be quite normal. Dr Gordon thought so, didn't he?' Leonard spoke slowly and carefully.

'Well, I'm sure you and Dr Gordon are right. But I had to insist that he stopped riding after he fell off his pony again last month. That didn't make me the most popular father in London, I can tell you. But he's so accident prone, always falling over, knocking into things, sometimes breaking them. Bea can get quite sharp – and I can't blame her, really – when he smashes something especially treasured. She has so few of her mother's things.' Jack sighed. 'He always seems to fall on his left side. But nothing much to worry about, I'm sure. He'll manage and he certainly won't be coddled.'

Penelope and Leonard again exchanged glances.

'Jack, you must not imagine that we are interfering. We only wish for the best. But Penelope and I also noticed how Tom favours his right eye. Forgive me, but he almost seemed to squint during that magic lantern show we gave here after his last birthday. I don't think he realized that anyone had noticed in the dark.'

'What are you saying?'

'I think that you might take him to see Gordon again. Or

even to another eye specialist. Sight is too precious to risk. He might need more than spectacles.'

Jack looked long at them both. He had met – several times – Leonard's greatest friend, Gerd, who had been a brilliant translator until he lost his sight. Gerd now scraped a living proof-reading in Braille. He shivered. 'I will. We will. I promise.' He wanted to change the subject. 'What other news?'

'House is going to be completely chaotic for the next few weeks. Don't know how we're going to manage,' said Penelope brightly. Jack looked up enquiringly. 'Viennese friends, Johann and Claudia Jacobs, are coming to camp here. Could hardly put them in the Mission, could I, darling?' She looked fondly across the table.

Leonard explained, 'Johann and I were childhood friends. We've managed to keep in touch all these years. In fact, we've seen them several times in recent years, whenever I've had to go to Vienna for a conference or Penelope has joined me for a holiday. Claudia is wonderful. Rather scatty, I think you would say, but enchanting. So we have to make room for them, cases of Johann's books, as much of their furniture as they can ship out and all of Claudia's fripperies. Their apartment on Wipplinger Strasse is enormous but as stuffed and cluttered as any Victorian parlour. It drives Johann mad. He was Bauhaus-trained, you see. Likes to keep things simple.' Leonard laughed.

'And why do they want to come to London?' Jack was puzzled.

'Don't you listen to anything, my dear boy? Don't you see? The last place they want to come to is London. They want to stay in their home, in their city, in their country. It is with the greatest reluctance that they leave Vienna and so

we must welcome them with special warmth. Things have
not been easy for them in Vienna recently and Johann fears
that they can only get worse. All those threatened – those, I
mean, with the wherewithal and the courage – are making
plans to leave. Claudia had been informed, you see, that her
work as an illustrator for one of the national newspapers
was no longer required and Johann's partners have been
excluding him from participating in a number of tenders for
large-scale community housing and factory projects towards
the East. They have both felt restricted and stifled. So I am
trying to find a proper permanent home for them here in
London. I think they can probably afford one of the mansion
flats in Bedford Avenue and I know of a lease which is about
to expire.'

Penelope was watching Jack's face. She knew that after
Leonard's comments about Tom her brother had only half
heard what Leonard had said about the Austrian couple. She
turned to her husband. 'He's not being dense, darling.' Then
she tipped her chin towards Jack. 'Very simple, Jack, and
very sad. Johann and Claudia are Jewish. They are coming
to us to escape.'

CHAPTER FOUR

'I can hardly believe it. You, Leonard, at last,' said Claudia.

'Neither can we, either of us. Been nearly three years now.' Penelope looked fondly at her husband. 'It wasn't that I'd become resigned to spinsterhood. I positively relished being by myself. Still faintly astonished by it. Marriage, I mean.' She patted her hair, almost skittishly.

'And you, too, were on the ledge, Leonard, until you met Penelope.'

He beamed at her. 'That's not quite the right idiom, Claudia, but pretty close. Also, and most unfairly now I come to think about it, it is only single women here who are said to be on the shelf.' Leonard picked up Penelope's hand. 'And I'm delighted that two of my oldest and dearest friends have now met my wife.'

'A pity the circumstances could not have been different,' began Johann, before drawing breath and brightening, 'but let us not dwell on such things tonight. We must have a toast. To friendship.'

'To friendship.' Four glasses clinked. The reds, ochres and umbers of the Golders' dining room were mellow. Candlelight flickered softly over dark, polished wood, over slightly sagging bookshelves and Leonard's collection of framed Spy cartoons. The table was littered with the lovely

48

detritus of dinner and petals from the tulips, which drooped like a corps of dying ballerinas from a low-cut glass vase. A faint cloud of scented cigar smoke floated above them, mingling with the last of the densely evocative smells of caraway, red cabbage and goose. Penelope had tried to help Min re-create as Central European a meal as ingredients available in the markets and shops of Soho could supply.

'Speaking of friends, my dear chap, do you ever see anything of that young man we met with you in Vienna all those years ago? Do you remember that Bauhaus seminar? There were such disagreements about form and function and the place, if any, of decoration in our new buildings?' Johann scraped through his memory and winced. In one way it was joyful to remember such times; in another it was agonizing. 'His name was Hugo, I believe. I thought he was rather brilliant.'

'If I remember correctly, *liebchen*, you were rather taken by his ravishing, captivating, brunette girlfriend as well.' Claudia smiled at Johann. The Golders exchanged glances and laughed simultaneously.

'Hugo? Yes, we see him quite often. You'll probably meet him one evening next week as he's coming to supper. And the "ravishing" girlfriend is now my sister-in-law.'

The Jacobses looked puzzled and Penelope said, 'Evangeline Eliott. Sister's married to my brother Jack, d'you see?' She went on to explain, tactfully and discreetly, how after Evangeline had declined Hugo's offer of marriage for the third or fourth time and had moved to Paris to preside over the Hôtel d'Eliott in the Rue du Faubourg Saint-Honoré in the early 1930s, they had rather lost touch with Hugo. 'And then he suddenly sprang this child bride on us. Sweet girl, awfully pretty. Name of Martina. Surprised you don't know her.

Slap, bang, wallop, and that was that. He seemed hell-bent on getting married, and between ourselves we both – that is Leonard and I – thought this was going to be a doomed what-the-hell-might-as-well sort of arrangement. At least they didn't waste too much of each other's time. Can you remember her last name, darling?' Penelope turned to Leonard.

'Schoenberg, was it? Something like that. Anyway, the marriage didn't even last a year. Poor girl had hardly any English and it must be said that Hugo made little effort to help her settle in. Can't really blame her for fleeing back to Mutti in Vienna. No real harm done. They're divorced now and both still young enough to make a fist of it with someone else. More coffee, anyone?'

'But recently we've been seeing him again. Still troubled. Still brilliant, too,' added Penelope.

'Do you think he still carries a candle . . .?'

'Carries a torch or holds a candle. No reason why you shouldn't be corrected about the ridiculous idioms of the English language, Claudia, if you're going to be here for any time.' Leonard immediately cursed himself for such tactlessness and Penelope called loudly for Min, then rescued him.

'For Evangeline? Yes, I'm certain he does.' She looked flustered and tucked a loosened iron-grey strand behind her ear. 'You will tell us if there's anything else you need, won't you? I do hope you will be comfortable here with us.'

Half an hour later Leonard and Penelope were in bed, he drafting a letter to the *Architects' Journal* in his neat, crabbed hand and she rereading the first chapter of Elizabeth Bowen's most recent novel. She set it down on the sheets. 'Leonard?'

'Yes.' The pencil flew, uninterrupted across the lined yellow legal pad.

'I was just thinking.'

Leonard set his pencil and pad aside. 'What?'

'Well, suppose we ask Evangeline here for supper next week, too? It would be perfectly logical. She knows Johann and Claudia. Might be nice.'

'It might be nicer if you didn't try to facilitate such crassly obvious match-making. If Hugo and Evie are going to stage a rapprochement they should be able to do so without artificial aids.' Leonard reflected for a few seconds. 'But I agree that it's silly that they don't even see each other occasionally as friends. Best, don't you think, if I call Hugo tomorrow and suggest that he calls Evie to see if he might bring her here that evening – you know, just offer a lift or something? Much better if the move comes from him. They are neither of them children, after all, and they'd both be rather angry if they felt that their meeting had been deliberately orchestrated by us.'

'Hardly ever saw my mother,' mumbled Penelope into the crook of Leonard's shoulder.

'What the hell are you talking about?'

'Saw a lot of Nanny, though. She used to say, "If you can't be good, be clever." Didn't know what she meant till I met you. Beastly man, you're both.' She beat his chest with her fists. Leonard folded his arms about her.

'Evangeline. Evie, is that you?'

'This is Evangeline Eliott, yes. Who is speaking, please?' Evie was in no doubt.

'It's Hugo. How have you been, Evie? Ages since I saw you.'

'Hundreds of years. And I've been fine, Hugo, busy. You know. How nice of you to call. Quite a surprise. Was there something . . .?' Her voice trailed off.

'No, nothing important, anyway. It's just that I was speaking to Leonard the other day and we fell to reminiscing about old times and it made me wonder if you'd like to have lunch. Thursday, perhaps.'

Evangeline tightened the sash of her robe. The very timbre of Hugo's voice evoked memories of times, years past, when she would have dissembled, cancelled, double-booked and parked the Alvis in a private square on the off-chance of spending twenty minutes with Hugo in the darkness or the trembling, frantic ecstasy of a hallway or her bedroom. 'I'm not sure. Let me just look in my diary.' It was on the table next to the phone. Lunch was arranged with Harriet Grainger. Her pencil was poised and ready to postpone it but she hesitated. 'Sorry, Hugo. Thursday's impossible. Some other day, perhaps? One day next week?'

'You can't make Friday?'

'Sorry, no,' she lied.

'When, then? Monday, Tuesday?'

'Hugo, I haven't seen you for nearly four years. Why does it have to be such a rush? We could have lunch next month.'

Hugo bristled. 'Do forgive me, Evangeline. I should explain. Leonard rather put me up to this. I know it's a bore but they have a couple of Viennese staying with them for the time being – do you remember Johann and Claudia Jacobs? – and Leonard and Penelope are trying to help them settle in. You met them with me, years ago. They just thought it would be nice for them to meet some familiar faces. That's all there is to it.'

'So why are we to have lunch?'

'Clearly we're not. But I did think we could play ourselves in that way. Avoid all the and-how-have-you-been nonsense on the evening of the supper. But it doesn't matter. You speak to Leonard or Penelope and I suppose I might see you there.'

'I'm free on Tuesday.'

Evangeline dressed and made up very carefully. In the four years since she had seen Hugo a little map of faint lines had appeared around her eyes and now that she was in her early thirties there was, she noted despairingly, a slight thickening about her waist even though her legs and ankles were as slender as ever and not even the most vicious critic could fault her jaw-line or shoulders. Old, troubling memories flooded through her mind as she bathed and rubbed frangipani oil into her elbows and over her knees. Why was she doing this? A silver-grey crêpe dress with a little bolero jacket hung waiting in her dressing room. The beading was jet and the tiny hat that went with the costume was tipped with an impertinent cockade of feathers and had a small veil which blew about her throat on breezy days. It was a merry widow's ensemble. She decided at the last minute to wear a severe navy wool suit, no jewellery, and to throw a neat little cape around her shoulders instead of the long, draped cloak, unexpectedly lined with scarlet, that looked so well with the silver grey. And now I look like a Salvation Army sergeant on her night off, she thought, too late to consider a third choice, as she left the mews house in Knightsbridge.

'You look wonderful,' said Hugo as, twenty minutes later, he rose to greet her in the small French restaurant in Sydney Street, deliberately chosen as somewhere they had never been together – neutral ground.

'And you look exactly the same.' This wasn't quite true. There were creases around Hugo's eyes that Evangeline did not remember and his face was even leaner. 'I remember that suit when it was new. Looks even better now.' It was tweed. Hugo was one of the few men who could get away with wearing tweeds in town. As always, the points of his collar turned slightly upwards. She felt a rush of the old tenderness and desire.

They asked and answered each other's shallow, stilted questions, addressed their menus in the silences and were relieved when the waiter came to take their order.

'Asparagus soup and blanquette de veau,' said Evangeline.

'Pâté . . . and the trout.'

When Hugo first mentioned his marriage Evangline felt a fierce stab of possessive jealousy. She wanted to know more yet she wanted to know nothing at all. Hugo felt the same about her brief sketch of the time she had spent in Paris after they parted. He had not realized how raw that wound remained – Evangeline's decision to run the Paris House rather than marry him. Superficial, uncontroversial exchanges of news and opinions sped to and fro across the table, neither Evangeline nor Hugo concentrating fully on the spoken words.

'It must be rather fun living in Pimlico. Quite a change from Marble Arch, I should think.' Why didn't I wear a hat with a veil, after all? Evangeline was thinking. I feel so old. 'And do your parents still have that lovely house by the river in Henley?' This is unbearable, it's impossible. If I was meeting him for the first time today I'd be flirting like mad. But it's impossible. He fell in love with someone else. People don't change. It's hopeless. You can't look back.

'Marvellous about Bea and Jack. I always thought that they'd make wonderful parents. Three nippers now, eh? Bet you're a perfect aunt.' Evangeline rewarded him with a grim smile. Damn, he thought to himself. Now she's going to think I mean that she's some sort of pathetic spinster creature who's invited to see her niece and nephews under sufferance. And damn again, why does she have to be prettier than ever? There was another pause. 'I'm hoping to go into partnership with someone called Spence. There's a chance we'll be asked to tender for one of the new university buildings in York.' She still has that habit of tilting her chin to the left and looking sideways under her lashes. It's adorable. It's impossible. Damn.

'York? How nice.' Evangeline glanced at her tiny watch. 'Good heavens, gone two already. I'm sorry, Hugo, but I really will have to fly soon. Could we have some coffee and—'

'Yes, of course. I'll ask for the bill at the same time.' Hugo braced himself. 'I'm sorry you're in such a rush, Evie, because we haven't really talked, have we?'

'Nonsense. Of course we have. Delicious catching up, and it's been awfully good to see you, Hugo, it really has. We absolutely mustn't leave it another four years.'

You know perfectly well what I mean, you wretched, graceless woman, thought Hugo. Well, two can play at that game. He leaned back in his chair after signing the chit. 'About that evening at Leonard and Penelope's . . .'

'Best not, don't you think?' answered Evangeline.

'Quite right. I agree. Best not.'

Five minutes later, on the pavement, they shook hands. A charge hesitated between them, each wishing to kiss the other, at least on the cheek. Instead their hands locked fractionally longer than might have been considered proper between chance acquaintances. 'Lovely lunch, Hugo, thank you. So good to see you again. You must come to one of my cocktail parties. I may be having another before Christmas.'

'I'd be delighted. Goodbye, Evangeline.' Hugo watched her back as she clipped down Sydney Street in her strapped shoes, their heels high and curved. The muscles in her calves moved beneath the sheen of the silk stockings and her back was long, straight and narrow. She climbed into her Alvis with a little wave of a suede-gloved hand and pulled away. Straight and narrow indeed, he thought. Then so be it. Damn you.

The Alvis kept stalling. Evangeline crashed the gears again. Ruddy, flaming, damned stupid car, she thought. Twice she took a wrong turn on her way to Mayfair and once she had to brake so sharply to avoid a nanny crossing the road with a pram that the Lanchester behind her almost brushed her mudguards.

'Idiot,' she called back to the innocent chauffeur at her tail. It was no good, she reflected as she waited for some lights to change, Hugo was the past. She did not deny the sexual frisson she had felt with him but neither could she pretend that he had shown any desire for her. Besides, if that's all there is to it, Evangeline told herself, there are any number of dishy young men in London. She glanced upwards to the rear-view mirror, saw to her horror that there was a tiny smear of asparagus soup on her chin, licked a finger and wiped it away. The lights changed and the Alvis lurched forward. No, the future was the thing. Perhaps she would think more carefully about what Viola had suggested. Sunshine, Hollywood, a break, a change. She pulled into the kerb outside the House of Eliott.

'Good afternoon, ladies,' she called as she entered the workroom. 'Doris, could I have a word with you in my office?'

'Of course, Miss Evie. Right away.' With disguised irritation Doris laid down the piece of nettle-green cloth she had been working on. Tailor's chalk had a tendency to rub away or fade fast, especially on the wrong side of velvet, and tacking the darts from mark to mark was an essential preliminary process which took skill and concentration. The Misses Eliott, she thought to herself, did not take kindly to being interrupted when they were in meetings or presiding over a fitting. They neither of them seemed to realize that down in the bee-hive similar respect was desirable for the requirements of delicate work. Doris chastized herself as she followed Evangeline upstairs: on the whole Miss Evie and Miss Bea weren't bad sorts. She knew plenty of other people who worked in real sweat-shops and never got a word of praise, let alone a decent wage.

Evangeline closed her door. 'I just wanted to ask you how you feel Connie is getting on.' Connie Taylor had joined the work-force about six weeks earlier. She had come from a factory near Brick Lane and was used to working fast but during her first two or three weeks had made a couple of mistakes in her machine-stitching. Evangeline had had to ask Doris to speak to her.

'Oh, Miss Evie, I think she's got the hang of it now. No

more blunders. No more wasted sleeve-lining cloth, I'm glad
to say. Seems funny, doesn't it, to have to ask someone to
slow down? More haste less speed, I suppose.'

'So none of you fear that she might be a passenger in the
workroom?'

'Heavens no, miss. She'll never be a specialist, if you
know what I mean – too impatient for fiddly things like
embroidery or appliqué – but a good little worker. Like a
demon on the straightforward stuff that some of the other
girls find a bit, well, dull. And she's a good sort. Always
cheerful and willing.'

'Good. I'd like her to stand in for one of Miss Nightingale's fittings tomorrow afternoon? I should say her measure-
ments are almost exactly the same and Miss Nightingale has
had to cancel an appointment even though she insists that
her dress be ready to collect on Friday.' Evangeline waited
and watched Doris's face for a reaction. 'And I'm sure it
wouldn't cause any disruption downstairs among the other
girls if she was used as a model in the final fittings.'

'Shouldn't think any of the others would want to have
pins stuck all over them, Miss Evie. Don't give it another
thought.'

'Excellent. Just what I wanted to hear. Would you send
Connie up to me, then? Thank you, Doris.'

Three minutes later Connie Taylor entered Evangeline's
office and the situation was explained to her.

'You mean I can put on Miss Nightingale's ballgown?
Me?'

'Yes, you, Connie. You must stand very still, pretend
you're a dummy, and you must make sure that you wear
clean underthings. It won't be very enjoyable, I'm afraid,
because you'll be tweaked and turned and possibly pricked

with pins and you won't be allowed to exclaim as Miss Nightingale would because her mama will be here. You must keep your mouth shut and act as if you are made of stone.'

'I don't mind, Miss Evie. If the ladies can put up with their fittings I'm sure I can.'

'That's settled, then. Tomorrow morning. You can go now, Connie. And thank you for being so co-operative.'

Something happened to Connie Taylor when Phyllis Nightingale's dress was slipped over her shoulders. It startled both Beatrice and Evangeline.

'Funny old turn this, eh?' Tilly had said to Connie as she led her into the fitting room, robed, as if for surgery, in a plain white cotton shift over her underwear. She smelled of carbolic soap and starch. The pink silk-satin dress was held carefully by Elsie who followed two steps behind.

'Thank you, Elsie. Leave the dress there, if you would.' Evangeline indicated the frame upon which the dress was to be draped. When Connie was in the dress little fragments of sartorial and cosmetic wisdom clashed in Evangeline's mind. Blue and green should never be seen, freckles should be bleached away with lemon juice, hair should be slick and neat . . . Connie could break every rule – she was magnificent, glorious.

In putting on the ballgown some of her thick red hair had broken loose from its pins. The long strands that curled away gave her a wanton look. Her skin was as white as marble and as smooth, her throat and chest freckled like a thrush's. The delicate pink of the cloth – according to all the fashion rules certain to be a disaster with Connie's colouring – gained the glow of dawn. Moreover, standing still as a statue, with chin lifted and shoulders braced, Connie acquired an extraordinary presence with the dress. Even Mrs Nightingale gasped. 'My goodness, Evangeline. This dress is a triumph. Phyllis certainly will be the belle of her ball.'

Evangeline nodded her thanks. She quickly slipped off her shoes, plain grey suede pumps. 'Connie, would you mind? We should see how the dress looks with proper slippers. I think you're about my size.' She turned ruefully towards Mrs Nightingale. 'Very much doubt if Phyllis plans to wear sensible lace-ups like Connie's when she wears the dress.'

'My dear, if she looks half as lovely in it I shan't care if she wears wellington boots.'

Connie obediently stepped into Evangeline's shoes and turned, bent, stretched and walked just as she was asked to. Before this fitting, Evangeline would have described the pink dress as pretty, more than serviceable, but less than inspired. Yet on Connie, standing and moving to order like a clock-work toy, it had come to life. The simplicity of the bias-cut bodice and the modesty of the high halter neckline contrasted with the deep plunge of the back and the rippling layers of unevenly cut chiffon that spread from a diagonal seam at the hip.

Evangeline tucked here and pinned there. 'This should be fine for Phyllis now, Mrs Nightingale. It'll be ready first thing on Friday.' She turned Connie round one last time and looked at the white back and the perfect architecture of her bones. 'This may sound crazy but I'd suggest that, instead of wearing any jewellery proper, Phyllis should have someone paste diamanté on to her skin here,' she indicated Connie's spine, 'or perhaps in a slanting line from her left shoulder to the bottom seam at her right hip.'

'I think that might be taking things a little too far, Miss Eliott, but I appreciate the advice. Thank you so much. A triumph. Phyllis will be thrilled.'

Connie came to life as soon as the door clicked shut behind Evangeline and Mrs Nightingale. 'Did I do all right, Miss Bea? I tried ever so hard to remember everything you said.'

'You did wonderfully, Connie. Thank you. You can get dressed now and go downstairs. Don't forget to change your shoes.'

Beatrice waited impatiently for her sister to return, and when she came in, said, 'What *did* you think of that?'

'Extraordinary. She's wasted downstairs.'

'Are you thinking what I'm thinking?'

Evangeline nodded. 'It's the natural thing to do. We've been talking about getting a house model for months.'

'How can you do this to me now? *Now*, of all times.' Beatrice's eyes were blazing. The tip of her nose was reddening. Evangeline forced herself to remain calm.

'What do you mean by "of all times"? We're always in one crisis or another. And we always weather them.'

'That's so typically selfish of you, Evangeline. What do you know of anything, of responsibilities? I suppose your flighty way of life prevents you from understanding. Wait till *you* have an absentee husband and a child who is losing his sight. Then see if you can run away.'

Evangeline stiffened. She had been expecting something like this. 'But, Bea, I haven't got a husband. Or any children. Don't you see that's part of the reason why I have to go? I'm devoted to Jack, I love Tom dearly and', she threw back her head to drain away tears in a gesture that Beatrice mistook for defiance, 'you're my sister and I'll love you completely and for ever, but', Evangeline steeled herself, 'I have to go. It's time for my life to start again. Not ours, mine.'

CHAPTER FIVE

'Our Connie's a marvel, isn't she?' Beryl was watching the smoothly seamed legs climb the stairs from the workroom for an unexpected call of duty in the fitting room. 'One minute she's having a laugh down here with the rest of us and next thing she can switch to being a mannequin like a proper lady. And do you know, she stayed on for nearly two hours the other night to help Bronya sort out some muddle she'd got herself into with that green linen suit for Lady Pamela – even though it made her late for her meeting with that posh new chap of hers.'

'Shouldn't wonder if I couldn't do the same for the extra bunce she's getting. Wonder how much lolly they pay her for swishing and swanking about?' Doris mumbled sulkily. She had changed her tune about Connie somewhat since realizing that the fitting for Phyllis Nightingale's dress wasn't going to be the only one. There was a silence and one or two stifled giggles but everyone forbore from pointing out that Doris, with her heavy frame and flat feet, would scarcely be offered the opportunity.

'Rather less than you might think, Doris.' Marjorie Palmer had stepped into the bee-hive. 'And there's little swishing to it and no swanking at all. I doubt if you'd enjoy having to stand stock still and freezing cold, keeping quiet while pins are being stuck into you until you have to take off the lovely clothes and get back into everyday overalls. Must be like being Cinderella every day. Think about it.'

Doris thought. 'I suppose so, but I still don't understand why the Misses Eliott decided they needed someone to model the clothes at fittings like that.'

'I do – at least, I think I do,' said Elsie. 'Once when I was up there, tidying up, Miss Bea and Miss Evie were talking. They said that fitting the clothes on a real body made them come alive, "Gives them expression," Miss Bea said. And then Miss Evie said something about creating an illusion – that's the words she used – for the lumpen daughters of the shires.'

'You mean all the fat Fionas think they're going to look just like Connie when their dress is ready? Fat chance,' Beryl shrieked.

'That's part of it, yes,' said Marjorie. 'And that will do, ladies. To work, if you please.'

'You mustn't blame Evie, Bea.' Jack was away on location and as it was the cook's night off Cyril had offered to come round and prepare supper. Beatrice had expected the usual bachelor's 'cooking' – smoked salmon and slices of game pie bought from Jackson's – and most appreciative she would have been, too, but Cyril had surprised her by bringing all the makings of a shepherd's pie and cabinet pudding. 'My mother's recipes. What's the point of eating restaurant food at home? These are the real treats, don't you think?'

She took a forkful of shepherd's pie. 'What in heaven is that extraordinary flavour?'

'The oregano, probably.' Cyril had brought back seeds from a recent holiday in Greece and was nursing the herbs in his conservatory. He replenished their glasses with an iced, sharp, pine-flavoured wine that Beatrice had not tasted before. 'About Evie, Bea. You must allow an old woman to give you advice and try to make some allowances yourself. Evie's had rather a ghastly time these last few years, hasn't she? It wasn't her fault, but she takes the blame for it all going wrong in Paris for a start.'

'I've told her often enough that she shouldn't.'

'Doesn't matter. Doesn't make any difference. Guilt seeks culpability just as water will find its own level. Then she thought it was all her fault when you didn't get Princess Posh's wedding tackle. The endless unsuitable men . . . I did have some hopes of Cameron but these days he's so publicly brisk with her that I want to slap him.'

'I'd noticed that too. He's almost rude. I'm surprised she takes it.'

'She takes it because she's not strong enough at the moment to invite confrontation.' Cyril waited for Bea to finish. 'The only unqualified success she's enjoyed recently has been her work on Viola's costumes. *Nell Gwynne* was a pretty awful film but everyone said how sensational Viola looked in it and that's probably why she's been scooped up by those studios in Hollywood.'

'And that's partly because of Evie's work?'

'Of course. It was a personal triumph for Evie – her first. It's not surprising that she wants to go down that road, at least for a little while. Besides, she and Viola are such friends now. I think they need each other, too.'

'I understand all of that, Cyril, but I still can't help thinking that she should be here with me now. I blessed her when she ran away before, wished her every last tiny bit of luck in Paris. I'm afraid I don't feel so generous this time. We're so busy,' Beatrice sipped and paused. 'And I'm so worried about Tom.'

'Evie's not to blame for Tom's eyes, Bea. No one is. Don't make her carry that particular can. Don't carry it yourself.' Cyril took her wrist and kissed it, just above her bracelet. 'Don't you think you should wave Evie off with a hug and a smile and an open return ticket instead of one of your cross little frowns?'

Beatrice looked up gravely. 'Yes, Cyril, I do. You're almost always right about these things, aren't you? But I will miss her most painfully,' she sighed.

'This girl has really got something. Who is she?' Priscilla Dawlish narrowed her eyes and tilted some of the prints from Cyril's latest session this way and that. 'Of course, she has the advantage of knowing the Eliott sisters' clothes well, after all these months. Understanding them, I mean, wearing them instinctively, not allowing the clothes to wear her as so many of the other model girls do.' She laid the pictures down and turned again to Cyril. 'I asked you a question, Cyril. Who is she?'

'Name of Connie Taylor. Used to work for the girls as a seamstress. Now spends virtually all her time upstairs. Nice girl, quite simple and unspoilt despite the look of *hauteur* that she can assume.'

Priscilla clapped her hands. 'I love it. I just adore it. This is *Pygmalion*. This is *The Green Hat*. Beatrice and Evangeline deserve full credit for discovering this treasure, but between us we can create her, really launch her.' A faint sheen of perspiration was breaking through Priscilla's *maquillage*.

The late summer of 1937 had become unexpectedly warm. She reached for the phone and asked to be put through to the Paris office. 'I shall insist that Louis comes personally to the Eliotts' next collection. That girl is wasted in a London house. However clever the clothes are, there is still something, sometimes, a little parochial about them. So much emphasis on clothes for dowagers and dowdy daughters, I suppose. It's amazing how many of the really elegant women still prefer to dress in Paris. Anyway, this Connie, she may need a little grooming yet, but between us we are going to make her.' She placed another cigarette in the ivory holder and inhaled. 'Model girls, you see, Cyril, will become the new stars, the new icons. Just you mark my words.'

'Constance Travis,' said Connie a few weeks later when Louis d'Abville asked her to dinner. 'My name is Constance Travis. Please don't call me Connie.'

Fluent though his English was, Louis was unable to detect Connie's slightly elocuted vowels, or identify some of her more colourful London idioms. They were dining at the Coq d'Or in Stratton Street. 'Do you remember my friend Pierre, from Lanvin? You were introduced to him at that little party we gave at the Connaught after the collections.'

'Of course. A charming man.'

'Quite. Pierre would like you to work for him in Paris. Do you think Mesdemoiselles Eliott would lend you out for a season or two? This is a delicate matter, I realize. Should I make the approach? Should Pierre? Should you?'

'You've got quite a nerve, Monsieur, to assume right away that I want to go to Paris. Don't I have some say in it?' Connie laid down her spoon. She could eat mounds of whipped cream and slabs of chocolate marquise the size of small paving stones without her figure suffering.

'A nerve?' Louis thought for a moment. 'I think this means courage or, perhaps, impertinence? Yes, I have got a nerve. My apologies, Miss Travis.' Louis was relieved to see Connie's face break into a wide, unrestrained smile that displayed strong white teeth. It was refreshing, enchanting, Louis thought, to see a beautiful woman smile like that. More usually they offered a narrow simper and a glimpse of predatory little rat's fangs. Connie's skin glowed in the pinkish light shed by the little lamp on their table, and her oyster-coloured satin dress fell in dark, heavily shifting folds about her shoulders and breasts. Priscilla was right, he thought. This one is a pearl. 'So would you like to come to Paris, Miss Travis? I can make arrangements for your accommodation, of course.'

Connie smiled a little more dreamily. 'Paris? Yes, I should like to spend some time there. I've often thought about it. I never really knew my mother – she died when I was a baby, you see – but she was French.'

'I knew it! Where did she come from? Which region?'

'Whitechapel. Her family were weavers, had been for generations since the first lot came over with the Huguenots. I think those families stuck pretty tightly together, around Elder and Fournier Streets, mostly. There was quite a rumpus, apparently, when she wanted to marry my dad. They'd met through the rag trade. But she was French, all right.' Connie forgot for a moment to mask her humble social background, but for Louis, Whitechapel had exactly the same ring as Whitehall and to be a weaver was no disgrace. Had not Jean Patou's father been a tanner?

'So it is settled, then. And who will tell the Mam'selles?'
'I will.'

In some ways breaking the news to Beatrice and Evangeline
was not as difficult as Connie had feared. Evangeline looked
positively relieved. Although she had her own plans to leave
London for several months she was uneasy with the thought
of Connie being around in her absence. She knew it was
illogical, dog-in-the-manger and unworthy, but ever since
she had heard the rumour of Hugo's flirtation (some said
fling) with Connie, Evangeline had felt ambivalent pangs of
jealousy whenever she saw Connie's flawless young skin and
faultless figure. Once, when she had noticed a tiny bruise
low on Connie's neck she had wanted to slap her and felt
ashamed. Two or three times she had heard giggles and
shrieks in the workroom as she descended the stairs, noises
which had abruptly ceased as she appeared in the doorway.
Each time Connie had reddened and looked downwards.
Once, in a cinema, she had been almost certain that a
couple, shoulder to shoulder a few rows ahead of her, had
been Hugo and Connie. She would recognize the shape of
Hugo's half-slump anywhere, and she did not stay to watch
the end of the film. They might, she had supposed, have met
at one of those parties to which Connie was increasingly
often invited, her gloriously beautiful presence by now
considered by some hostesses to be something of a *coup*.
Evangeline finished, 'It's a wonderful opportunity, Connie.
Just don't forget us and come back safely. We'll manage
somehow.'

'Yes, of course you must go, Connie. You'll learn so

much. And if you do want to come back to the House of Eliott in a couple of seasons we'll be delighted. Except you'll probably be too grand for us by then.' Beatrice spoke with amused warmth.

Connie almost cried. 'You're both being such toffs about this. You've taught me everything. I feel so ungrateful.'

'Nonsense,' said Beatrice. 'Life doesn't offer many chances like this. They must be seized.' She hesitated. 'Is your father happy about it? Will you stay with relatives? Didn't you tell me that your mother was French?'

Connie seemed uncomfortable. 'Dad thinks modelling is one step away from the street. I can't stay with relatives because there aren't any that I know of, but I didn't dare tell him that Monsieur d'Abville has found rooms for me. He'd think I was a kept woman. He doesn't even know that I'm Constance Travis now – he'd think I was ashamed of him or something.' She looked even more miserable, twisting her fingers.

'So what *have* you told him?' Beatrice was alarmed. She felt a sense of protectiveness and responsibility towards the girl.

'Oh, I think it'll be all right,' Connie blew her nose and brightened. 'Only a white lie, really. He knows the House of Eliott had a branch in Paris. Don't think he's ever twigged that you closed it down long before I started here. I've not exactly told him but rather let him understand that I'll still be working for you and I've promised to write to him every week.'

Beatrice was uneasy. 'I don't much like the sound of that, Connie, but you've reached the age of consent, and it's your business, not ours. Even so I think it would be better if you were honest with him.'

White lies. Always the most dangerous ones, mused Evangeline as Connie left the room.

Beatrice watched sadly as her sister folded the slippery silk of the dove-grey peignoir and laid the final sheets of tissue paper over it before closing the lid of the last and smallest trunk. The other two, her hat-boxes and her little calf travelling case were already waiting downstairs.

Evangeline looked up and saw her sister arch her back, hands pressed into the small. 'Are you sure you want to come?' she asked. 'Goodbyes are awful. I'll be perfectly all right by myself.'

'How can I want to come when I don't want you to go? But I wouldn't think of not sending you off. Besides, I'm getting horribly used to farewells and partings, what with Jack going away nearly every week, and even Connie going was a strain. You're only my sister – it'll be a breeze.' Beatrice sniffed and began to cry again.

Evangeline rushed to her and put her arms round her shoulders. 'Look at it the other way, Bea. Think of all the welcomings and homecomings. Think of how you feel when you hear Jack's key in the door every time he returns. I've seen your face light up.' She hugged Beatrice more tightly. 'It's only for a few months and they do have the telephone in California, you know.' Evangeline grappled for more words of comfort. 'Molly will take care of everything at home, and you know that Cyril is your slave, social and otherwise. And', she added, 'the way we've been working recently, the next collection is as good as finalized. I'll be working on the one after that from California and I'll send all my ideas and sketches back. Connie's a tough act to follow but Dagmar, or whatever it is that Deirdre calls herself now, will be wonderful. She's got just the right Nordic ice for the times, even if one does not particularly care for her. You can't like everyone, Bea. Sometimes relationships just have to be purely professional.' After Connie went to Paris the sisters had appointed a rangey blonde from Dagenham as their house model. The fact that Deirdre was splendid until she opened her mouth had nothing to do with her Essex accent but, as Beatrice and Evangeline agreed, the girl was paid to pose and to show off their clothes, not to be an agreeable conversationalist. It was a pity, however, that the women downstairs found Dagmar equally disagreeable. 'Anyway, you've got enough good friends to keep you going. And the family. It'll be all right, I promise.'

Beatrice could not repress a contemptuous laugh. 'Dagmar, indeed. Somehow I never regarded it as pretentious when Connie became Constance. I suppose we already knew her as the sweet warm soul she is. But Deirdre becoming Dagmar and brooding about as if she were Miss Garbo is almost comical. Do you know,' she looked up at Evangeline with a glint in her eye, 'downstairs they refer to her as "Dagenhamar". But Evangeline's reference to the family swiftly caught up with her and Beatrice's eyes filled with tears again, just as Evangeline had dreaded. 'Poor little Tom. Did I tell you they are talking about surgery?'

'Yes, Bea, you did. And I know you'll keep me posted—' Evangeline was spared further discussion of Tom when her doorbell chimed. 'That'll be the cab. I'll get the driver to take this last trunk downstairs. Chin up, Bea.'

The cab wove through the late-morning traffic and arrived at Waterloo in good time for Evangeline to oversee her luggage unloaded into the boat train. The *Normandie* was due to sail at four. The sisters were uncharacteristically silent in their first-class compartment as the train hurtled through Reading, Basingstoke, Petersfield and Lyndhurst on its way to Southampton. Evie carried a small leather vanity case and an oxblood clutch purse, made to match her shoes, which exactly echoed the deep brownish red velvet of the tiny Juliet cap that was shaped snugly to her crown. As the train began to lose speed Beatrice opened her more capacious bag and handed Evangeline a small parcel, wrapped in stiff vellum. 'For the voyage, my dearest Evie.'

The little box was made of white cardboard. It had corrugated sides and a shallow lid which fitted tightly over the rim. Inside Evangeline found a mass of tiny blue pills. 'For seasickness,' explained Beatrice with a brief smile. The pills were packed too tightly to rattle for nestling in their midst was an even smaller parcel, wrapped in a fragment of gold silk. It contained an oval locket on a chain, engraved on one side with an exquisitely worked bee and on the other with the date. Inside was a single, perfectly pressed forget-me-not. Evangeline could not speak. After a minute she looked up, her eyes round and wet. 'Do you remember, Bea, how when we were children – or rather when I was a child and you had to play with me,' she gulped, 'Molly used to retrieve boxes like this from Father's litter basket? We used to make dolls' hats out of them? Now, there's an idea . . .' She tried to smile but broke down and let the tears flow freely.

Beatrice leaned across the carriage and took both her sister's hands, not crying now but Evangeline's support and solace once again.

*

The sisters were almost the last to leave the train, both composed at last, make-up repaired and hats straightened. As a result they avoided most of the boarding crush and were being led to Evangeline's cabin within twenty minutes. The steward assured them that Miss Eliott's luggage would be dealt with, her larger trunks stowed and the small one, together with the little calf case, waiting for her in her stateroom. The *Normandie* was a magnificent ship, fitted with care and style. She reminded both Beatrice and Evangeline of the Savoy Hotel. Both gasped when they were shown into Evangeline's stateroom. Not because of its opulence and size, or the banks of flowers massed around the room, or at the sight of champagne chilling in a silver bucket and of the dozens of telegrams. They gasped because Jack was there, with Cyril.

The four drank champagne and decided not to lunch in the restaurant, preferring to order from the steward smoked salmon, caviar and perfect, tiny cheese gougères which presaged the extraordinary culinary standards of the *Normandie*'s kitchens. As the second bottle was finished, Evangeline's steward knocked politely and said that those not sailing would have to vacate the ship within twenty minutes. Their easy conversation faltered. Beatrice's joy at the unexpected delight of seeing Jack and gratitude for Cyril's presence turned once again to pain. Evangeline, like Jack, caught the stricken look on her sister's face.

'Look after her, won't you?' She tried to give Jack a champagne smile. 'Both of you look after her, d'you hear?' She took Cyril's hand. 'And be off with you now. You've got a train to catch.'

'We'll wait till the last minute, Evie, and then you can wave from the deck like they do in the pictures.'

'You'll go now. I can't stand these protracted farewells. I can't tell you how happy I am that you three have seen me off, but it's better if you go now.' Evangeline was pacing herself. She knew she could only last another minute or two before collapsing in tears again. She hugged them all and bundled them out of her stateroom, leaning against the door when they had gone and breathing the scent of freesias and roses.

'I wonder who will look after *her*,' murmured Cyril as they walked down the gangplank.

Evangeline had intended to wave goodbye from the deck and spent the next few minutes leafing through her cables, waiting until it was time to merge with the crush and jostle of other first-class passengers for a last call, a last smile and a last mouthed message. But just as the low, slow blow of the funnel signalled the first, almost imperceptible sliding of the *Normandie* from her mooring she read her final telegram.

MY LOVE TO YOU EVIE HERE THERE AND EVERY-
WHERE AND ALWAYS AND NO STOPS IN THIS CABLE
HUGO.

CHAPTER SIX

There was a light thud, a rustle and a clatter.

'It's my turn,' said Beatrice. Neither she nor Jack had ever lost the sense of excitement and anticipation that a child feels upon the arrival of the post. For children, who seldom receive letters or packages, unless from absent parents or for an imminent birthday, envelopes and parcels exemplify the thrilling, longed-for state of being grown-up. She tightened the sash about her waist and hastened to gather the scatter of mail from the tiles in the outer hall. Those which were clearly bills she put aside on a small table near the umbrella stand but brought into the breakfast room a small sheaf of others. 'A nice little cache this morning,' she said, leafing through them. 'These are for you,' she passed Jack a small handful and, with delight, 'this looks like one from Evie, another from France, and, Jack, there's a card from Leonard and Penelope. They must have sent this from Greece weeks ago.' Beatrice poured more coffee and buttered another slice of toast, luxuriously prolonging the morning ritual.

Breakfast, these days, was often the sweetest, most intimate time in their day. Sometimes, under the table, Beatrice would warm her feet in the fur-lined leather slippers Jack always kicked off when he sat down. Then, when he was ready to rise, he would find her narrow foot and affectionately eject it. 'We may not hold hands any more, Bea, like soppy young spooners, but at least we—'

'Rub along. Fit each other like soft old shoes.' Her tone, too, was light. Neither Beatrice nor Jack often cared to admit to themselves, let alone confront the other with, the vaguely troubling fact that the crackling fire had softened to a quieter glow. Perhaps, each thought privately, all marriages are like that. Perhaps we are lucky to have retained even this. There was, however, a rare, special intimacy this morning: Jack had driven up from Bristol the afternoon before even though he was due in Cardiff for lunch today with some trade union official for his film, having quite forgotten that Molly had taken the children to see her sister in Bognor Regis. Beatrice was startled and delighted to find him at home. They had dined early at the Ivy and retired before ten, slept late and woken starving. The night before, Beatrice had asked the cook to prepare kedgeree, Jack's favourite breakfast. 'Eat it up. You've a long drive ahead and little prospect of much more than a sausage roll and a curly sandwich when you get to Cardiff.' She looked at him over the rims of the metal half-frames she had to wear for reading these days, setting down her own letters. He was still a handsome man, she thought. A little grey here and there, a little more lined perhaps, but still curiously boyish. His eyes were creased in amusement. 'Something interesting in your post?' she asked.

'This one from Mother. It's killing.' He pushed the sheets of cream writing paper across the table. 'She's a pacifist, a socialist, a Fabian, a vegetarian, for all I know a Keynesian and an agnostic but she's also a tremendous gossip. She's really rather wicked, the way she describes some weekend they've just spent in Oxfordshire – ghastly modern expressionistic dancing, or posing as she calls it, pale young men and raddled old women getting into huddles and talking about curtains.'

'That'll be Syrie and Guy, I expect. I'll read it all later, if I may, but I'm saving this one from Evie till last. You can read it now if you like.'

Jack glanced at his watch. 'Bea, darling, I can't. I must dress and make some telephone calls and fly if I'm to hit the valleys on time.' He rose and kissed the top of her tousled auburn head. 'Will you still be here when I leave?'

'I doubt it, Jack. I'm beastly late already.' She pocketed the rest of her post. 'I'll read Evie's and then leave too.' Beatrice got up and rested her head in the crook of Jack's shoulder, sniffed him and tightened her arms.

'It won't be long this time, darling. I'll be back for dinner on Friday. The children will be home, won't they? Perhaps we'll all go to Lyons, and then to the cinema on Saturday afternoon. What do you think?'

'Marvellous idea. And perhaps we'll find some time to talk about—'

'About Tom? Yes, Beatrice, we must.'

Beatrice placed Evie's hastily scanned letter in her bag but didn't find time to reread it until the late afternoon. It was always the same when she allowed herself to be a little late in the morning, she reflected. In her absence one kind of hell or another would invariably break loose. She stifled a grudging half-thought that Evangeline's absence didn't make things any easier. This time there was a catfight in the workroom followed by Marjorie Palmer's recommendation of the dismissal of both squabbling parties. A bolt of urgently need vicuna wool – quite the wrong colour – had been delivered by one of their more reliable suppliers and Pamela Inverness changed her mind three times about the sleeves of her dinner dress during the course of one fitting. She was also unforgivably rude to Dagmar, treating her as if she was made of wood and comparing her loudly and unfavourably with Connie.

'You must try to ignore that sort of thing, Dagmar. They don't—'

'Don't say they don't mean to be rude, Miss Beatrice. And please don't say they don't know any better, either. But don't worry about it. Sticks and stones, you know . . .'

Beatrice was discomforted. 'Thank you for understanding, Dagmar.'

Dagmar replied with a directness that bordered upon disrespect. 'Oh, I understand all right, Miss Beatrice. But understanding isn't always the same as forgiving, is it?' Dagmar buttoned up her own dress and stepped into her boat-like, stretched old shoes. Beatrice had often noticed how even the best mannequins frequently had calloused and bunioned feet. It must be all that standing around in ill-fitting shoes designed for mincing and dancing and posing indoors, not for running for a tram or waiting for one in the rain. She watched Dagmar leave the room, asked for some tea to be sent up and instructed Tilly to take messages rather than put calls through to her. She heaved a sigh and knew she would have to be back on duty before long but for a blissfully peaceful twenty minutes she would catch up with Evie's news.

'My Dearest Bea' . . . Beatrice could not resist again scanning through the eight sides of paper, thin as gossamer and almost as transparent. The new air mail service was certainly a wonder: Evie had dated this less than a week ago

– her earlier letters had been sent by sea mail and had sometimes taken nearly a month to reach London. Certain names jumped off the paper – Viola's, of course, Shirley, Mr Selznick, James . . . *James?* She took a sip of tea and forced herself to return to the top of the first page, to read slowly, to savour.

Evangeline was still missing London, the family and all her friends like mad, she wrote. Like hell you are, thought Beatrice with a rueful smile as she went on to read of how her sister's time was taken up. She and Viola had been sharing a little house in a place called Laurel Canyon, which Beatrice had always thought rather a pretty name for a surburb. Pausing for a moment, she reflected that an American might think the same of many a London suburb, from Child's Hill to Brook Green . . . But Viola's English actor friend, increasingly celebrated in Hollywood, had an apartment in some complex nearer to the centre of Hollywood and she spent most of her time there so Evangeline was often alone. Beatrice frowned, not just at the idea of her sister's solitude and, perhaps, loneliness but at the very idea of people living somewhere called the Garden of Allah. It sounded like some sort of louche camping site.

But you're not to worry, Bea. I still love it here. I'm so exhausted most evenings that it's wonderful to get back to our little house. You've no idea how beautiful the night skies are. I sit out most evenings and watch the stars – the real ones, I mean. And then in the morning the light is blinding. It's clear, it's pure and it's divinely warm. I'd forgotten how wonderful it is to feel heat on the skin. The neighbours look after me and allow me to use their swimming-pool. You'd be surprised how many people out

here have them. The water never gets really cold. I'm up
to twelve lengths every morning.

She wrote of work at the studio, of Viola's costumes, of
parties and press agents, of huge cars and the absolute plenty
of life there.

Honestly, Bea, I don't know what a Californian would
think if they asked for a beef sandwich in London. They'd
think some sort of mistake had been made. Here you can
hardly open your mouth wide enough to take a bite. And
the sandwich will sometimes come with a great field of
salad and chips, as they call potato crisps over here. And
there are restaurants which sell Chinese food. Imagine! It's
bitty and spiced and delicious. That's why I need to swim
every day – at this rate I'd be grotesque if I didn't.

She wrote again of an enchantingly pretty child, Shirley, who
had been very successful in a number of recent films, and of
her mother.

Bea, you would have laughed. I nearly had an accident.
This mama had got the idea that because I'm English I
must, obviously, know the Royal Family. She said she
wanted her little Shirley to look just like Princess Elizabeth
– they are almost twins, you know. At least, only a few
months' age difference. Anyway, I agreed to ask you about
making the poor little brat some coats and dresses.
Sketches coming separately. See what you think. Daft, isn't
it? Little Shirley would be much more comfortable in this
climate in the sort of sun-dresses that we used to wear.
Do you remember that one lovely holiday we had with
Nanny's family in Shanklin?

Bea read on, happy that her sister seemed so exuberant but missing her with increasing, almost palpable pain at every paragraph.

> I've been taken out to dinner quite often. American men aren't all gangsters, you know. I was a bit disappointed!!! They're all safe in taxis and unnervingly courteous. There's one, an actor called James, who has asked me to spend a weekend with him at his house on the beach at Malibu. Don't worry, Bea dearest, his housekeeper will chaperone. But truthfully things. here in *that* department are much more relaxed than they are in London. Practically everyone I've met has been divorced at least twice. Viola, for example, could never attend functions with you-know-who as freely in London as she does here ...

The letter concluded with enquiries about the children, Jack, Beatrice herself and various friends. Evangeline asked about business, clients, the girls in the workroom, Connie. Lastly she asked Beatrice if there was any news of Hugo.

> He did send me that very sweet wire before I left, as I told you, Bea. And despite myself and my better judgement I dropped him a line when I got here. But I haven't had a reply. Never mind.

She went on to mention some of the films she had seen. Beatrice laid the letter down and finished her tea. Oh, Evie, she thought, how I wish you were here with me now. But you deserve, so richly, a time of freedom and self-indulgence. She braced her shoulders. And make the most of it while you can because I'm sure all our worlds are going to change before long.

Beatrice's reflective mood was disturbed by a light tap at

the door. It was Tilly. 'Sorry to bother you, Miss Bea, but Lady Blanche and her mother arrived a minute ago. Are you ready for them? Shall I fetch Dagmar?'

'Of course, Tilly. Show them up and tell Dagmar to stand by.' Beatrice put her sister's letter in the drawer where she kept her compact. She powdered her nose, dabbed at her eyes and applied a lick of rouge. The door opened and she rose, hand extended, her eyes and smile bright. 'Countess. Lady Blanche. How good to see you. May I offer you some tea?'

Cyril settled Beatrice's stole around her shoulders. 'Are you sure Jack doesn't mind about this sort of thing?' A taxi, its engine running, was waiting for them at the kerb outside the Maddoxes' house in Upper Brook Street. It was early summer and the street lights had only just come on.

'Heavens, no. If anything he's relieved. He likes the idea of me being occupied and amused while he's away.'

'And perfectly safe?'

'If you say so, Cyril.' Beatrice patted his hand. 'You know by now that Jack dislikes, almost despises, this sort of function – all trivia and gossip, he says. And all gossip is malice, he maintains.'

'But where would we be without it, my dear?'

Beatrice deliberately misunderstood Cyril's question. 'That's exactly what I've tried to explain to Jack. While I'm doing smiley-smiley and offering my most tinkling laugh to the most odious bores I am really working. It's essential for the business that I'm seen – and seen to be well connected at that. And I can't tell you how often Lady Muck or the

Dowager Dull has made an appointment the very next day for a dress "rather like the one you wore at the Shallow-Tediouses' last night".'

Cyril laughed. 'Rare for you to be humorous, Beatrice. You should try it more often.'

Only slightly piqued, she smoothed the finely pleated bronze silk of her gown and checked that beneath the fox wrap the narrow silk bands that criss-crossed its bodice to create a Grecian impression were firmly in place. 'Didn't really want to have these stitched down. Against the spirit of the dress somehow, but slippery silk just tied against slippery silk was a disaster. It looked like my nightie after five minutes.'

'You – and the dress – look divine, my dear Beatrice, as I said when I collected you. You have no need to fish.'

'Sorry, Cyril. It's just that I can barely talk about my work with Jack any more. He finds it so unimportant compared to his. And what with Evie being away I need a sounding board . . .' Her voice faded and faltered.

'And I suppose there's no small talk in Jack's world? No subtle ways of opening doors that are important to him? No guile? No murmuring in corners and clubs? No, it's all big talk where he's concerned, isn't it?' Even in the dim light of the car Cyril could see Beatrice's features set into a loyal frown. She withdrew her hand from his arm. 'My turn to say sorry now, Bea. It's just that I'm irritated when people dismiss our work as valueless, or decadent. What's wrong with helping to make people make the best of themselves? So what if they usually happen to be rich? It can be inspiring and helpful to everyone.'

Beatrice smiled at him wanly. 'The trouble is, Cyril, that sometimes I think Jack's right.' The cab pulled to a stop outside a tall, stuccoed house in Eaton Square. 'Look, we're here. Chins up. Here's to fawning and flattery.'

'I wonder if she saw her. Maybe they even spoke,' Beryl said excitedly. 'I heard the Countess tell Miss Bea to be sure to arrive early last night, before Him, she said. And then she gave a little cough and lifted her eyebrows. Didn't say anything, mind. Does she think the likes of us are idiots, or what?' Beryl ran her finger down the newspaper columns, silently mouthing some of the words. She called out in triumph to those other members of the House of Eliott work-force who shared her interest in matters aristocratic. 'Yes. Here it is. He *was* at the Countess's. Blimey. Miss Bea might even have danced with him.' Beryl was much taken with one of the Scandinavian crown princes, currently visiting his British cousins.

'I don't think so, Beryl. They only dance at balls, I think, and this was – what? – a reception.' Elsie was bending over Beryl's shoulder. 'Still, if that fiancée of his was there she might have talked to Miss Bea,' she straightened and clasped her hands before her, 'and maybe we'll be making her dresses soon.'

'From what one hears, that is most unlikely – as you would realize, Beryl, if you made a proper study of the news. The lady in question is no longer in the country.' Marjorie Palmer had affected her briskest voice. 'Now, may I point out that you are all here to work and not to idle in gossip about personages whose private lives are no concern of yours.'

'Silly cow,' muttered Beryl as she stuffed her newspaper in the waste paper basket.

*

Upstairs Beatrice was trying to telephone Cardiff. When she eventually got through, the line was terrible. 'Jack, can you hear me? Ah, that's better. I'm sorry to interrupt you, darling, but it's just that Leonard and Penelope have asked us over to supper on Sunday and they need an answer today as they're going off to some hiking centre for a couple of days tomorrow . . . No, rambling, they call it. Why are you laughing?'

'Rather them than me, that's all, Bea. I've met some of their fresh-air fiends and, yes, they can certainly ramble.'

Bea was bemused but did not ask Jack for clarification. These lines had a habit of breaking down or suddenly fading. 'Well, will you still be in London on Sunday evening or will you have to have left by then?'

'I have to be in Scotland first thing Monday. But, let me think, I suppose I could take the night sleeper from King's Cross. It leaves at midnight and I can get to the station directly from Gower Street. So, yes, why not? It's been far too long since the four of us spent any real time together – time without the little blighters, I mean, so that we can talk properly.'

'Yes,' answered Beatrice slowly. She preferred family lunches with the children even though they sat in awed silence at the table and only broke into brief giggles when Leonard told them a short, funny story. Their presence, however, limited opportunities for serious conversation or the intellectually intense debates that invariably developed when the little ones were absent. 'Yes. Well, I'll tell Penelope to expect us, then. Good.'

'Must go now, Bea. Love to you all. See you on Friday evening.' He rang off before she had time to reply.

Beatrice paused for a minute or two in rueful thought. It

wasn't just that Jack avoided some aspects of her world – she, after all, was just as guilty of that as he. Quite often, recently, she had made excuses and not joined him on visits to Leonard and Penelope or to joyless, forbiddingly serious socialist friends. When they did make jokes, she didn't understand them. Neither of them had aired the issue but Beatrice felt certain that Jack sensed as keenly as she that in some aspects of their marriage they were leading increasingly, alarmingly separate lives. So it was excellent, she thought, that they should see Penelope and Leonard together on Sunday. It occurred to her that the Golders might have invited other people: if so, cultured they would certainly be but also rampantly political. However, she felt this was unlikely from the way in which Penelope had issued the invitation. In any case, she could always try to steer her in-laws into an account of their spring holiday in Greece and the Balkans. Knowing Leonard there would be sheaves of photographs to leaf through and Penelope would place some visually dubious but delicious food on the table made from a recipe she had coaxed out of some rustic innkeeper. Bea smiled to herself. It would be all right.

Tom and Clare were allowed to stay up for supper with Bea and Jack on Friday evening, having hovered in the hall playing their own mysterious version of fives – a disgruntled Ned allowed only to look on – until they heard the twist of their father's key in the lock. Beatrice sat on the stairs, watching fondly as Jack set down his cases and scooped up his children one by one, ruffled their hair and kissed them. He burrowed in his pockets for little surprises: an optimistically bought Airfix balsa-wood model plane kit for Tom, a tiny Welsh lace dorothy bag for Clare and a bag of glass marbles for Edmund. Beatrice clapped her hands and commanded the elder two to wash and be ready for supper in fifteen minutes. She hugged Jack and settled a sleepy Ned on her hip before handing him over to Molly. 'Goodness, this boy's quite a weight now. Over to you, Molly. He's so tired. I think he can miss his bath tonight. We'll both come up later when he's settled.'

Jack had time for one small whisky before supper. There were signs of strain on his face. 'Tom's got another bruise, hasn't he? That one on his knee. Oh, Bea, I'm not sure if those new spectacles are doing him much good.' He sighed. 'It'll be a miracle if he can manage that model aeroplane.'

'Not now Jack.' Tom and Clare, scrubbed, hand in hand and proud to be joining their parents, appeared at the door. The family walked down to the dining room where the cook shortly arrived bearing a tureen of Cullen Skink and where the air was filled, furthermore, with the promise of a perfectly baked ham.

On Saturday there came the promised expedition to a Lyons Corner House. Little Edmund had to be left at home with Molly but not before a morning of games in the nursery with his siblings and Jack. Beatrice let the four of them rejoice in each other – the children had seen so little of their father lately – and worked for a couple of hours in the dressing room she had had converted into a small, bright study. After lunch at the Corner House near the Strand, during which the children were delighted to indulge in treats forbidden at home, including tomato ketchup and Coca-Cola, they went to one of the big picture houses in Leicester Square. All four sat enthralled and enchanted and neither of the children uttered a word during *Snow White and the Seven Dwarfs*. Afterwards even Jack had to admit that the animation was masterly. But perhaps for Tom and Clare the greatest treat of the day was to ride home on the bus.

'What a lovely day,' Beatrice smiled tiredly after the children had had their cocoa and poached eggs and been, not unwillingly, dispatched to bed.

'Wasn't it?' Jack poured a decent-sized whisky this time. 'Can't wait for supper. Why do children always want to eat such disgusting things?' He set his glass down. 'Bea, I really do want to talk about Tom. You don't seem to be very interested.'

'That's not fair, Jack, and you're wrong. Maybe I should have organized another appointment for him sooner and I don't really know why I delayed because I'm not usually cowardly about facing up to unpleasantness, am I?' Jack shook his head and Beatrice continued. 'I'm taking him to see O'Brien, that new specialist in Harley Street. He has an appointment on Tuesday.'

'Good girl.' Jack walked over and kissed the top of her head. 'What's for supper?'

'Yesterday's soup, yesterday's ham, cold with some salad, and the rest of yesterday's blackberry and apple crumble if Molly hasn't polished it off.'

'Perfect.'

Sunday passed in quiet, contented serenity with a walk on Hampstead Heath being foreshortened by a rainstorm. Jack and Beatrice played card games with the children, helped them with jigsaws and listened to music on the radiogram. After the seventh time that they had roared and screamed along with 'The Laughing Policeman' even Jack had had enough. There was a long splashy bathtime before Beatrice began to get ready for the evening and Jack spent an hour or so with paperwork and repacking his bags.

'You look nice.' Beatrice had chosen a plain white cambric blouse in startling contrast to a deeply flounced scarlet skirt with a tight embroidered belt at the waist. 'Not one of yours, surely, though?'

'No, indeed. You can't imagine, Jack, the odd little pleasure of sometimes going into a shop – a *shop*! – and buying something rather wild like this, something for which I bear and take no responsibility. Ready?'

Beatrice had been right: there were no other guests – the Jacobs were settled in a new block of flats near Regents Park. She had been right, too, about the photographs, pored and laughed over in the mellow light of the Gower Street drawing room, and right about dinner. There was a curious dish of beans, drenched in olive oil and some tough, rather hard bread. Afterwards came a strangely flavoured stew. Penelope said, comfortingly, that it was lamb. It was an eccentric but delicious and lively meal, served early because of Jack's train and finished well before nine.

Leonard drew upon his cigar. 'Well, Jack, my dear fellow. You've told us something of your work now. How do those factory people you're working with react to all this talk of appeasement? And are they pleased that even so there's probably going to be another war? Have their bosses told the poor saps that it will mean more work and better pay and neglected to add that they'll be the cannon fodder, as usual?' Leonard went on to muse about Mr Chamberlain's recent visit to Germany and his promise that there would be no war as long as he and Herr Hitler saw eye to eye. His voice thickened. 'I'm very anxious, Jack. It is, of course, the last thing I want but I fear the worst. No one should trust the promises of such a man – the German Chancellor, I mean, of course.'

Penelope saw Beatrice stiffen and noted her expression. 'Shall we take our coffee to the other room?'

'No, absolutely not. I just hate all this talk. Why can't we simply have a nice evening? Why does politics always have to intrude?'

'It must. These things must be addressed and understood, Bea, if we have any hope at all of continuing to have nice, simple, warm evenings like this in the future. I think Penelope understands.' Leonard glanced at his wife and she nodded. 'Don't you see?'

Jack knew that Beatrice was largely in sympathy with his politics and with his broad aims but was often exasperated by her unwillingness to confront the logical consequences of the social conditions he deplored. Beatrice was actually far from indifferent. She was, rather, painfully disquieted. He spoke more tenderly. 'We must all realize that munitions factories are being built in Germany again and here as well. It may not happen but all the signs are there. And there is such a thing as a just war, you know.' He looked at Leonard.

'I'm afraid Jack is right, in every way. Since Johann and Claudia arrived here there have been many, many others. Soon there will be a flood so I thank my God that the housing projects were well under way so early. You yourself have found employment for some of our visitors in your workrooms. Penelope and I, Beatrice, have not hesitated to exploit any friend of ours who is in a position to help in some way. I cannot believe, however, that you have been dissatisfied with the work of those whom I directed towards you.' Beatrice shook her head. Leonard went on, 'Some of the immigrants, Beatrice, have tales to tell, rumours they can hardly bear to repeat. I will not elaborate upon those this evening. Let us just say that people are fleeing evil. We will welcome them and if necessary we will brace ourselves to fight that evil.'

'But you're a pacifist, Leonard. Both of you are.' Beatrice turned to Penelope. 'I never thought I'd hear you talk like this.'

'Never thought I would, my dear Beatrice. But extreme times demand extreme measures and, believe me, I think those extreme times will shortly be upon us.'

Beatrice raised a stricken gaze to Penelope whose brow was furrowed and whose eyes were damp. Then she turned it to Jack. 'Do you mean bombing?' Her eyes widened in terror. 'An invasion?'

He nodded. 'I'm afraid it's possible. We mustn't assume that diplomacy can avoid it. And perhaps we should not assume that avoidance is desirable. We must face things. You said only yesterday that you didn't shy away from unpleasantness. None of us must.'

Beatrice's gaze had not wavered from her husband's. 'But the children. The children.'

CHAPTER SEVEN

'What about Canada? We could send them to Canada. They'll be safe there, won't they? I heard about some other people who . . .' Suddenly Beatrice was unable to open a newspaper, overhear a fragment of conversation in the workroom or speak to friends without learning more about the dangers or hearing about people who were preparing to face the possibility of parting with their children. 'Molly says that if we like she could take them back to her parents' farm in Ireland. They'd grow up like little peasants but . . .' Hearing her own panic Beatrice fought to introduce a tone of levity to her voice.

'Bea, darling, we simply cannot discuss this on the phone. I'll be home the day after tomorrow and we'll make some sort of plan then. In the meantime you are not to worry so. King George has pints of German blood in his veins – he won't want to encourage a war. No one wants this, Beatrice. It's only twenty years since the last Armistice. I can't believe it will happen so do please try to remain calm.'

Beatrice had veered between states of chilled disbelief and near-hysterical terror since sending Jack off at King's Cross just before midnight on Sunday.

'How did you get on in Harley Street with Tom? Could the doctor give you any news?'

'No, Jack. Not really. We'll have to go back in the morning.' Beatrice's voice threatened to crack again. 'He asked Tom lots of questions and made him do all sorts of exercises with his eyes. O'Brien was very kind but poor Tom must have been so bewildered. He was very brave. He hates those glasses. All he said to me when we left – I took him on a bus for an ice at Fortnum's for being so stoic and patient – was, "Mummy, will I be able to play football again now?"' She started to sob. 'Oh, Jack, am I breaking down or breaking up?'

'Don't be so bloody ridiculous, Beatrice. Just tell me what the doctor said.'

Tom and Clare were at their lessons when Jack slammed the door behind him the following day. Beatrice, emerging from the drawing room, put a finger to her lips as he crashed his bags on the floor. 'Ned's asleep, Jack. Let's try not to disturb him.'

Jack drew breath, attempted to regain composure. 'Ned's asleep. Good. Ned's always asleep. What about Tom? I must know.'

Beatrice, too, breathed deeply. Her voice was measured and quiet, her words stilted. 'You beseeched me, Jack, to be calm. This is what I am trying to be. I hope to maintain a steady sort of feel in this house. I do not want any more tears and recriminations. I want peace.'

'Don't we all?' Jack wiped his brow after removing his coat. 'Tell me, Bea, were you impressed with Dr O'Brien? What did he say when you saw him again today?'

'Come in here and sit down beside me.' She led him back into the drawing room where letters and papers were scattered all over the chair seats and carpets. There were forms and applications, notices and newspaper cuttings. She settled stiffly in a chair by the window and tried to keep her voice level. 'O'Brien says that Tom has already lost most of the sight in his right eye and that, as it is unlikely that any surgery can correct this, it would be pointless and possibly dangerous to put him through the trauma of an operation. Apparently spectacles may help to save what sight he still has in that eye but O'Brien isn't optimistic. I was rather relieved when he said that surgery was not advisable.' Beatrice gulped. 'He says it's a detached retina. Not much they can do about that.' She looked up at Jack. He was well aware that to lose the sight of one eye might never really trouble his son yet could not help but fear for him should destiny or accident damage the other. Then a minor disability would change to tragedy, an innocent world be permanently proscribed and a curtain of darkness drawn across all of Tom's bright chances and potential. Jack handed Beatrice a handkerchief before nodding to her to continue.

'Obviously, when Molly had taken Tom away, I asked O'Brien about the other eye. I believe he's an honest man, Jack, he didn't spare me the bad news so I trust his opinion about the good. He said that there's no reason why that eye should be damaged. Just one of those things, he said.'

Beatrice began to cry and Jack leapt to her side. 'I know what you're thinking. That silly accident. O'Brien would have asked you if Tom had had any infant crises. Did he?'

'Yes, and I told him about measles and whooping cough and all the rest. And yes, I did tell him how he'd struck his face on the tiles that time when I dropped him after his bath.' Beatrice shuddered again into sobs. 'He said Tom's sight wouldn't have been affected by that.' She lifted her face. 'But I shall never believe him.'

Jack stiffened himself and took both her hands. 'Tom's a fine lad, smart as paint. We both know that.' He lifted one of Beatrice's hands and placed it over her right eye. 'Now, open the other one. What can you see?'

She looked about the room, slowly, and then at her husband. 'Almost everything.'

'Well, then. We shall have to take special care of our Tom but we must never treat him like a cripple or an invalid. Losing the sight of one eye does not prevent a child or an adult from seeing practically everything they need or want to see.' Jack's mouth set into a tight line. 'I will not have my son mollycoddled. He'll go to School, to Eton, just as I did, and be strong. We know we can make that happen, don't we?' His eyes were as damp as Beatrice's.

'Not so sure about the School bit, Jack, darling. Don't forget there's something else we need to discuss.'

Jack was prepared for this. 'I was being alarmist on Sunday, Bea. Try to forget about it.'

'How can I? It will break my heart but I think we must send all the children away from London if your fears are even half founded. They could, I suppose, stay with your parents, but Malvern is too close to the aviation factories in Cheltenham for my liking. I think we should consider other options. Molly's suggestion is kind but obviously impossible. I read in *The Times* today that Southern Ireland is all for war and although that might mean that the small towns and farms won't be bombed I'd hate the children to live in that kind of atmosphere. They'd be bullied at school, for one thing.'

'I agree with you, Bea. How quickly you have become politically astute. Forgive me, darling, but I do sometimes underestimate you, I know.' Jack squeezed his wife's hand

and took another long draw on his whisky. 'But what, then?'

Beatrice collected a number of lilac-coloured sheets of paper. These days, in California, dainty translucent airmail paper was printed in every shade. 'This is from Evie. You don't have to read it all. Just take a careful look at the last two pages.'

Jack was familiar with Evangeline's bold, lucid hand, knew well her habit of underlining and exclaiming. He was also more attuned than Beatrice to the unconscious, but bravely miserable sub-texts that her feverishly sunny letters sometimes contained. As he scanned, unbidden, the first few sides of the letter he caught a glimpse of a sad spirit again astray and adrift. This time there was no sub-text: it did get cold, after all, at night in California. Viola, these days, treated her less as a friend than as a dresser. James, her actor friend, was seeing at least two starlets as well as her. She missed the family. She was lonely. Moreover, film rights to Cameron's recently published novel had just been bought by a neighbouring studio. Casting discussions were already under way.

I don't know how I will bear it, Bea [Evie wrote]. I always suspected he might vilify Vi, but it was a terrible shock to see how he savaged me in it, too. He just seems to have used everyone he knew in London, everyone whose drink he drank, every table at which he supped, every pillow where he laid his head . . . I don't even want to be on the same continent as Cameron now, let alone in the same town, but I suppose I must . . . There are still a number of outstanding work commitments that I don't want to duck out of but I need a little sanity in my life to counterbalance the pricks, if you see what I mean.

Jack did not read the next few pages properly – she was clearly back in brave and brash mode. Then, three sides later, Evangeline changed tack.

I'm told, Bea, that the newspapers here can be much freer in what they print than the London ones. What do they call it? D Notices or something? Anyway, I worry dreadfully about you all and, despite everything, I have a plan. Send the children over here to me. They'll be safe, warm (most of the time!!) and loved. I'm rich by London standards. I haven't even bothered to tell you what I'm paid for an alteration let alone a design. I know I'm being selfish as usual but won't you let me have them, at least until the emergency is over? It'd certainly take my mind off Cameron . . .

Jack laid the letter down. 'What do you think, Bea? It's not such a terrible idea, is it?'

Beatrice riffled among the debris on the carpet. 'I'd have been inclined to agree with you until I read this. It only arrived half an hour before you.' She handed a telegram to Jack.

CAMERON NOW HERE PERMANENTLY STOP UNSPEAK-ABLE AND TOO AWFUL STOP CAN'T POSSIBLY TAKE CHILDREN NOW STOP ALL IS SCANDAL STOP IN-TEND TO SAIL QUEEN MARY NEXT TUESDAY STOP WE CAN DISCUSS CHILDREN WHEN I ARRIVE HOME CAN'T WAIT STOP ALL MY LOVE TO ALL OF YOU STOP EVANGELINE

Jack read the telegram twice. 'Well, something at least seems to be settled. We must welcome her very warmly, yes?'

'Very warmly indeed. It's been nearly two years. She

went in, let's see,' Beatrice counted back on her fingers 'spring 1937. She deserves a party.'

'A party for someone who is running away after running away in the first place? That's an odd thing to celebrate, Bea.'

'No, it's not. Do you imagine Evie will skulk back here with her tail between her legs, all defeated and failed? I know my little sister a bit better than you do, Jack. She's done wonderful work – triumphant – in Hollywood, as you know. But the greatest triumph is that she's coming home to us. It's so typical of Evie, swimming or sailing defiantly against the tide. I always wanted some little snip of her guts.' Beatrice was emphatic.

'Then a party it is. The best one.' Jack paused and his voice, unintentionally, lowered. 'Don't underestimate yourself in the guts department, Beatrice. Courage is in the family blood. But a party, certainly. Perhaps the last one for a while. We'd better make sure it's the best.'

Evangeline was lean and limber but as Beatrice hugged her, moments after she stepped off the boat train at Waterloo, she noticed that faintly etched into her skin – pale gold from the Californian sun – was a new and deeper network of tiny lines, particularly around her eyes. The sisters clasped hands and stretched arms, standing back from each other for a second before embracing. From this distance she's more ravishing than ever, thought Beatrice. Oh, my poor Bea, you look so tired, thought Evangeline. She stooped. Clare and Tom were tugging at her jacket. 'How's my leading lady? How's my best boy?' She laughed and seeing her sister's smile flicker, added quickly, 'Film term. Means something technical.' She skipped towards Molly who was holding Edmund's hand a few feet away and planted a kiss on both of their cheeks. 'I can't say how wonderful it is to see you. To be back.' She tickled Ned's chin and exclaimed at how he had grown. 'Jack here?' She turned back to Beatrice.

'Over there,' Beatrice pointed to a porter struggling with a castle of cases on a trolley. 'He'll take the man to the car. We're parked just outside but, actually,' Beatrice assessed the number of bags and trunks, 'I think we'll need at least one extra taxi. Did you have to charter a separate ship for that lot?'

The Eliott sisters stole sidelong glances at each other as Jack drove to Evangeline's home. It was less than two miles from Waterloo but the lunchtime traffic was heavy. The plan was to settle her in, having waited for her luggage to catch up, and collect her later for dinner. Beatrice and Molly had spent a furious – in every sense – few days straightening and cleaning the mews house: Evangeline's tenant, perhaps understandably dismayed at being told she would have to leave several weeks before the lease was due for renewal, had left the place in filthy disarray. Now Beatrice nursed Edmund on her lap while Evangeline had her arm about Clare, who was squeezed between them. Tom had the special honour of sitting next to his father. He called out loudly every time he spotted a Riley, the car that currently obsessed him. He kept turning round to announce his score.

When he had turned back for the fourth time Evangeline laid a hand on her sister's wrist. She pointed to her eyes and twisted her face into a pointedly puzzled expression. 'Not now, Evie. Over dinner.' Beatrice took a less furtive look at her sister. 'Your hair is lighter. Little glints here and there, anyway.' Beatrice flicked at stray fairish tips. 'Is that the sun or some sort of Californian alchemy?'

'You can buy it in a bottle over there. Good stuff, Bea, not just tarts' peroxide. You'd be surprised what you can buy in a bottle over there, actually.' Evangeline suddenly seemed weary. She looked up. 'Don't worry, Bea. It's all that sea air. Makes a girl impossibly sleepy.' She turned her head away and peered out of the window, conscious of Bea's worried scrutiny. 'London. How I love it. How I've missed it. All damp and grey and dirty. It's wonderful to be home, Bea.' The car drew into the mews and Evangeline turned again to the window. 'And it's wonderful to see my little house again. Hope those blighters looked after the car properly.' Her large grey eyes filled with tears. 'Will you come inside with me, Bea? I need to be alone with you. Just you.'

Beatrice, too, felt herself begin to choke. 'Oh, Evie, it's been so awful lately. So awful without you. Thank God you're home.'

They waited for the other taxi to rumble into the mews. As Molly stood by with Edmund, Jack and the driver heaved the luggage into the hallway and then Evangeline stooped to kiss Tom goodbye. 'I'll see you later, young man.' She slipped a tiny scented tablet of *Queen Mary* soap into Clare's little hand.

Beatrice took Jack's broad dry hand and Tom's slightly damp paw. She looked from her husband's face to her son's. 'I'll see you later, Jack dear. I won't be long, Tom, sweetheart. Clare, my pet, help Molly with Ned, won't you? Just going to help Auntie settle in. I'll be back in time to read you all a story this afternoon.'

Tom cast a puzzled look at his father. 'Women's talk, old man. You'll get used to it one day. They can't help themselves, poor things.' He led Tom to the car, waited while Molly and the other children climbed in, and drove away.

Beatrice and Evangeline walked through the small hallway into a long narrow room which smelled of beeswax polish and flowers. There was a bottle of champagne in a silver bucket with two gleaming glasses set beside it.

'To us again,' said Beatrice, as she poured, a tear now trickling down her cheek. 'And now, tell me all that you've been up to.'

'To us, always,' replied Evangeline, wiping her face with the back of her hand. 'There's so much to tell you, to hear, to talk about. We can't possibly do it all at once. You go first.'

Evangeline listened intently and without interruption as her sister elaborated upon Jack's fears for the future. 'He's been making light of things, Evie, but I know that's only for my sake. He meets a lot of politicians and journalists, you know, at his club and through his work. I think we had better prepare for the worst and make the best of it when it – whatever it proves to be – happens. Anyway, I just knew I couldn't bear to send the children away. At least not now while we still really don't know what will transpire. Not now that . . .' Her voice lowered to a whisper.

'I'm not going to hurry you, Bea, but can you tell me about Tom? You told me a little in your letters but always so obliquely. I felt that something must be badly wrong.' Evangeline filled their glasses in the silence that followed.

Bea's angular frame began to shiver and she busied herself for half a minute more, searching in her bag for a handkerchief. 'Rather cold in here, I'm afraid, Evie. I don't really trust central heating yet, do you?'

'After quite a long time in North America I trust central heating, I trust hot showers, lifts that don't break down and aeroplanes. Not much else.' She gave a light laugh and waited. 'Come on, Bea. Please talk about Tom. How much does he know?'

'Very little. He's fed up, of course, about having to wear spectacles all the time now but that's nothing new, only more of the same. I know that his eye problem isn't a really bad one but I can't help fretting, feeling responsible.' Beatrice saw how her sister's lips pursed, and hurried to explain everything that Dr O'Brien had told them, and that the disquieting news had been confirmed by another, an equally brilliant but far less pleasant, specialist. It all tumbled out in an incoherent rush. 'Jack and I can't agree about how to handle it. He wants to tell the poor little chap exactly what the situation is – treat him like a man. But, Evie,' Beatrice turned to face her sister, 'he's still just a little boy. I feel we should let him realize gradually, in his own time. Answer his questions as honestly as we can when he asks them.' She sighed. 'I just don't know what's for the best.'

Evangeline picked up Beatrice's hand. 'You're distraught, Bea, and you're running way ahead of me. I think you'd better explain slowly, properly. And I mean everything. About you and Jack, too. When you don't see people for a long time you notice changes that would be imperceptible from day to day. You two seem to be losing something too. There was something different about the way you behaved towards each other at the station. It was different.' Evangeline paused. 'It was almost too polite.'

It was nearly three-quarters of an hour before Beatrice, with many repetitions, had fully explained to Evangeline the heavy responsibility that Jack was now carrying which made him easy to irritate and her desperate to avoid confrontation, Tom's condition, her residual guilt about the babyhood accident and fear that they might have taken the wrong decision about the slim chance that surgery could help. Evangeline was calm and firm. 'I don't think so, Bea. We're not a doctor's daughters for nothing. Even though things have advanced in recent years I think you and Jack were right. Don't mistake me – I'm not putting in a good word for Father, heaven forbid – but even I remember him saying darkly how risky and literally shocking it was. How it had to be a last resort. If Tom's condition is now stable, as you say, it would be better to wait until he can cope better, I'm sure. And as for you and Jack – well, I'm not surprised you're jumpy with each other sometimes. That's nothing to worry about, I'm certain.'

Beatrice smiled weakly. 'Thanks, Evie. We're not making much headway with this champagne, are we? Would you like a cup of tea instead?'

'Thought you'd never ask. Somehow it never tasted the same in California, even made with the Jackson's tins you sent over. Must be the water, I suppose.' She followed Beatrice into the small kitchen that Beatrice had had stocked with basic provisions, including the makings of Evangeline's breakfast in the morning. If she knew her sister at all well the Alvis would be parked in a side-street behind Harrods the following day, ready to be loaded with boxes and packages from the food hall. Evangeline had always preferred to shop personally and choose than to telephone her order. When the tea was ready, Evangeline carried the tray back into her sitting room. 'Tell me about London.'

'You haven't told me about yourself yet. I want to know about you.'

'You will, I promise, and very soon. I'll tell you all about the work, about Viola, about the extraordinary place that California is – and I went to New York a few times, did I tell you?' Beatrice nodded. 'And I'll tell you about impossible men. But not quite yet. Talking hard as you just did is tiring. But so is listening. Can we have a little rest and talk about something light? It can wait for a few hours, can't it? I'm here for ever now, Bea.'

Beatrice gave her a long, grave look. 'Such certainty. But you're right. We must all be sensible and we mustn't give in to doubts and fears. I suppose there's a sort of wilful cussedness in the air of London at the moment. You'll notice it.'

'What do you mean?'

'I suppose it all began when the King, I mean the Duke of Windsor, went to France and married Mrs Simpson, just after you went to America. You'll remember that the parties had really got going in May '37 around the time of the Coronation, just before that and it's been non-stop ever since. King George and Queen Elizabeth aren't much fancied by society or vice versa, I feel. So there's been rather a reckless spree of balls and parties and dances to compensate, I suppose, for what is regarded as a rather dull royal imperative. Everyone still adores the little princesses, of course.'

'Go on.'

'Well, you obviously know some of this. More, perhaps,

than I do as the newspapers here are censored and you said that the American ones aren't. Everything seems to have collided – the Abdication, the new Royal Family, these dreadful rumours of war with Germany, an awful lot of political bickering.' Beatrice pulled a face. 'The result seems to be some kind of hedonistic frenzy. The order books have never been fuller, neither have the restaurants and theatres. It's as if people want to dance, drink and distract themselves into oblivion.'

'This all sounds quite beastly, Bea. Really grim. Like the last days of Ancient Rome – you know, Nero and his fiddle and all that – or the collapse of the Austro-Hungarian Empire in Vienna – and that was less than fifty years ago.'

'Awful. I suppose it is, in a way. But you can understand it. And pessimism is often unfounded, isn't it?' Beatrice sounded hopeful and doubtful, all at once. 'Speaking of Vienna, have you . . .?'

'No, I haven't.' Evangeline rose and walked to the window. She turned to Beatrice. 'Listen, Bea, I really do feel utterly exhausted now. Would you mind terribly if I took a little nap? I'll be fine later and can be over to you for dinner at what, eight? Someone will collect me, won't they?'

'My dear, I'm so sorry. I didn't mean to tire you.' Beatrice reached for her coat and hat. 'Shall we try to make it seven thirty? Clare and Tom would love you to kiss them goodnight.'

She left. Evangeline, still by the window, saw her sister climb into a cab at the top of the mews two minutes later. She walked to the phone and dialled Hugo's number.

A stranger answered. Hugo hadn't been to his house for months.

California, 1938

She tried to settle on a wooden chair but its slats cut into her bottom and the back was angled in such a way that her neck ached. It was impossible to relax. Evangeline thought ruefully of English striped-canvas deck-chairs, smelling faintly of creosote, mould and paint from a winter in the shed. She remembered how comfortably, as a child, one could curl up in them with a book. Her hand dipped down for her glass. Before she could locate it a maid appeared with a jug. 'More soda, Miss Eliott?' With every crash of distant foam and with every squint against the sun, Evangeline felt worse.

It was bad enough being left alone, here on the beach where she had anticipated a day or two of fevered love-making and indulgence. The watchful presence of Horatia made things far worse. Evangeline didn't even feel able to loosen her bandeau top, let alone remove it. The Jantzen two-piece had been considered very daring, even on Mulholland Drive, despite its high-cut waist. Now she felt like a trollop every time she went into the kitchen and inspected the contents of the refrigerator, tall and humming in the corner. Horatia was always there, seated and crisp in her starched white cotton and all too ready to help and advise. 'Course, you English people never had to worry about no Prohibition, did you? Guess you never got out of the habit like us folks did? Can I fix you anything, ma'am?'

The sun scorched her skin. Heat made Evangeline drowsy and she decided to go indoors. She really did not want to sleep as James had promised to be back by lunchtime. His note that morning had been apologetic: an important agent was in town and he really had to see them at once. 'The beach is yours and yours alone. Enjoy it', the note had concluded. Evangeline wondered if he had considered the inhibiting presence of Horatia and mused next on why he had not told her of this appointment before they had driven to his house on the beach at Malibu the night before.

The propeller fan whirled above her, clattering, but she could still hear the steady crashing of the ocean. It was as regular as breathing. In the cool bedroom Evangeline stripped and saw how, even after only an hour in the morning sun, her body was banded red and white. It stung. A bathroom inspection failed to unearth any calamine or skin salve. She began to search in drawers and cupboards, not exactly rummaging but not being stealthy either.

She found nothing. Some shirts, bathing drawers, a muddled film script or two and a dozen odd socks. She was about to give up and return to the relative cool of the linen sheets when she saw the cami-knickers. They were made from apple green rayon and trimmed with pale brown lace. How very vulgar, she thought as she hooked a strap with one finger. Badly made and finished, too. As she lifted it she noticed that a scrap of paper had been pinned to the back, just above the crotch gusset where there was a little tear. 'You ripped these, Baby James. And now you owe me another one, or maybe a pair.'

As Evangeline stared the door opened. 'I heard you stir, Miss Eliott. Can I get you anything?' Horatia's gaze was cool. Evangeline dropped the green cami-knickers, startled. 'No, thank you. I was just looking for some calamine or something.'

The maid stared at Evangeline, slowly looking her up and down. Evie had forgotten that she was naked. She flushed and reached for a robe. 'You won't find that kind of thing in here, Miss Eliott. There's some skin cream in a jar on the porch if that's what you're looking for. Those yours? Mighty pretty.' Horatia looked at the green rayon. 'Guess not, now I remember. I do believe the last young lady who came to stay left them behind. Mr James, he sure does have a lot of pretty ladyfriends.' Horatia left the room.

Evangeline took a hard, cold shower and pulled on some loose trousers and a shirt. She sat in the shade on the steps of the porch and wondered what to do next. James was handsome, flirtatious, monied and gallant. Why was she bothered that he had other girlfriends when she hadn't the least interest in settling down with him? It made no sense. They could easily have a pleasantly erotic and uncommitted fling, after all.

No, we can't, thought Evangeline. He has deceived me. He lied, even about my small place in his life. Deception was not always forgivable but it could sometimes be understood within the context of a serious relationship. It was contempt-ible within the small parameters of one such as theirs. Suddenly, in this blinding, hard noon light, Evangeline missed England, damp and grey and green. Not quite enough to decide – yet – about returning, but quite enough to pack her small bag and to ask Horatia to call for a taxi.

'Goodbye, Horatia. Thanks for all your help,' she called from the window when the car was about to pull away from the beach house. 'Do tell Mr James that I'm sorry I had to run and that I'll see him around.' She had resisted the temptation to pin a second note to the apple-green synthetic, expressing some sort of superior pique. That would have made it all appear more important than it was. None the less, Evangeline had to dab at her eyes during the taxi ride back to Laurel Canyon.

She thought of Cameron, and of their tense, brittle dinner a week or so earlier. Evangeline was half proud and half ashamed of the memory of her own metallic appearance and responses. I slept with this man, she had thought to herself as he paused to catch a waiter's eye, I believe I screamed out loud at times when he touched me. I actually considered marriage. She remembered how he had attempted to excuse himself and his wretched novel, the one which was shortly to be filmed.

'Cameron. You are in danger of becoming a bit of a tart,' Evangeline had said after he had reported a recent conversation with one of the Hollywood columnists. 'And it wasn't nice of you to model one of your characters on me.'

'Tart? You know what they say, Evie. Takes one to know one. And as for libel or slander, if that's what you've got in mind, they also say that the greater the truth, the greater the—'

'Libel,' finished Evangeline. 'And in this country the greater the bill at the end of the court case. Don't worry, Cameron, I won't sue. But I won't forget, either.'

They had shaken hands. 'All nice again, now, Evie?'

'Yes, Cameron. All nice. We must have lunch sometime.'

He had grimaced. 'You know how that phrase translates in this town?'

'Of course. It means, "Get out of my life for ever." Good day, Cameron.'

The cab drew to a halt and Evangeline paid the driver. She sat on her terrace until dusk fell and longer. It was a wonderful clear night. The fragrance of mimosa and lemon balm and the hibiscus near the door was almost intoxicating. Evangeline checked through her post and thought of London.

CHAPTER EIGHT

'You know, I'm not sure if I want a big party. Does that sound awfully rude?'

Jack sliced across the Stilton and offered a slender wedge to Evangeline with the point of his knife. 'No, not rude. Not rude at all. Maybe for me it's a relief. But it's baffling. We'd be only too happy. There are dozens of people who want to welcome you home and, Evie, you never used to shy away from parties.'

'That was then, Jack. Maybe I've changed a little bit. For a start I've been to enough parties over the last year or two to find that they can pall. And, in a way, the most ghastly ones were those thrown by the British enclave. They were so self-regardingly nostalgic and snobbish in the way they tried to personify "breeding" and "class" and "society". There was even some wretched cricket team captained by C. Aubrey Smith – you know, the actor.' Evangeline looked up. 'And their "little tea parties" were some of the worst.' She grimaced and continued. 'And then, again, I know this sounds vain but here in London I suppose I was on what the Americans call the A List. I found it quite startling to find that – despite being English and having all that specious status – I just wasn't as important as the film people. They look over your shoulder here, of course – some people always did – but in Hollywood they don't even bother to murmur a polite excuse if someone more interesting has entered the room. They just bolt. It all contrived to put me off big parties, I suppose.'

'It wouldn't be like that here, Evie,' Beatrice chided gently. 'We'd only invite people who really want to see you. All the friends who've missed you.'

'I think that's part of the reason, too, Bea. I want to savour and cherish and nurse each of those friendships again. See people quietly, play myself in with them, you know. Do so at a sane pace. Proper talking, proper listening.'

'I can understand that, Evie. And if you want to use the house here for supper parties that might be a little too large for your tiny dining room you can always do that, can't she, Bea?'

'Of course. And we won't mind if you don't always want us to be there. This is your home too, Evie, your house. Treat it like that. Jack and I can always hide in our own little sitting room, that is, if we're both here. Your home, remember . . .'

'I've always felt that. But bless you both for saying so.' She got up and kissed Jack's cheek and then her sister's. 'So, business as usual tomorrow, is it? There on the dot?'

'Certainly I shall be there by nine but I shall be furious if you are. Evie, don't be unreasonable.' Beatrice stretched out an arm. 'You have unpacking to organize, personal business to attend to and, from the looks of you, sleep to catch up on. Give yourself a day or two and leave it until Wednesday at the earliest. Please.' To her surprise Evangeline shrugged and nodded. 'Now, what can I tell you about our news here?' Evangeline leaned forward as Beatrice outlined some of the details of clients and clothes, moments of drama and hilarity in the workroom and changes of staff that she hadn't always thought to mention in her letters. She spoke of new recruits, including Bronya, Anya and Ruth, refugees referred to her by Penelope and some of the best workers imaginable. This evening she spared her sister news of some of the tensions that their arrival had caused in the workroom.

Evangeline was riveted and relieved. 'At least we still have Beryl, Elsie, Coral, Doris, Marjorie and Molly, of course. And our dear Tilly, despite all those supplications from Derry's. How could they have imagined that Tilly would have wanted to be put in charge of their alterations service, if you please? I nearly choked when you wrote to me about that, Bea.' She sighed. 'At least we have some stability. I hate it when there's none. Pity about Dagmar never quite matching up to Connie, I had high hopes of her. I suppose we shall have to look for a new house model quite soon, then.' Beatrice nodded, not unhappily. 'And do you ever hear from Connie?' Evangeline finished.

'We did at first but not now, not for ages. Cyril was quite shifty about it when I asked him if he happened to know anything. I'm sure he does but he told me that if I needed to learn how to snoop I should take advice from Priscilla.' Beatrice laughed. 'I shan't ask Dagmar to go just yet – some of the clients like her and she can't leave anyway until all those fittings are completed. She'll never have Connie's glamour but she has done quite well. Actually her looks seem somehow more in tune with the times – you know, lofty, aloof, slightly supercilious . . . I wonder if we ought to keep her on, after all?'

'No, you don't. Be honest, Bea, you can't bear the girl. Not my type either, as a matter of fact. Always looks to me as if she's just eaten a bowl of prunes,' muttered Jack, perhaps the slightest bit worse for wear. 'But I grant you that she's one of those women, almost like certain actresses', he glanced across at Evangeline, 'by whom the camera is seduced. In the flesh all her *hauteur* seems phoney and forced to me. But it is utterly convincing in the picture.' He pulled on his cigarette. 'I don't want to introduce a grim note into this happy evening but now that you're back, Evie, I think you girls should think hard about how you may have to adapt if there is any, er . . . unpleasantness.'

'What do you mean, Jack? You've not taken much interest in the designs recently.' Beatrice's words were sharp but her tone was fond.

'Clothes? Good Lord, no. I wouldn't presume. I was just thinking about the workforce. If it's anything like the last bash you'll lose some of the girls to the factories, even to the forces and the nursing service. You'll have to think about working with a smaller staff. Might need to invest in some modern machinery, that sort of thing.'

'But maybe we should also be thinking, whatever you say, Jack, about different sorts of clothes. Perish the thought and please God it won't happen, but women have always got to have clothes. And you've often said that wars and revolutions affect the way people dress.' Beatrice caught her sister's eye and saw something of the old gleam. 'What do you think, Evie?'

'I'm ready for a challenge. Another one. Ready for several, in fact.'

'Wonderful about Miss Evie. Being back, I mean.' Doris was stitching the last button onto the left cuff of the primrose yellow jacket of the costume the Hon. Mrs Caroline Falkinir would wear for her second daughter's christening. She held it up when the last button was fixed. 'Funny, isn't it, how some women get fatter and fatter when they have children and others just melt away. I'm sure she's smaller now than she was before she got knocked up the first time.'

'Doris! That's not like you. That's disrespectful.' Elsie was indeed shocked although Doris had slowly but inexorably been developing a sense of humour and mischief. 'Pity she only ended up as a Mrs after all that débutante season hoo-ha. I mean, that's no better than if one of us got married, is it?'

'Depends if you become Mrs Millionaire and your old man owns half of Rutland, I suppose. No doubt she'd have preferred to have married a lord or a baron or something but she seems happy enough. Much happier than that Lady Pamela. Now she always was a catty b—'

'What is catty, please? Is this not a nice thing to be? A cat is a beautiful animal.' Bronya spoke little and seldom but she listened hard as she finished buttonholes, hoping, one day to understand English.

'A cat is a filthy animal which should not be given houseroom, a flea-ridden, good-for-nothing who at least understands a few good English words like "Shoo" and "Push off."' Maureen looked up from her work with contempt. Anya and Ruth exchanged glances and were about to get up to stand behind Bronya. All three were from Poland and the older two were quietly protective of the sixteen-year-old whom they tried to coach in English in the park outside on fine days while they shared their lunch.

Bronya simply nodded and smiled but Beryl interrupted, 'I'm much more interested in Miss Evie. Don't you think she looks sort of sad?' Beryl's personality had mellowed slightly too. None of the other women in the bee-hive could work out why she had become so much quieter, more reflective and thoughtful. Her good humour remained but some of the old cheerful malice was absent. 'Maybe she's got another one of her Broken Hearts.' A flash of the familiar levity returned. 'Maybe she's run away to escape a scandal.'

'She's just come home to help Miss Bea. Missed London. Doubt if she really liked that silly heathen place, despite what she wrote on the postcards.' Doris still regarded any community without a flourishing Methodist chapel as virtually pagan.

'Anyway, it's about time,' Coral joined in. 'We could do with her here again. Sending drawings over and even talking on the t-t-t-telephone isn't the same. I think Miss Bea missed her an awful lot. You know how even we can sometimes sort something out without t-t-t-telling Mrs Palmer that we've got a problem? Just by t-t-t-talking. Bet it's the same with Miss Bea and Miss Evie. They n-n-n-n-need to work t-t-t-together.' Coral's stammer had improved but she still had trouble with Ts and always fell at the last fence of a long speech.

'You may be right, for once, Coral,' replied Doris. 'Now, Beryl. You're the eyes and ears of the world, or of this place, anyway. What did I hear about Miss Day coming back? I'm sure Tilly, I mean Mrs Finch, was making an appointment with her when I was last upstairs.'

'Well,' said Beryl, relishing the full attention and her floor. 'From what I hear Miss Day is coming back to London for the première of her film. You know, the colour one they did in Hollywood? And we're to make her dress for when she's presented to the King and Queen. She'll be meeting them, you know, at that big picture-house in Leicester Square. So that's quite exciting, I suppose. But there's probably going to be another historical film next and that's going to mean more farthingales and silly pointed medieval hats, I shouldn't wonder. Why can't she be like Ginger Rogers – or Jessie Matthews? Be fun to make some nice modern dance stuff.'

The basement door slammed and Ivy Watson, recently employed with her friend Maureen Grey as a seamstress, hoped that she did not reek of the Woodbine she had smoked on the basement stairs as she rushed to her bench just before Marjorie Palmer entered the room and began to speak. 'She doesn't choose to dance, she doesn't sing and it would not be appropriate for this House to make costumes of that sort. And, Beryl, you are required upstairs. At once, if you please.' Marjorie had heard most of the conversation but had stood at the bottom of the stairs and was now contorting her features in an effort to look fierce. She addressed the workforce, twitching her nose and sniffing several times. Ivy kept her head down. 'Miss Evangeline will indeed be producing designs for Miss Day's costumes in a forthcoming motion picture. It is, as Beryl said, another historical story – William Shakespeare, I believe. Large bolts of heavy cloth will need to be cut. You know what this means, of course?'

'The big table. We'll have to keep the big table clear, won't we, Mrs Palmer?' muttered Doris.

'I don't mind. I'll be in charge of keeping it ready. I like the b-b-b-big table. I like to spread out a bit,' Coral chimed in.

'So we heard, dear, so we heard.' But Doris smiled.

'Find that it's affecting your business, Beatrice?'

'At virtually every level, I'm afraid, Penelope. Only last

week I had to dismiss two of my best seamstresses because they were taunting Bronya. And Anya and Ruth – you remember them? The inseparables, you called them. So I'm in need of two more good workers if you can arrange it again.'

'I'm not sure that I'd want to place anyone else at the House of Eliott, Bea, if that sort of thing goes on there.' Penelope, better than any of them, knew how unpleasant things had been in the East End. The Whitechapel riots had been bad enough, fuelled by the alarmingly charismatic Oswald Mosley and brutishly undertaken by his Black Shirts. Anti-semitism was rife in Britain, especially in the cities, and the taunting of Jews had become worse since Mr Chamberlain had returned from Munich with a promise of peace, which tacitly consented to Adolf Hitler's policies of racial segregation.

'Now, Pen, be fair,' exhorted Jack. 'There aren't any more bad apples. In fact, it was the other girls downstairs who complained about the bullies to Tilly, wasn't it, Bea?'

'Yes, and Tilly came to me with it. I've scarcely ever seen her so agitated. I had to give Ivy and Maureen a hearing, of course, but it was obvious from their manner that Tilly had been right. They were almost brazen. Said that outsiders were taking jobs away from proper English people and that if Bronya, Anya and Ruth wanted to eat their sandwiches together and talk in their own language they should do so among their own kind. I ask you! If I'd simply been trying to get to the root of some routine workroom squabble or even admonish them for almost any other misdemeanour I might have half admired their brass. As it was, I told them to go there and then.'

'Good for you. And yes, of course I'll see if I can find

you two more. You could ask around, too, couldn't you, Leo?'

He agreed. In fact Leonard had just found an apartment off the Finchley Road for a tailor and his family. He was sure that while he built up his business in London Dieter could spare two of his daughters. 'I gather they were never allowed to be seen in the shop itself in Danzig but did wonderful work in the room at the back. I had it in mind to mention them to you anyway, Beatrice, so this is fortuitous.' He opened a bottle of wine, sweet, red and warming, but nothing could lend real cheer to this evening's supper. 'You said it had affected every part of the business, Bea. What did you mean?'

Beatrice didn't answer for a moment. Then she said, 'A couple of clients lost recently. Not a tragedy as we've been struggling to keep up with the orders and neither of the defectors were exactly favourite people of ours.' Leonard raised an eyebrow, waiting for her to continue. 'You know Lady Cohen, of course?' Leonard nodded. 'These two women, Sybil Farmiloe and Helen Urquhart, truly ghastly, both of them, are thick as thieves. Mrs Farmiloe was apparently seated below the salt at some dinner party while Lady Cohen was seated next to the host. For someone like Sybil Farmiloe this placement was a sort of social Siberia. Anyway, Lady Cohen was wearing that rather beautiful ivory panne-velvet gown we made for her. This, it seems, added insult to injury as Sybil, too, was wearing one of our gowns. I think it's a very nice dress but she insisted upon having it made in a colour that really does not suit her. I believe she felt thoroughly outshone by Lady Cohen and complained about feeling slighted to Mrs Urquhart the next morning.

'Both of them have cancelled appointments and withdrawn orders. When I ventured to ask Mrs Farmiloe if we had displeased her in some way she had the appalling manners to say, in an absurdly lofty tone, I might add, that she did not care to patronize the same dressmakers as Jewesses. Dressmakers, indeed.' Beatrice bristled. 'She also made some lightly veiled threat about advising her friends to do the same.' Now Beatrice almost giggled. 'Good riddance, I say. I'm not terribly worried. Mesdames Farmiloe and Urquhart are simply bad apples of another kind, aren't they? London cannot have many such rotten, sick people.'

'I wish I could share your confidence, Beatrice. These are truly terrible times. And sickness is often contagious.'

Beatrice dabbed at Jack's eye with a flannel moistened with iodine. He winced. 'Sorry, darling. I know how it must sting. But it really is getting better – you know it's fading fast when it reaches the yellow stage.'

'Do you think Leonard noticed it?'

'Of course he did. It doesn't look near normal yet. Probably just too polite to ask how you acquired it.' Beatrice laughed. 'Maybe he thought I'd taken a swipe at you.' She laid down the cloth and bowl. 'But I think you should have said what really happened.'

'No, Bea. The conversation tonight was gloomy enough as it was. Anyway, I did tell Penelope while I was helping her to refill that Roneo contraption of hers in the back room, so she'll tell Leonard in her own time if she thinks he ought to know.'

'You could sue that horrid man, you know.'

'What would be the point? It would only make him feel

important and give free publicity to him and his loathsome kind.'

'I still don't think it's right that someone can actually talk about "Jewboys", let alone insult Leonard in his absence and you personally for having a "Jewboy" as a brother-in-law. And at the Reform of all places. I thought that place was founded upon Liberal principles.'

'So it was. Things have changed, Bea, and they will continue to do so. Not for the better, I fear.' Jack fell silent and then his face suddenly broke into a wide grin and his eyes glinted. 'Besides, Beatrice, I was not insulted to be reminded that Leo is my brother-in-law. On the contrary, it's a source of pride. And you forget that I was boxing champion at School. Even if I'm asked to resign from the club as well it will be a small price to pay. That fellow got more than an honourable shiner like this.' Jack pointed to his eye. 'I believe I broke his nose and, with any luck, cracked a couple of ribs as well.'

'What on earth's been the matter with Tilly today? She's a bag of nerves. Do you think she's quite well?' Beatrice laid down her pen.

'Look out of the window,' suggested Evangeline.

Leaning against the door of a small black Ford parked near the railings opposite the House of Eliott and a few yards to the south was a man Beatrice recognized. She was startled. 'Why, it's Mr Grant. What the devil is he waiting for? Our appointment was over soon after four. I remember, because I was worried about keeping Maudie Carstairs waiting.'

'Keep looking.'

Beatrice was baffled but stayed by the window, feeling a little prurient. It was certainly none of her business if the man chose to stand by his own car and smoke a cigarette in the golden dusk of a late summer evening. 'Good heavens, there's Tilly.' A small, slight figure dressed in dark green patterned rayon stepped across the road, the light breeze causing the folds of the best-quality artificial silk to flutter slightly in the rush of air. In some recess of her mind Beatrice remembered how the old Tilly would have scuttled rather than stepped and would have patted away stray wisps of her bun rather than confidently pinning a cheeky little hat in place. 'She seems to be going to speak to Mr Grant. Good God, Evie, she's getting into his car.'

'Bea, you can be very dense sometimes. Haven't you noticed how often Mr Grant arrives early for appointments? How often he contrives to be here while Tilly is having a tea-break? I think they've become quite friendly. In fact, something tells me that tonight they are going out on what would be described in America as their first "date".'

'Really?' said Beatrice. 'Good. About time too.'

When she was widowed, five years earlier, Tilly had displayed a misguided stoicism after her husband had been knocked down by a tram near their flat in Southgate. She took no time off work except the day of his funeral, in Finchley. She worked furiously, still downstairs, lost weight and acquired a hectic colour to which she would always refer as evidence of her good health whenever anyone expressed concern. She coughed often, long and with almost audible pain. Both Beatrice and Evangeline feared that Tilly displayed the characteristic high colour of the consumptive.

When, after some months, Tilly had requested a private meeting, both sisters feared the worst.

Tilly entered the office and asked if she could sit down. She twisted her handkerchief and seemed close to tears. 'I don't quite know how to begin.' She looked first at Beatrice and then at Evangeline. 'It's just that I think I have to go away.' The Eliott sisters exchanged worried glances. 'You've done so much for me . . .'

'Tilly, please, it is we who should be grateful. Is there anything, anything at all that we can do?'

The speech came out in a confused rush. 'Yes, Miss Bea, Miss Evie. Would you let me go on a little holiday? Truthfully I mean a long holiday. Quite a few weeks. Of course I'll understand if you won't want to have me back after that but it's the only thing I can do, you see. Go there.'

'Go where, Tilly?'

'Oh, I'm in such a state.' Tilly coughed for half a minute before catching her breath. 'It's like this. When me and the old man got married someone gave us this lovely plate. It had mountains painted on it, and snow and a blue sky and fields with cows. The writing at the bottom said, "A Present From Zermatt". We had to go to the library to find out where Zermatt was. Switzerland, isn't it?' Beatrice and Evangeline nodded. 'Anyway, there was a funny little wooden house and a beautiful girl standing by the door. She was wearing a red gathered dress with an apron over it and a frilly white blouse. Well, the old man and I loved that plate and we hung it over the fireplace. When we didn't have enough money for coal we'd still sit in front of the grate and look at the picture on the plate. We had this daydream, you see, that one day we'd live in a wooden house like that with cows in the garden and mountains behind us. He said he'd plait my hair every morning. Whenever one of us was miserable the other one would just point to the plate.'

Evangeline felt tears prickle behind her eyes. 'Go on, Tilly.'

'Well, now, can you believe it? The tram company have sent me a cheque. Suppose I'll have to open an account at a bank now, won't I? Seems my husband had some sort of life assurance policy which he never told me about but his brother knew all about it. Anyway, they've sent me some money. Compensation, they call it.' Tilly sniffed. 'I'd rather have him back than any miserable eighty-three pounds but I've got it now and that's that. So what I mean to do is go to Zermatt. And I'll stay for a few weeks in a pretty little wooden house with cows and do all those walks we used to dream of taking in the mountains. And in a way my old man will be with me – we'll be together again in our daydream. Do you understand?' She broke into another alarming and by now familiar cough.

Beatrice looked up, clutching her own handkerchief. 'Yes, I think so, Tilly. Of course you must go and may Switzerland bring you help, peace and maybe a little joy. You need have no fears about your job here. It will be waiting for you. We'll manage, with difficulty, without you.'

'Quietish period coming up, anyway.' Evie's voice was choked and thickened.

When Tilly returned to the House of Eliott two months later she was changed in a dozen ways. Her eyes were bright and her complexion rosily tanned from wind and sun, the deep, dark pink patches on her cheeks had vanished. Weeks of rich, creamy food had built her up and her cough had vanished. She had picked up a few words and phrases of French and was now determined to study the language at a night school. Travel to a place where only the most sophisticated of innkeepers or non-British tourists could distinguish between a Bermondsey accent and a Belgravia one had lent her an astonishing new social confidence, especially as Beatrice and Evangeline had thrust into her hand a small case of clothing 'samples' to include in her packing. She was cheerful, alive, rested and confident. 'You see, I could say goodbye to him properly at last, Miss Evie. I took the plate with me and buried it in some snow. I said goodbye to him on a mountain. I'm all right now.'

'You always were, Tilly. Even more so now. Welcome back.'

Within a year both Eliott sisters were agreed; Tilly was ready to become their assistant *vendeuse*. Less than a year after that, Tilly having shown an aptitude which surprised Evangeline less than her sister, when the chief *vendeuse* left Tilly was promoted. It was shortly afterwards that Harold Grant, who supplied the House of Eliott with many of their buttons, facings, trimming, beads, embroidery threads and other notions, began to take a keen interest in the pretty, assured, efficient yet somehow approachable young widow.

'You'll have to forgive me, Mr Grant . . .'

'Harold, please. And what have I to forgive you for?'

Tilly pulled at her skirts as tightly as she could. Their folds touched the floor of the Ford. 'I haven't done this sort of thing before. Not since . . .' She looked at Harold Grant both nervously and beseechingly. 'It's just that I'm a bit rusty at stepping out, you know, courting.'

'Courting, are we?' Harold Grant laughed. 'One step at a time, my dear. Early supper at the Corner House suit you, then the pictures? We could go and see that one with Cary Grant and Mae West. What do you think . . . Tilly – if I may?'

'You may, and that would be just the ticket,' replied Tilly.

'Well, I'm glad that someone's going to be happy, Evie,' said Beatrice, as she moved away from the window.

'Don't be too sure. We may still have to look after Tilly. He's married.'

CHAPTER NINE

'Thank God it's over.' Jack poured himself a large whisky, and for once Beatrice nodded as he raised the bottle and she simultaneously raised an eyebrow.

She took her glass. 'Over, Jack? You heard what the King said. We're at war.' She sobbed. 'It's only just started.'

'Beatrice, you are the love of my life but that doesn't mean to say that at times you aren't a very literal-minded woman. This horrid, funny period is over.'

'I shouldn't have thought this was a time for jokes. What on earth are you talking about?'

'Darling, I'm sorry. Sorry, sorry, sorry.' Jack moved to sit next to her on the sofa, flinging an arm along the back and cupping her far shoulder. 'What I meant was funny-peculiar, the tension. That, at least, is over now. We know where we are.' A terrifying low moan began outside, its frequency becoming louder and shriller.

'My God, surely not so soon. The children. I must get the children.' Beatrice and Jack raced from the room but by the time they had brought their three bewildered and blanketed little ones downstairs and collected the survival-kit case they had had in readiness for weeks at the cellar door, another noise pierced the night.

'I think they call that the All Clear, Miss Bea,' said Molly.

She had felt more able than Beatrice to bone up on what might be expected in the event of the outbreak of war and, in any case, her friend who was going out with a bank clerk who also trained with the Territorial Army had hooted out and decoded the different sounds of the sirens many times recently, to the consternation of other customers at the ABC café where they usually met. 'Means I can take the nippers back to bed.'

'No, Molly, please.' Tom caught Molly's glare and turned to Beatrice. 'Mummy, please can we go into the cellar – *please*?' Beatrice almost laughed. Tom had been longing for this moment, had packed his own private bag of treasures in anticipation of a siege. She had noticed how most of his drawings recently had been of aircraft and ships. 'No, darling. Back to bed. Take care of Clare and your little brother. Look how sleepy they are.' Clare was rubbing her eyes and the thumb stuck in her mouth threatened imminent tears. Ned was beginning to grizzle.

'Oh, all right. I suppose so. Come on, silly.' Tom took Clare's hand. He turned back to Beatrice and Jack as he left the room. 'Do you promise there'll be another air raid soon?'

'Yes, my boy. I think I can promise you that,' said his father.

Beatrice picked up her glass and took it to the drinks cabinet. As she poured out another measure, and one for Jack, she tried to regulate her breathing. 'I wonder if we were wrong to keep them here in London. It's not too late, surely?'

'I think, Bea, that perhaps it is. I couldn't stand the idea of the children being in some boat that was struck by a torpedo in the North Atlantic, could you?'

Beatrice shook her head. 'They wouldn't even have us

with them. You're right. But what about Molly's offer? We could see them every few weeks if they were in Ireland, couldn't we?'

'I think not, Bea. Forget about the children growing up like little hooligans – fine by me, actually. But you know already, the Irish have no sympathy for Britain in this war. I wouldn't want our little blighters there.'

'Molly would protect them.'

'She'd do the best she could, I know. Remember, Bea, that she might be compromised herself. In any case, it might not be enough. No, let them stay under our roof, in our house. Everyone says this won't last long, not like the last time.'

'Do they? Do they really?' asked Beatrice, in a flash of perspicacity poised somewhere between optimism, realism and dread.

Some weeks later Evangeline was on the telephone when the small grey-haired man was shown into her office. She was both bemused and annoyed and indicated her irritation with a sharp look at Beryl who merely shrugged as she closed the door behind her. Evangeline placed a hand over the mouthpiece and told her visitor that she would be with him shortly and then she continued with her telephone conversation. 'I agree with you, Hugo. Now is not the time for grudges or misunderstandings. But really I can't talk any more now. I have someone in my office.' There was a silence. Evangeline noted that her visitor looked closely at some of the photographs that lined one wall of her office. He got up to stare hard at one or two of them. 'I really must go now, Hugo. And, yes, I'll see you at Le Caprice tonight.' She sat down but did not invite her visitor to do so. She had learned to hate surprises.

He stood before her with his hands clasped. Evangeline noticed that his suit was shiny but freshly pressed, his collar frayed but his shirt immaculately laundered and that the leather of his shoes was cracked but polished. She noticed, too, that his hands were freckled and that in the light of the window near the photographs there was a reddish tinge to some areas of the grey hair. 'I'm Evangeline Eliott, as you probably know. Can I help you Mr . . .'

'Taylor. Samuel Taylor. I believe you knew my daughter.'

Evangeline's brain raced. 'Connie. Connie is your daughter? Mr Taylor, forgive me, do. Sit down, please. How is the dear girl? Would you care for a cup of tea?'

'Thank you, no. Unfortunately, Miss Eliott, I can give you no news of Connie. I was rather hoping that you could supply it to me.'

'I don't understand.'

'Neither do I, believe me. When she first went to Paris she wrote to me every week, but for months now there has been no word. But as she is or was working in your Paris office, I felt sure – or at any rate I hoped – that you would be able to give me news of her.'

A chill of guilt and fear settled over Evangeline like a crêpe shroud. She hoped that her face betrayed none of this. 'What did she say when she last wrote?'

'It was a strange letter. It did not sound quite like my Connie. She wrote almost in riddles and said she was going on a little holiday but I was not to worry because although it was not as she had hoped with the House of Eliott she could easily find other work.' He looked up into Evangeline's startled face and continued. 'I at first formed the impression that there had been some small dispute, that she had gone away to calm down. Her mother would sometimes pretend to leave me after a little spat and she would always return. Then I started to think that perhaps there was some disgrace – that my daughter had caused trouble for you in that way. I have no wish to be a supplicant, Miss Eliott. It has taken much of what remains of my pride to come here. If my daughter has disgraced you I apologize and will make good in any way that I can.' He paused again and studied Evangeline's face. 'But I see that she has not. And that my last hope is fading . . .'

Evangeline felt herself flush and remembered the conversation she and Beatrice had had with Connie before she left. She tried to remain calm and reassuring but knew that she must be honest with Samuel Taylor now. 'Connie didn't exactly go to work for us in Paris. We closed the business there some time ago. She went to work for some trusted friends of ours. I'm sorry, Mr Taylor. My sister and I didn't feel we had any right to interfere with her plans or', Evangeline stumbled, 'family arrangements.'

'I quite understand, Miss Eliott. Connie is nearly twenty-four years old now. She has always been headstrong.' The elderly man paused. 'I had guessed as much and have spent all the time that God allows and all the money I possess in trying to trace her. But I have had no success. You were my best hope and my last one because I had hoped not to embarrass you like this.' He fell silent.

'You don't embarrass me. At least, not in the way you fear.' Evangeline braced herself. 'Perhaps you didn't realize that Connie's professional name had been Constance Travis for a while before she went to Paris. I now feel terribly guilty about not asking after her. Things have been in such terrible upheaval lately.' She heard herself sounding inadequate. 'But I'm sure you'll trace her now that you know the name she uses. We'll do all we can to help.'

'I am grateful, Miss Eliott.'

The conversation could have finished there and then but something impelled Evangeline to prolong it. 'These are dreadful times, Mr Taylor, but although I'm sure you long to have Connie back here with you, she had good friends in Paris and I doubt if she's in any danger. This Phoney War goes on and on. I don't believe that British citizens are threatened yet in France. They are under Red Cross protection, remember.'

He winced. 'Connie is indeed a British citizen, Miss Eliott. But she is also a Jew.'

'What are we going to do, Bea?'

'We're going to track down Daphne and Renée, that's what. They might be able to help.' Daphne and her French West African friend Renée were torch singers and cabaret dancers. They had been friends in London years ago, years, even, before Beatrice and Jack had married. 'And Louis must know something. One of us might call, or write to him at once – Priscilla and the *Mode* offices can help with that. Even Cyril may be able to give us some leads. I feel so responsible. He was muttering something the other day about going to Paris to visit a friend. Incredible, isn't it? Now I know why it's called the Phoney War.' She unhooked the telephone and asked for a number in the seventh *arrondissement*.

*

Later Evangeline met Hugo. The restaurant was so crowded and overbooked that they had to wait nearly an hour at the bar before their table was ready. Deeper lines were etched around Hugo's mouth and eyes and some new ones had appeared on his brow. His hair was a little greyer. After all, it had been three years. Why couldn't that odd, adorable little nest of freckles beneath the left side of your jaw have faded away? Why couldn't your hands have coarsened? God help me, why must you still be the most attractive man I've ever seen, Hollywood notwithstanding, Evangeline thought, only half hearing what he was speaking about.

'If London is bombed, as it certainly will be, it will be primarily a tragedy for human life and spirit but also a disaster for buildings – unique and historic buildings. I'm not talking about the palaces and the cathedrals, although they matter too, of course. I really worry much more about the little residential terraces, warehouses, particularly those near the river, the bridges and the small churches – places people use all the time, shops, schools, cafés ... Beautiful places that Londoners take for granted ... and quite right too. We should all accept as our right the lovely bricks and stones of our city, not stand awestruck.' Why does that little strip of ribbon have to keep falling off your shoulder? Why do you have to have that ridiculous smudge on your cheek? I suppose you were messing around with the mascara brush in the taxi. Why didn't you ever get that little gap in your teeth fixed? Why couldn't you be less pretty rather than more?

'So what will you do, Hugo? Join up?'

'Possibly. Probably. But there's something I may have to do first.'

Evangeline was about to enquire what that might be

when a waiter informed them that at last their table was ready. The long narrow room was dizzy with music. Couples had already danced through two sets of sirens. The lights were low, flickering and flattering. Hugo drained his champagne glass and took Evangeline's arm. 'It'll be easier to talk when we sit down. I booked that corner table over there. They're talking about rationing and we should make the most of this. Hungry?'

Evangeline turned to him as they had threaded half-way down the room. 'No, Hugo.'

Without moving his hand from Evangeline's arm he turned her neatly, the look over his shoulder explaining everything to the head waiter. 'Then shall we go home?'

'Evie, listen to me. Or do I have to box your ears?'

'Sorry, Bea. Didn't get much sleep last night.'

'You dined with Hugo, didn't you?'

'No, actually. I didn't dine at all.'

'I'm sorry, Evie. I didn't mean to pry. I just thought it was rather nice that—'

'Thanks, Bea. I'm fine, though, or will be after one more cup of coffee. Now, what were you saying?'

Beatrice explained again. Priscilla Dawlish had asked all six of the most distinguished London fashion houses to submit designs for new uniforms for the women's armed forces. 'She says we can do designs for all three or just for one. What do you think, Evie? Shall we?'

'There's no question about it. We must.' Evangeline was suddenly awake and alert. 'I suppose we'll need to work within all kinds of restrictions. Type of cloth, yardage, practicality, of course. And within a budget?' Beatrice nodded. 'Well, that's fine. There's the challenge. Anyone can make a lovely frock out of perfect silk. We must try to create something worthy, practical and attractive from sow's-ear serge. Give me a few days.'

Beatrice and Evie decided to submit, finally, only their design for the Wrens uniform. Those for the WRAC and the WAAF were serviceable enough but seemed, somehow, to incorporate touches, detail and devices that had been rejected for their Wrens designs. It didn't seem proper or correct to offer anything other than their best work or ideas.

The suiting had to be navy, of course, but Beatrice knew of a miller in Scotland who had managed to blend a certain amount of synthetic silk into his serge. This meant that the skirt – assuming most Wrens would wear slips anyway – would not need to be lined. It hung straight both front and back, with no centre pleating to pull and unpress. Instead there were deep pleats at each side. 'Most of the poor girls will be sitting down all the time. Box pleats sag behind and get pulled loose by the great British bottom. And they crease over the tummy at the front. This way they can sit comfortably and spread the slack of their skirts across the sides of the chair.' For warmth's sake the jacket had to be lined, but its square-cut neckline echoed the shape of the snug, horizontally striped fine woollen blouse (devised in favour of a mannish shirt and actually the most expensive item in the ensemble: Evangeline remembered too much about the itch of coarse wool against the skin from her childhood), intended to be worn beneath it. The jacket also eschewed a pale replication of masculine tailoring and fitted neatly to just below the hip. 'It's a fallacy that a long jacket disguises a big backside. So long as the skirt is cut well everything will be seen to be in proportion,' she told Beatrice on the evening before the designs were due to be submitted.

Every detail had been considered: pockets, suitable areas for medals and other decorations or marks of rank, ease of movement, decorum and warmth. 'You see, Bea, if we place a very discreet button here,' Evangeline indicated a place at the back of the jacket's neckline, 'they can fix the scarf on the loop during the winter and tuck the ends quite severely into these loops inside the jacket front. They won't get cold necks and they can pack away the scarf and wear the same jacket during the summer, with the cotton top.'

'And the hat?'

'My triumph, Bea, I think you'll agree.' Evie had sketched all angles of a hat, each drawing on a different shape of face. It looked like a tiny bird with wings on each side and a little beak dipping towards the forehead. 'A wren, do you see?'

'I certainly do. Why should women in uniform have to look dowdy? Marvellous, Evie. I'll put these in a cab for Priscilla first thing.' She looked at her watch. 'Supper time. Will you come back and eat with us?'

'Thanks, Bea, but I can't. Got a date, you know.' Evangeline smiled. So did Beatrice.

'Beatrice, my dear, I'm so very sorry.' Priscilla Dawlish sounded, for once, sincere. 'Those idiots at the High Command. We've got a bloody war on but they won't shift their attitudes by one little inch. Disgusts me.'

'Priscilla, please be a little more specific. If you're saying that the House of Eliott Wrens design hasn't won then I'm sorry and disappointed. But it's not the end of the world. I'd like to know why, of course.'

'Well, they wanted something rather more military than the sketches that you and Evangeline produced. And they seemed to take no notice of all your clever practical considerations. None at all. And no notice, either, of my recommendations. I really did think your Wrens look was outstanding in every way – but what can you do? They grudgingly admit women but want them either to look like men or like tarty barmaids in a Plymouth pub. Evie won't be too upset, will she?'

'She'll be very disappointed. More so than I am since she put so much thought into the designs. But she'll live. She has other things on her mind at the moment.' Beatrice smiled to herself and waited for Priscilla's inevitable enquiry. 'Don't ask me. Haven't a clue, as they say.' Careless talk, she thought to herself, echoing the new slogan which admonished gossip or unnecessary use of the telephone, can indeed be costly.

Somewhat piqued, Priscilla could not resist adding that the House of Eliott had not done themselves any favours by specifying that they would not charge anything for their designs and that they would show them, moreover, at their next collection. 'Those old men at the Admiralty, my dear, old gits if you ask me, simply could not understand. All the other houses presented a fee with their designs. Those silly old fools still adhere to the principle that you get what you pay for. True in peacetime but not, surely, when we are in the grip of *force majeure*?'

Although Beatrice laughed, all indignation spent, after replacing the telephone receiver when Priscilla had at last finished, she was not looking forward to breaking the news to her sister. Evangeline, however, was dreamy and sanguine. 'Don't worry, Bea. It wasn't a waste of time. Nothing ever is. I fiddled around with some drawings for land-girls' outfits as well, actually. Now that Ethel's signed on I think we'd better make them up for her. A sort of "going-away" ensemble, don't you think? She'll be the most chic land-girl in the country and if she doesn't end up on the top of a haystack, married to a blossom-cheeked farmer with several hundred acres, I don't know who will.'

One morning early in 1941 Beatrice slit the tops of her letters with a knife much less sticky with butter and jam, honey or marmalade than it would have been a few months earlier. There were several bills, a bulky envelope that she recognized by the handwriting to be from a friend, and an interesting-looking aerogram from Singapore. She set these aside and read first an announcement about the forthcoming issue of clothing coupons and wondered how it would affect the business. She would have to make enquiries. They would certainly need to think again about party frocks requiring yard upon yard of silk or tulle if cloth, too, was to be rationed. She made a mental note to telephone her friend at Liberty's. He would know. And she would cable Mr Lee who had often supplied them with startlingly beautiful bolts of silk from his warehouse in Hong Kong. She continued to muse. Would coupons simply buy a jacket or skirt whether it came from the House of Eliott or from Derry's or Bourne and Hollingsworth? It was baffling and worrying. She started guiltily when Jack spoke.

'Bea. Beatrice.' Jack took her wrist and set down the

knife. 'Are you listening? Are you awake? Will you listen to me, please?'

'Jack, my love. I'm so sorry. Miles away, you know.'

'And so might I be. Bea, I've decided to . . . in a manner of speaking . . . enlist.'

Beatrice shuddered into a painful and total clarity. 'That's ridiculous, Jack. You can't. Also, in a manner of speaking, you're too old, thank God. You can't.'

'Too old to be a soldier, perhaps. After all, I am a little over forty, I grant you.' He gripped her other wrist in excitement. 'Bea, it's the most marvellous, marvellous and totally correct thing. The War Office has asked me to make newsreels from the front. I want to do it. It's as if I've simply been in training for this with the work I've been doing for Pathé. I must. Don't you see?'

'Yes,' replied Beatrice slowly, dabbing at her mouth.

CHAPTER TEN

It was a Saturday morning and Evangeline lay in bed. She had woken to the sound of the milkman's dray horse clopping across the cobbles outside. After getting up briefly to draw the curtains and to make coffee and toast she had returned to bed. Autumn sunlight flooded into the room and outside the low murmur of Knightsbridge traffic was pleasing, reassuringly familiar. She brushed some crumbs from the pale counterpane and stretched diagonally, luxuriously, across her sheets. How lovely it was, she thought, to be back in my own bed. How wonderful it was to please oneself.

The doorbell had pealed earlier but she had ignored it. Neither had she lifted the phone on any of the three occasions that it had rung. She stretched again and wondered what she would wear to lunch. She was meeting Viola at Solange's and then they planned to spend the afternoon at an exhibition – or even two. Viola felt she had a lot of London to catch up with and Evangeline remembered the feeling. They would decide which ones over their aperitifs.

Remembering the arrangement, it occurred to Evangeline that Viola might have been trying to telephone with news of some change of plan, so she dialled the Freemantle number. Viola answered at once. 'No, not me, Evie darling. I've spent the entire morning trying to memorize my lines. Been up since dawn. Well, about nine o'clock, anyway. Must rush now. We can do all our jabbering later. A girl's got to fix her face. See you in an hour.'

Evangeline glanced at the clock by her bed. Viola was right: it was approaching noon. She reluctantly ran her bath, tipping in Oil of Chypre from Floris, and let the thin silk robe slip over her shoulders, down her back and settle in an almost weightless heap on the tiles. She was not given to false modesty and was well aware that her figure was far better than that of most women approaching their mid-thirties but Evangeline was none the less pleased that steam from the bathwater misted over the mirrors and that the blur obscured her very slightly thickened waist. Her mood of perfect contentment cracked a little wider when the phone rang again just as she settled back into the perfumed clouds, and vanished completely when two minutes later it trilled again. She ignored it. The long, slow soak that Evangeline had intended turned into a quick dip. Within little more than thirty minutes she was dressed, made-up and heading towards St Martin's Lane in the Alvis. As she drove she cursed herself for not suggesting that they meet at twelve thirty. Viola invariably operated socially on Actress Time, which meant she never set foot from home a moment before she was due at her destination. Evie waited, sipping a gin and tonic, for half an hour before Viola arrived, stunning in the swaggering fuchsia wool-crêpe coat and slender dress beneath, finished for her only the week before. A scarlet tricorn hat trimmed with a fuchsia edge broke all the fashion colour rules and made her look like a chic highwayman.

'I know, I know, darling. It's outrageous, especially with my colouring. But let me tell you, my cab driver told me just now that he wouldn't mind if I asked him to stand and deliver some dark night. Cheek!' She laughed as she settled herself in front of Evangeline. 'Why the long face? He didn't mean any harm.' She glanced at her watch. 'And I'm only French late, you miserable blighter. That's what Renée always called it, anyway.'

Evangeline looked up. 'Sorry, Vi. I'm not cross with you. Only with myself, if anything.' She brightened. 'Lovely to see you. I'd forgotten you knew Renée. Do you ever see her?'

'Not really. Don't think she's been in London for years. Hear a bit about her, though. I gather she and Daphne are still la toast de toutes les lower dives de Paris.' She thought for a moment. 'I suppose we ought to be a bit worried for them. Put some feelers out, shall we?' Evangeline nodded and Viola leaned forward. 'But now, Evie, I want all your news. There's never time for a jaw after fittings. You girls seem busy as ever, I must say.'

'We are,' said Evangeline, picking up her menu. 'Shall we get this over and done with first?' When the waiter came for their order she asked for the soup and the rack of lamb. Viola astonished her by eschewing poached fish or salad and asking for pâté and roast pheasant.

'Got to make the most of it – in England, anyway. It's not going to be long, one gathers, before restaurant food will be rationed as well.' She patted Evangeline's hand. 'Never fear, Evie, when I'm back in the States I'll send you a little care package every week. You must make out a list for me of all the non-perishables you'd like me to post. Cookies, Dime bars, things in tins, fruit cake, bully beef, you know, that sort of thing.'

Evangeline smiled. 'Thanks. I certainly will. But I don't think it's going to be as bad as all that – at least, not for those who can afford to eat in restaurants.' She caught

Viola's arched, enquiring look. 'There could be all sorts of dodges around this five-shilling-maximum meal rule that they are going to impose. Someone told me that you'll be able to have oysters, then fillet steak and then trifle, perhaps, or some Stilton at the Ritz for your five bob but that you'll find when the bill comes that you're charged a pound for your roll and another for your coffee. I suppose it's unfair, really.'

Their first courses arrived. 'Since when has life been fair, Evie? Me, I want as much unfair as I can get. Second helpings of it, please.' She laughed. 'Do you, truthfully, want life to be fair?'

'I don't know. I just don't know.'

'My, oh my, we are in serious mode today. Come on, Evie, tell Auntie Vi all about it.'

Evangeline took a sip of her wine. 'It's Hugo, really. I'm in a bit of a muddle about him.'

'Thought as much.'

'It seems so dreadfully shallow to be preoccupied with one's own selfish concerns at a time like this but I just can't help it. We've seen each other once or twice recently, first time for years.' For once Viola was able to remain silent, merely nodding for Evangeline to continue. Her features, in fact, tightened and knotted but Evangeline did not notice. 'I find him, well, if anything, more attractive than ever. And I still like him enormously, although I think he'll always be what you might call "difficult". Anyway, I suppose you could say we had a bit of a spat a couple of days ago.' She hesitated.

'Go on.' Viola's expression relaxed slightly.

'Years ago, I don't know if you ever heard about any of this, Vi, we didn't know each other then, Hugo wanted to marry me. I was very young and had rather enjoyed simply being his mistress, lover, call it what you will. At the time I didn't realize what a huge step Hugo had taken in asking me. Anyway, we had a rather chilly parting after that. I went off to Paris. Remember? Wasn't it around that time that I first met you – while I was on a visit to London? And he went to work in Vienna? And now, just recently, Hugo suggested marriage once again, in an oblique sort of way. I told him I'd become too used to being by myself and that this was the worst of times even to think about it. Quite apart from the fact that we've only just started to pick up the old threads and get to know one another again, everything is so uncertain just now. I said I'd prefer for us to see each other often but casually, you know.'

'What did he say?' Viola was examining her finger nails.

'He was rather cross, actually. Very huffy. But we made it up and I think everything's all right again. In fact I'm seeing him tomorrow. We're going to hear Myra Hess play at the Wigmore Hall and, if the weather holds, afterwards go up to Hampstead and we'll have the last picnic of the year on the Heath.' She paused. 'So that's it, really. Part of me is sure that I'm doing the right thing, saying the right things, but a tiny fragment of me wonders. What do you think?'

'I think you're a perfect little fool.'

'I thought you'd say that.'

'I'm glad you weren't in, or didn't want to answer the phone on Saturday morning.'

'Why?'

'Because I was going to suggest we called this off. And if I had we wouldn't have had such a lovely time, would we?' The afternoon's music had been exquisitely played and suitably spiritual for a Sunday. Now Evangeline and Hugo were sitting on a woollen rug finishing the last of their bread and cheese and the red wine in a gathering dusk, which introduced a light, brisk wind. Evangeline pulled her coat about her shoulders.

Hugo sniffed the air. 'I suppose we should have picnicked first but I love this place in the early evening, at this time of year. The smells and the shadows. I think London is an autumn city, don't you? It's at its best then.'

'As Paris is a spring city, you mean?'

'Ah, yes. Paris.' Hugo drained his glass. 'You were quite right, Evie, the other day. Much better this way.' He smiled thinly. 'Even so, I wish I'd never asked you to marry me in the first place, all those years ago.'

This seemed contradictory and Evie was confused. In the fading light she could not see his face clearly. 'I don't understand.'

'Then let me tell you. If I had not proposed to you and you had not refused and we had not quarrelled about it you might not have gone to Paris and I certainly would not have gone to Vienna with Leonard. So I would not have met that pretty little fool Martina and married her instead. I would not have made that poor girl's life such a misery when I dragged her back to London and she would not have run home, understandably, to her parents when we divorced.' By now shadows all but obscured Hugo's face. 'I still feel responsible for her, Evie. Her parents are Jewish which means that Martina, fair and Aryan though she may look, is in terrible danger. I have to go to Vienna and bring her back to London. Friends of Johann and Claudia were her guardians. They will take care of her here.'

Evangeline felt an uncomfortable and unaccountable twinge of jealousy. 'You said it was stone dead. That you didn't love her any more. That you never really had. Why take such a risk?'

'Because I must. A sort of debt of honour, I suppose. If I'd tried to love her the marriage might have worked and she might still be here with me, or at least safe with friends in London.' He sighed. 'But I didn't really love her in the first place and I was too selfish to make an effort later.'

'When do you leave?' Evangeline spoke quietly. She felt sickened, but why should she care if this mission led to a rapprochement for Hugo and Martina? Wasn't that unworthy and awfully dog-in-the-manger of her? The idea of Hugo being hurt or detained himself then crossed her mind and she felt as if her chest had been struck by a brick. She tried to keep her voice level. 'I wish you luck, Hugo. It's a very decent thing that you're doing, very decent indeed. Will you let me know when you get back to London?'

'Of course I will.' Now Hugo shivered. 'Let's get packed up. Time to get you home.' They found a cab, eventually, in Spaniards Lane.

'Will you come in for a while?' The cab had drawn up outside the mews house.

Hugo hesitated. 'Best not, Evie. Not tonight. I'll take the cab on.' He coughed. 'One other thing I should mention. I've decided that, if they'll have me at the advanced age of thirty-nine, I shall enlist as soon as I get back. I've been thinking about it since the start.' He feigned not to hear Evangeline's gasp. 'Out you get, meter's running. Take care, Evie, and don't worry. I'll be fine and so will you. We'll have one of those five-shilling dinners soon, shall we?'

Evangeline could not speak. She clambered out of the cab and, for her neighbours' sake, was glad that a siren howled almost as soon as she closed the door behind her. It was far louder than the sound of her sob.

'You're not going to believe this.'

Beatrice was used to Priscilla Dawlish's dramatic preambles. She held the phone under her chin and continued to scan through the column of figures which the accountant had just passed to her. 'What is it, Priscilla? Has violet nail lacquer been invented? Are we to start putting bustles in our frocks?'

Priscilla was oblivious to the sarcasm. 'It's Cyril. He's joined up, in a manner of speaking. He's been taken on as an official war photographer. Isn't it just killing? Imagine! Cyril, of all people, in the thick of it. He keeps saying he loves to see a man in uniform – the sort of remark you'd expect Cyril to make – but for once I believe he's serious.'

Beatrice remembered, as she did every few minutes, how soon Jack was due to leave and sighed deeply. He wasn't sure when he and his small film crew would be ordered to sail. They had to behave as if every day and evening together in London might be their last for the foreseeable future. 'So I was wondering, Beatrice dear, if we might have a little farewell dinner for the sweet boy. There's no one else to arrange one for him. What do you think?'

'Good idea, Priscilla. Where shall we go?' Priscilla ignored the almost imperceptible hesitation in Beatrice's voice.

'Well, I wondered, Beatrice, if it could be held at your house? My dining room is so poky while yours is charming and it would be better, don't you think, to send the dear boy off from a real home with real friends. I can bring some of the food, of course.'

Beatrice brightened. Dinner parties were a bit of a struggle these days, not just because of food rationing but because the cook had enlisted in the WRAC. However, Molly quite liked to turn a hand in the kitchen if she was asked to, and this way it would at least mean another evening at home for Jack. Moreover, a number of her country-based clients had shamelessly offered her eggs, game and pork joints in return for early appointments or an extra inch of braiding. Only yesterday Cynthia Clement-Powell had arrived with a brace of pheasants declaring that she wanted the feathers used to trim the shoulders of a wrap and that Beatrice could do exactly as she wished with the birds themselves – just so long as the wrap was ready for dispatch by Friday. 'Beatrice. Beatrice, are you there?'

'Yes, Priscilla. I'm so sorry. It's a wonderful idea. Shall we say the day after tomorrow?'

It was a small party, eight people altogether. To Beatrice's surprise Jack was not at all displeased by the plan. 'It stretches my departure away, somehow. I know that the evening before I have to go we'll be by ourselves, the whole family, so an evening like this puts it off. Besides, as you know, I've always been rather fond of Cyril. He's a rascal but a talented and amusing one and I admire him for volunteering. It's right that we should send him off properly. After all, he hasn't got a family, like us, to do it for him.'

'But admit it, Jack, you're longing to get away, too, aren't you?'

'In some ways. Not in others. Funny how you can sometimes dread the thing you desire and vice versa, isn't it?' They were dressing, the day before the party. Jack was late for a meeting with the Pathé people: his other work had to continue until he went abroad. 'You're a wicked woman, Beatrice Maddox. What kind of a war effort do you call that?' He nodded towards their rumpled bed.

'I was lying back and thinking of England,' she said crisply, 'among other things.'

All things considered the dinner went very well, Beatrice thought afterwards. Between them she and Priscilla had managed to put on the table some asparagus (begged by Beatrice from a client who had patriotically turned over her lawns for the growing of vegetables but who insisted that she retain the right to choose which ones and to keep her cherished asparagus bed going), Molly's soda bread, a salmon trout for which Priscilla had traded a fashion puff in the magazine, the pheasants and a rather nasty pudding made largely from dried fruits and for which, fortunately, no one had much appetite. Evangeline brought several bottles of wine to add to those from Jack's cellar and Viola produced an enormous slab of her favourite chocolate, sent to her by a friend in California and saved for a special occasion.

Cyril, as guest of honour, had been invited to bring two friends of his own and a charmingly shrieking pair they were, causing Cyril to touch his funniest, shrillest heights. One of the young men, Philip Davenport, had worked in the theatre with Viola and the other, Frederick (no one quite caught his surname), seemed to work in the police force and regaled the party with outrageous slanders concerning a number of public figures. Priscilla became a trifle lachrymose towards the end of the evening but forced herself to perk up when even she noticed that Cyril's bravura was flagging. As the evening hours passed he spoke ever less loudly about how much he was looking forward to joining the action with boys and ever more frequently showed the seldom seen serious side of his nature. At a perilous moment when his own tears seemed about to spring he slapped his own wrist, admonished himself and called for a final toast.

'To us. To all of us. May we all meet again soon.'

By two o'clock everyone had left and Beatrice and Jack slept too heavily in each other's arms to hear the sirens or the rumble of explosions far to the east of London where the docks were taking yet another hammering.

'What are we to make of this?' Elsie held out two long bolts of heavily embossed brocade.

'That's Mrs Carstairs's drawing room curtains, that is, and what we are to make of them, Miss Bea says, is an evening gown. Very patriotic of Mrs Carstairs, Miss Bea said, for Mrs Carstairs to use her curtains instead of buying cloth while we can still get it. Very mean, in my opinion. She wants a little cape if there's enough cloth left over.' Beryl giggled. 'Talk about optimism. Might manage it if evening dresses were cut as short and straight as daytime clothes are these days. She'll have to make do with that terribly, terribly ancient velvet coat we made for her all of two years ago.'

'I think it's very sensible, all this. Tests our initiative,' said Doris.

'Tests Miss Evie's, you mean, don't you? Wonders she did with that bedspread of Lady Pamela's. I copied it, actually.' Beryl lowered her voice and spoke behind her palm. 'I memorized the pattern and cut up my bedspread at home. It's only candlewick, not silk like Lady Pamela's, so it doesn't hang as nice and I couldn't get any lining for it but it still makes me feel like Greta Garbo when I go downstairs to make my cocoa.' She fingered a mound of fragile cream silk. 'This would have been just perfect for the lining, though. Fat chance of some Jerry parachuting down into my back garden, though, worse luck. Still,' Beryl heaved a philosophical sigh, 'nice that some can still get married in silk dresses, I suppose. Makes a change from all those uniforms and suits. Anyone know who it's for?'

'Well, it isn't for Tilly, that's for sure,' Ruth piped up from the back of the workroom. 'I believe her romance with Mr Grant is over.'

'How do you know?' demanded Beryl.

'She got bored. He was married already and Tilly tell me that she thought he was just a flashing Harry. All trousers and no mouth, she said, so we don't think she mind much. Anyway, she got new boyfriend now. Mr Grant, maybe he just help Tilly to – is this right? – play herself in.' Anya shrugged. She and Ruth still spoke as one.

'But how do you know about this new feller?' Beryl demanded. 'And who is he?'

'We know because we watch and see. We are used to having to do that.' Ruth pulled a deliberately infuriating, mysterious face.

'And also we know because she told us,' finished Anya with a giggle. 'We like Tilly very much but we think that somehow she imagine that because we do not come from England we don't quite understand her if she want to unbosom her burden to us. Like the confession that some of our Catholic friends at home told us about.'

'Unburden her bosom,' corrected Ruth.

'Never mind that. Who is he?' Elsie shrieked.

'An American. That's all we know, isn't it, Anya? He take her to see *Cavalcade* and Tilly say he seem a little bored. In the air force, we think. A pity she didn't meet a nice Polish airman instead. Plenty of those in town.'

'Why can't we find any, then?' asked Anya. 'If your clogs are so clever.'

Jack had been gone for a month and Hugo not yet returned from Vienna. Evangeline and Beatrice were having tea one Sunday, the children walking in the park with Molly.

'At least they seem to be enjoying all this. Even Ned asked me the other evening why they hadn't had to go down to the cellar recently. There had been a lull recently in the bombing and everyone was hoping that the worst of the Blitz was over. He said it was boring sleeping in the nursery.' Beatrice laughed. 'He picked up that word from Tom. Everything bores Tom except Spitfires and explosions and his gas-mask – he loves carrying that about with him.' She sighed. 'Yes, everything bores him, especially me. It's hateful having to be the lone disciplinarian. He keeps asking when Daddy's coming back, keeps saying, "Daddy would let me." Clare's a bit the same but not half as bad.'

'You can't blame him for missing his father, Bea.'

'Of course I don't. And of course he's too young to realize that I miss Jack every bit as much. It's awful. I feel such guilt about Tom and it doubles every time I have to tell him off. Funny, isn't it, how it's so much easier with the other two?' Beatrice bit into another of Molly's shortbreads and looked up. 'You know, if I didn't know better I'd swear she'd made these with butter. Any word from Hugo?'

Evangeline shook her head. 'What a silly girl I am, Bea. If I'd married him when he first asked me he wouldn't be there now.'

'You can't blame yourself, Evie. You just weren't ready then. Perhaps it runs in the family. I was almost your age before I felt ready and able to marry. You should be happy that at last you know what you really want – ' Beatrice was interrupted by a clatter at the front door and the noise of the children returning home, changing their shoes and hanging up their coats. She called out to Molly to bring them in for tea.

Five-year-old Ned ran into the room first, the sight of his sturdy little legs encased in his first long socks causing a lump to rise in Beatrice's throat. 'Look, Mummy! The man was there outside in his blue suit. This is for you.' He held out a telegram. Beatrice went white as she tore it open. Evangeline motioned to Molly to keep the other children outside for a moment and then turned to her sister again.

Beatrice's face was lit with happiness and her eyes sparkled. 'It's from Jack. He's perfectly fine and he's got a twenty-four-hour pass. Should be home tomorrow after-noon.' She clasped the telegram to her chest. 'Oh, Evie, I'm so happy.' She took Ned's hand and called for Clare and Tom. 'Guess who's coming to see us tomorrow? Yes! Daddy!' As they danced in a circle of four around the rug in front of the fire Evangeline felt a great knot of envy, longing and pain tighten in her chest.

While Molly was preparing the children for their baths Evangeline told Beatrice that she was sure she could organize some theatre tickets through Viola for Monday evening. 'Thanks, Evie, but I think Jack and I would prefer to have dinner somewhere.' Beatrice frowned. 'But Monday is Molly's night off. I know she'd oblige under normal circumstances but she told me weeks ago that she'd arranged to meet one of her sisters and stay over in Kilburn. Some kind of family hooley, I think.'

'Don't worry, Bea. I'll come here and baby-sit. I promise you it will give me real pleasure. I'll do the lot, give them their supper, bath them then read to them. I'd like to, I really would.'

Beatrice had become used to Jack's short absences in the past. She was astonished, now, to find how fluttery and nervous she felt as she waited him to arrive on Monday afternoon. As the hours passed, excited anticipation descended into fear and gloom. By six thirty, when Evangeline rang the front door bell, she had changed her clothes four times. The last time, as it was now so late, she had decided to wear a Chinese yellow satin dinner dress with a draped and dipping back and a skirt which was cut to fall below the knee at the front but to slither about to almost train length at the back. The jewellery she had chosen was amber, its rich, dull glow lighting her throat, earlobes and wrist. Her face fell when she opened the door to her sister but she tried to brighten up and kissed her on both cheeks.

Evangeline stood back. 'What's up, Bea? You look marvellous, you're going to have a wonderful evening, so what's wrong?'

'Jack's not here, that's what. I was expecting him hours ago. Looks like you may be relieved of your night watch, Evie. They've had their supper already and Molly's put Ned in the bath. She's on her way out now.' Beatrice managed another wan smile.

'I'm staying, whatever happens. This is my treat, too, remember? I've been looking forward to playing Mummy all day. Are they upstairs?' Her sister nodded weakly. Evangeline flung her coat over the bannisters and took the stairs two at a time. 'It's your wicked aunt, chicks. I've come to wash behind your ears.' Beatrice remained at the foot of the stairs. Amid the sounds of splashes and happy squealing she heard a key twisting in the lock and saw her husband's shadow behind the dark, coloured glass.

It was like a bad dream. She wanted to rush to him but her legs wouldn't move. Instead Jack slammed his bag down and ran to her, clasping her so tightly that she thought she would break. 'Darling Jack, darling Jack.' She could only mumble as he crushed her and kissed her face, her neck and her throat.

Eventually he stood back. 'My Bea. My beautiful Beatrice. How I've missed you.' He looked up, hearing the bathroom noises. 'Darling, I've told the cab driver to wait – might have to wait ages to catch another. We are dining, aren't we?' Beatrice nodded. 'But I must say hello to the nippers before we go.' He was already mounting the stairs. 'I'll explain about this dashed delay when we're in the taxi.'

All three children, pink and glowing, were in the bathroom. Evangeline rose from her knees at the side of the bath and kissed Jack briefly as he and Beatrice entered and then closed the door behind her. The children were silent for a moment and then broke into loud and delighted screams. Beatrice remained near the door and felt that her heart might break with love as she watched her husband somehow encircle all three of their children in his arms, kiss and tousle all three of their damp heads.

The front door clicked shut. When the children were dried, helped into their night things and tucked up in bed Evangeline told them that she would be back to read them a story in five minutes. She checked that the black-out curtains were properly drawn across every window in the house and made a mental note to tell Jack and Beatrice that steam was causing the paper strips criss-crossing the panes in the nursery bathroom to begin to lift away. She searched the children's bookshelves for the story she knew they all liked best – the one about the princess and the pea. She knew perfectly well why it made them laugh so much but always read it with a solemn face and what Clare called her 'Viola voice'. Evangeline had taken her niece to one of Viola's matinées when she was a tot and Clare had been stage-struck ever since.

CHAPTER ELEVEN

Jack had booked them into Luigi's, the small Italian restaurant where he and Beatrice had dined countless times before they were married. A strain of misplaced nationalism meant that many Italian restaurants had had to close after the war began but Luigi and Carla were somehow exempted – their families had been restaurateurs and shopkeepers in Soho for generations and their children – waiters and desk clerks now – spoke with pronounced Cockney accents. Even so, the long, narrow room did not have its customary bustling pre-war clatter. Beatrice was pleased: they could talk easily, seated at their favourite corner table, and neither of them particularly liked the showy kind of restaurant where diners could take to the dance floor between courses and table-hopping friends rendered conversation difficult.

'This is a splendid treat for me, Jack, but you must have been eating wonderful food in France, surely? One hears that since the Fall in 1940 food restrictions are almost non-existent there.'

'One hears all sorts of things that aren't necessarily true, especially in war-time when a particularly virulent form of Chinese whisper can take hold.' Jack was studying his menu and looked up. 'In any case, I chose to be billeted, as it were, with the enlisted men. I don't see how I can portray their realities without experiencing some of them. I've shared their quarters, their conditions and their perfectly horrible food. Let's order, shall we? Quite a lot seems to have been inked out of the menu here but it still looks pretty good to me. I know it's only been a matter of weeks but it seems like years since I ate anything but hashed-up mince or stew and stale bread.' He opted for a rather unItalian lobster bisque and grilled sole. 'Thank God they haven't rationed fish here yet.' Beatrice, too distracted to be hungry and unwilling to waste time over the limited menu, said she would have the same. They had finished their split of champagne and a bottle of Frascati was brought to their table.

Jack seemed reluctant to speak of his work in France, partly because much of the detail concerning locations and procedures was classified, even to his wife, and partly because – for this evening, at least – he wanted to forget the front, to catch up with news of the children and to enjoy the incandescent presence of Beatrice. In the candlelight she glowed, her auburn hair burnished, and her pale shoulders and throat creamy against the slippery yellow satin. Beatrice expected that he would elaborate about his work later, after they had made love. That was usually Jack's way: she wasn't always at her most alert and receptive at such times but it was better, Beatrice considered, than being married to some-one who rolled over immediately and began to snore as she had heard some men did. While their love-making tended to send her into a deep, purring drift of contentment, Jack often spoke afterwards of difficult matters. One kind of energy was spent to be replaced immediately by something different, expressed with heightened clarity.

He tipped her chin with his index finger after she laid down her knife and fork, the bones of the sole left neatly at the side of her plate. 'I thought about you – about you all – constantly. Did you get all the cards and letters?'

'Nothing yet. But I know that deliveries from France are erratic. We'll probably get a sackload all at once. Did you miss me?'

Jack knew exactly what Beatrice meant. He leaned forward and cupped both her cheeks with his hands. 'Just a little bit. Just about once every twenty-four minutes. All right, maybe slightly more often than that.' Beatrice flushed as the waiter arrived with menus again. Jack had saved a small space in his stomach for some of Luigi's legendary cassata. Beatrice's flush had spread to the flat plain beneath her throat and above her breasts. Her face, conversely, had suddenly become very pale. She gripped Jack's hand with a fierce pressure that alarmed him. 'What's up, Bea?' The waiter still hovered.

'We must go, Jack. We must leave right away.'

'What on earth . . .?'

'I just know we must. Something dreadful has happened. We have to go home at once.'

Jack shrugged and asked the waiter to bring the bill. He glanced at it, left some notes on the table and took Beatrice's elbow. He had to bundle her fur about her shoulders as she was already on the pavement scanning the streets for a taxi and whiter than ever. There were no cabs. She began to run. The sky to the east was still and dark – the docks had been spared this night. But to the west there was a fearsome reddish glow cut, like a hideous false dawn, with flickering yellow blades of fire which the swaying columns of ARP search-lights illuminated before they died in the high cloud. And there were horrible sounds. There was the mingled rumbling of departing aircraft and that of buildings collapsing. A sickening, scorching smell was carried on hot gusts of a terrible wind. And they had thought the worst was over . . .

Jack followed Beatrice as she stumbled along pavements, shouting at cars, begging for transport, but most vehicles were heading away from the blaze. Only ambulances and fire engines seemed to move westwards. They ran faster and crashed into crowds of people huddled in doorways or racing for the shelter of the tube. Eventually, only a mile away from Upper Brook Street, Jack saw a cab unload. The driver hesitated for a moment after Jack thrust a clean white fiver into his hand, but then turned. Noise intensified and traffic thickened as the cab inched west. Beatrice was hunched forward, quivering. Jack leaned out of the window, his mouth covered with a handkerchief. 'It's no good, Beatrice. Traffic's at a complete standstill ahead.' Civilian vehicles were jammed and banked up so that fire engines and ambulances could cut through the streets. 'We'll be better off on foot.' He thrust a further pound note at their cab driver, grasped Beatrice's hand and they stumbled onto the pavement. They ran again, Beatrice oblivious to the fact that the low, curved heel of one satin slippers had twisted off and both of them unheeding of the increasing noise, stench and heat as they approached their street near the park.

A crowd had gathered on the corners as they turned into it, gasping. The gutters were overflowing, fire hoses were trained on houses at the far end and the air was thick with dust and cinders. 'It may be all right, Bea. I think they've missed us.' Jack was later ashamed of his reaction as he and Beatrice pushed through stricken groups of people, bundled in blankets and white with shock, people whom he dimly recognized as neighbours. Someone tried to bar their way. 'We live here. Our children—' Beatrice fisted her way past and kept running. The road had cracked and buckled. Water was spurting out of drains and the heat intensified as they approached their home. The stitch in her side felt like a twisting knife. At last she and Jack pushed their way through and stood in front of their house.

Further along the street, houses were still aflame and the firemen worked with what she would remember as a silent frantic calm. At any rate, she could remember no noise but her own scream.

The tall, narrow, flat front of their house had apparently escaped damage aside from blown-out windows and a ruined porch. Fragments of the slender supporting pillars were scattered amid other rubble all over the road. In slow motion Beatrice traced with her toe the number fifty-four, painted in black on the stucco. They had stopped for a second, panting. Acrid smoke made her eyes water and her chest heave and choke. She felt as if she was watching herself in a film. Seven houses along, the terrace had completely collapsed and there was a long, smouldering gap as if teeth had been brutally pulled from a beautiful mouth. Then she saw how the damage and dereliction fell in a long diagonal from their own chimneys to the houses which had been completely destroyed. In the next instant Beatrice saw that number fifty-two no longer had a roof or a nursery floor. That second time she didn't hear herself scream.

Jack and Beatrice hurtled into their house.

Every name was called, all at once, louder and louder. '*Tom, Ned, Clare, Evie!* TOM, NED, CLARE, EVIE!'

At last there was an answer. 'We're here. We're all here.' It was Evangeline's voice, thin and unsteady, and it came from the cellar.

Jack had grabbed one of the heavy electric torches they

kept in the hallway in readiness for emergencies. Its beam was broad and powerful. They descended the stairs. 'Here, in the corner.' Evangeline guided them. By the light of the torch Beatrice and Jack could see her face, chalk white except for black smudges of dust. Clare and Ned were wrapped in blankets, arms about each other, asleep. Evangeline's left arm was outstretched, encircling them as much as possible. Cradled within her right arm and with his head lying heavily against her chest, was Tom, fragments of pale wood clenched in his fist. Beatrice and Jack knew immediately that he was dead.

The electricity had come back on in some of the rooms and Jack had been told by one of the wardens outside that it would be safe for him to light a fire in the kitchen. Clare and Ned were still asleep in each other's arms, covered now by Beatrice's fox cape as they lay on an old settle in the kitchen. From time to time Beatrice distractedly ruffled their hair as one might stroke the fur of sleeping kittens. Jack clasped Tom's body to his chest, rocking it back and forth as if he were singing a lullaby. Tears cascaded down his face. He tightened his grip on his son. Beatrice was staring ahead glassily and Evangeline simply quivered and shook, her head slumped on the table and buried in the crook of her arms. Outside, the street was quiet now and it was getting light.

Molly did not speak when she let herself in from the basement stairs. She looked, lit the gas for hot water and made some telephone calls from the drawing room. Then she went upstairs to see where the children might rest. She decided on the drawing room as being the safest. While the tea was brewing she gently shook Clare and Edmund awake.

Drowsy and grumpy, they stumbled off with Molly tugging at their hands. She settled them on sofas only pausing to unstrap their shoes, tuck blankets around them, and to open a window. Then she climbed as many further stairs as she could before a fetid gust of morning air at the turn of the stairs leading to the nursery floor made her look up and see daylight and devastation. Timbers from what remained of the roof hung loose and creaked. Clouds of dust made her choke, and splinters of glass crackled beneath her feet.

The tea was ready when Molly returned to the kitchen. She poured four cups and laced each with brandy. Down here everything looked, or might seem, perfectly normal, apart from the unnerving silence and the nauseating smell of recent fire. Molly gently lifted Tom from Jack's arms.

'No.' It was his first word. 'No. You do not take my son.'

Molly breathed deeply and fought to control her own tears. 'God has taken your son, Mr Maddox. I have asked the doctor to come for him.'

'Jack. That's my name, Molly. Call me Jack.' He relaxed his hold on Tom, ran his fingers through the silky dark hair for the last time, removed the spectacles and placed them in his own pocket. He touched Beatrice's shoulder. 'Bea, darling, Molly says that Dr Blair will come for Tom in a minute. I suppose I'll have to talk to him about – ', he stumbled, 'about arrangements. Do you want to be there with me?'

'No. Not yet. Give him to me.' Beatrice took the small body and crushed it to her breast. Then she held it before her, studying it as if she wanted to memorize every detail of the small, limp and still sweet-smelling form. Only a cut near his left temple marred the perfect beauty of the child. He could still be sleeping, Molly thought. Beatrice kissed him, his hands, wrists, nose, grubby knees, his shoulders, hair and eyes. 'Goodbye, my boy. Goodbye, my dear little Tom.' She handed him back to Jack. Jack took his son and waited with him on the steps at the front of the house until the doctor arrived.

More tea was made. Jack was back in the kitchen. Evangeline had raised her head but was still shaking. Molly had gone to the scullery to cut some bread for toast and to warm some of yesterday's porridge. Beatrice sat, still and silent as a stone. Only Jack could speak. 'Can you tell us what happened, Evie?'

She lifted her face. She spoke slowly, every phrase punctuated with sniffs and hesitations and heaving gasps. 'I read them a story and stayed with them until I was sure they were all asleep.' She looked briefly into Jack's eyes. 'Tom tried it on a bit as he always does when I babysit. Claimed eldest child's privileges and asked for more cocoa and a biscuit. He put his fingers through the curly bits here, wheedling me.' She patted the back of her hair where it grew wavy and springy at her nape and sobbed. 'The siren went then and I told him we'd better get Clare and Ned down to the cellar. He was thrilled, excited. I think he felt very much the man of the house.' Jack nodded for her to continue.

'He was an angel. Clare was grumpy and started to cry and Ned was fractious too, but we got them downstairs, between us. The whole house was beginning to tremble. I was terrified. I could hear the explosions getting louder and louder – I knew it must be very near. I was trying to calm and settle Clare and Ned when I realized Tom wasn't with us any more. I'm so sorry, Jack. He'd been such a little man that I'd felt able to concentrate on the other two. I called out from the bottom of the cellar stairs. I screamed for him to come back down and I beamed my torch up. I just saw his little face – he was smiling, Jack, he was happy and almost exultant – and he said he had to fetch something from his room.

'I didn't know what to do. I looked back at the other two but decided I'd better chase Tom and haul him back down. I caught up with him in the nursery, just as he'd grabbed his balsawood plane.' Jack groaned, remembering the long, squinting and painstaking hours Tom had spent assembling it, refusing any help, remembering how heart-breakingly clumsy his effort had been. But Tom had, triumphantly, finished it. 'I took his hand and was bundling him out of the room when the house was hit. The roof seemed to sweep off in a fraction of a second, skitter off in blazing fragments in a matter of instants. I thought we'd both be pulled into the sky by the force of the heat and the pull of the air. I thought the floor and the stairs would crumble beneath us. I picked him up and dragged him down to the cellar again. Each time my foot struck a stair tread I thought it was a miracle.

'I didn't realize what had happened until I got him down to the cellar. The balsa plane was crushed in his little hand. I could see by torchlight. There was a clean, sharp shard of glass from one of the windows, I suppose, piercing his temple. I pulled it out. But he didn't bleed, so I knew he was already dead.' Her whisper was barely audible. 'I'm sorry, Jack. I don't know what else I could have done.' Evangeline was gasping again, gulping at fresh tea that Molly had stiffened with more brandy.

'You have nothing to blame yourself for, Evie. You must never think that.' Beatrice spoke for the first time. She rose and stepped towards her sister, cupping Evangeline's face in her hands and kissing both cheeks. Jack stood over them, an arm around each sister's shoulders. While they cried together Molly went to see if Clare and Ned were still sleeping peacefully on their sofas.

It wasn't a difficult decision for Evangeline. Beatrice and Jack had more or less insisted and she had no inclination to disagree. They had talked about everyone moving to Knightsbridge to stay with her in the mews house but it really wasn't practical, not for them all, and the house in Upper Brook Street was habitable. Besides, Beatrice and Jack would have felt that it was a second abandonment if they had left Tom's home. So, a few days later, she had backed the Alvis into the garage and locked the doors for the duration. Now she waited in the hallway, sitting on her biggest trunk and surrounded by several smaller cases. The taxi was due any minute. She made one last telephone call, to Hugo's parents in Malvern. She had written to him at home and to his regiment but had not heard back. Evangeline wanted to be sure he would know where to find her.

The taxi pulled up, the driver loaded her luggage, and turned out of the mews. As he drove towards Mayfair the short journey was punctuated with his observations about everything from the tendency of officers from the Polish air force to tip themselves out of his cab, mournfully drunk outside the Brompton Oratory, to his opinion of what he saw as the arrogance of the Free French. 'Talk about free, they all seem to want a free ride, if you see what I mean, miss, those Jean-Pierres. Make free with the girls in the back seat, don't tip and leave the cab stinking of garlic and God knows what. Give me a Yank any time. I had that . . .'

The traffic had thickened and the driver had to pull out of Green Street with a swerve.

Evangeline had not really been listening. 'What?' she asked, as the cab lurched. She saw the house. 'It's all right, driver, doesn't matter. We're almost here.'

'Whatever you say, miss. That'll be three and six,' he said as he dropped her.

'Evie, dear. I'm so pleased to see you. We were afraid you'd change your mind.' Jack kissed her and led her to the little white room on the third floor. 'There's a cold lunch ready and waiting so just take your time.' He left her with her cases. Evangeline sat on the edge of the narrow bed. The worst of the frightening scorched smell had already left the house and Leonard had helped to arrange for builders to repair the roof. The stair carpets had yet to dry out completely but the odour of residual damp was soon to be countered by that of fresh paint. Beatrice had roused herself to find some flowers and place them in a small Susie Cooper vase on the night table.

It had been the first time she had left the house since the funeral. There, with Jack at her side, his leave extended for compassionate reasons, she had finally broken down into loud, heaving sobs splitting the peace which filled St John's in Hyde Park Crescent with raw pain. Afterwards she had resumed an unnerving, blank-eyed silence, eating little and sleeping less. Even when she did begin to speak, mentioning something about returning to the House of Eliott offices, Jack and Evangeline – each of them also grief-stricken – remained worried, for Beatrice had yet to *talk*. At least Jack and Evangeline had managed to do that.

The calm and silence of the house, after the bustle of the West End traffic at noon and the cab driver's strident opinions, were oppressive – it was like being in a church. Evangaline wondered, not for the first time, if she had made a mistake. She unpacked and hung up a few things, splashed her face with cologne and smeared on a little lipstick before going downstairs.

Lunch was laid out on the table in the morning room. Molly had made some of her wonderful soda bread and instead of butter there was something quite sharp yet creamy which Jack said Penelope acquired from one of her refugees who had been billeted in Shropshire and looked after goats. There was a Woolton Pie and a few slices of salmon which some chef friend of Cyril's had dropped by in the expectation of Cyril being there. Jack, due back in France the following day, had spent the last of his coupons on a jar of mandarin oranges from Fortnum's. A grim little feast. He had brought up a bottle of Chablis from the cellar. 'This is an important occasion. We want to welcome you, Evie, don't we Bea?' The brave gaiety was countered by the hollow, blank expression in his eyes. Evangeline did not know how long she could bear it. Jack turned to Beatrice. She nodded and cut into the bread. After less than an hour Beatrice made an excuse and left to have a brief lie-down.

'She really needs you, Evie, especially now that I have to leave again. She's been very brave but I don't think she could manage unless you were here.'

Evangeline nodded. 'I want to be here. It's my place.'

There was a light click. Beatrice closed the door behind her. 'Actually, I don't feel tired after all.' She looked at Jack, not smiling but with something approaching animation in her face for the first time since that terrible night. 'I heard all that. Did you mean me to?' Then she gazed at her sister. 'Yes, Evie. This is your place. We're a family. We've always been a family when it mattered most. And so now, with you here, we really are the House of Eliott, good and proper.'

Jack sighed more with relief than pleasure to see some spark cross his wife's face at last. They were a family – the Maddoxes and the Eliotts bound now by hoops of steel. He did not feel excluded by Beatrice's remarks to her sister. He felt heartened and the first glimmer of cheer. Grief for Tom was not diminished, and would never lessen, but this first evidence of Beatrice's will to begin recovery was to be marked. Not celebrated but remembered. 'There's one more bottle of '32. Shall we?'

'Why not?' answered Beatrice and Evangeline together.

CHAPTER TWELVE

'I 'm sorry, girls, but I simply can't be doing with these itsy-bitsy, fancy-nancy hats. Give me a good wide swooping brim, any day of the week. Think of the Anzacs, for pity's sake.'

'But, Cyril,' Priscilla Dawlish admonished him, her scrap of a sense of humour once again deserting her, 'we're not talking of Ascot here, but of the Royal Marines.' Cyril Hunter, Priscilla, Beatrice and Evangeline were poring over pencil sketches in the *Mode* offices. Cyril, on leave, had agreed to help Priscilla decide which designs should be declared the most chic in her latest uniform competition. Since the Eliott girls had decided not to enter this time she felt that they could offer unbiased advice. 'We all love the Anzac hat with that adorable little flip on one side but we have to move with the times and also be practical.' She pushed some other drawings across the table. 'What do you think of these dinky little forage numbers, Evangeline? The Americans look well in them, don't you agree?'

Evangeline's heart was not in this post-lunch discussion. She wanted to get back to her desk and so, she could tell, did Beatrice. 'Sorry, Priscilla. I'm not the best of judges. I want to see men wearing trilbys, Panamas, even Homburgs or bowlers again. Cyril's your man for this sort of thing.' She smiled at him. 'Don't forget that supper date of ours, Cyril.

We have something TTI to ask you about. I'd better go.' She lifted a brow and Beatrice, too, gathered her things.

'What's up with Evie?' asked Priscilla after the sisters had left the room. 'And what in God's name does TTI mean? Is it a vital military code or some obscure social disease?'

'She's quite busy, I believe,' answered Cyril. 'No doubt she wants to clear her desk. And TTI means Terribly Terribly Important. Figure of speech, rather like SNAFU. You know, dear, Situation Normal All Fucked Up.' Cyril peered again at the sketches. 'This one, I think. Also she's frightfully in love this time, thank God.'

'Hugo?'

'Yes, at long last.'

'Thank heaven for that.' Priscilla took a long draw on her cigarette. 'Do you have any news of Constance Travis?'

'I think that might have been what Evie was alluding to when she mentioned TTI just now – and, as you know, Priscilla, I do have my contacts . . .'

'It's impossible, Evie. We'll have to wait until my next leave. But then, then . . .'

'Justice will be done.' She curled against Hugo's chest, nipping the fair wiry curls there with her teeth. 'Why did we waste so much time?'

'There's no such thing as wasted time, Evie. It's taken us ten years to know that this is the right thing. It wouldn't have been wasted time if it had been twenty. We're ready for each other now, ready for the complete caboodle, children and all, if you like. I wouldn't mind.' Hugo kissed Evangeline's hair and stroked the gentle curve of her belly. 'You're almost emotionally retarded, Evangeline, ten years behind most women.' He dodged the thump that she aimed at his shoulder, laughed and continued, 'Those years when you didn't do any proper growing up, after your mother died . . . You've had to make up for them in some other ways. Now you've passed through your spoiled-little-girl phase and I've been well past my stiff-upper-lip stage for a while. So here we are.'

'I'll try to organize a special licence. Can one do that? Caxton Hall or somewhere? So that we can get married the moment you're back in England?'

'I'm not sure. But we must look into it. That's what I'd like, soon as I'm home.'

'And when will that be? Any idea? Where will they send you next?'

'Haven't a clue about either of those questions but I have a nasty feeling it might be out East. The army tends to confuse architects with surveyors and civil engineers. There's a railway needs building in Burma and my colonel implied that I might get posted there. Seems like a structural impossibility to me, but at the moment they appear to want it to stretch right up through from Singapore.'

Evangeline stiffened. 'That's a world away. It could be months.'

'Yes, Evie darling. It could be months – if we're lucky.' Hugo gathered her into his arms again. 'But think about me sitting on some shady verandah, planter's punch in hand and some obedient native maiden attending . . . Could be worse, you know.'

Evangeline stuck out her tongue. Hugo opened his mouth and covered it with his lips. There were four hours before he had to report to Victoria station. In the hotel where they had decided to spend his last night of leave they did not care how much noise they made and every last minute, including the three that it would take them to walk to his train, could be savoured and cherished.

The following day Evangeline felt both exultant and bereft. Hugo had given her a small leather box at Victoria. 'Silly trinket, I don't really believe in these things, do you?' The box contained a plain white-gold band set with three square-cut diamonds of equal size. 'It was the simplest thing I could find yesterday afternoon. You don't have to wear it.'

She had slipped it on her finger at the barrier. 'Yes, I do,' she said. Then she kissed him above his collar and walked away.

'Are you listening, Evie?' Beatrice's voice was sharp.

'Sorry, Bea, miles away.' She twisted her ring: it was a little loose, and she turned to Cyril. 'You were saying? You've tracked Connie down, is that it?'

'Manner of speaking. Try to pay attention this time, Evangeline. I will say this only once.' All three laughed thinly and then Cyril spoke with an uncharacteristic intensity, his voice slipping at times back to the vowels he had used before success and society had put a gloss on his accent. He looked over his shoulder. 'I'll wait till Bea gets back.' Beatrice had risen briefly to take the soup plates and the considerable remains of the parsnip pie back to the kitchen. The only part of supper that any of them had really enjoyed had been the peanut-butter sandwiches – made with a jar sent to Evie by Viola and bread made by Molly. The National Loaf, brown, wholesome and unrationed, was one of the few easily obtainable commodities but somehow the soda bread tasted more of a better past and a richer future. Cyril looked covetously at the last crust. 'Thank God they haven't rationed flour yet. Times like this you really begin to appreciate what you actually like. Shame about butter, though, isn't it?'

'We manage pretty well for dairy things. I suppose it's little less than high treason but I find it impossible to refuse a lovely slab of butter and a few slices of bacon if one of the clients accidentally leaves a package here. We force ourselves, don't we, Bea?' Evangeline spoke in a high, almost prattling tone as Beatrice settled herself back at the dining table and placed the pot full of acorn and chicory 'coffee' in front of them.

Cyril cleared his throat. 'This might surprise you. Some of it might shock you. I say, Beatrice, do you have any of that brandy left? I only brought it here last time so that I could drink it myself, you know.' Beatrice rose and found the bottle and three balloon glasses. Cyril took a large gulp. 'It wasn't difficult to find out about Renée and Daphne. I've heard that they have a regular spot at one of the night-clubs that some of the German officers particularly like.' He cleared his throat. 'Given what those bastards have been up to in other parts of Europe, it's quite extraordinary how some of them express themselves in Paris.'

'What do you mean?' Evie sipped her Cognac.

'More, much more than the frisson that the erotic routine between a beautiful white girl with unmistakable breeding and a beautiful black girl caused here in London after the last war, the High Command are positively enraptured by Daff and Renée. It's the only reason why Daphne hasn't been interrogated or even interviewed as yet. You'd think that Renée would be in danger because of her colour but she's too smart. She plays the curiosity card. They think she's a pet, literally. Particularly since she obviously enchants the perfect, aloof Aryan English girl. Those two, they sail very close to the wind – and this situation *can't* last for ever – but so, I suppose, must some of the German officers who invite them over to share champagne after their turn is over.'

'Sorry, Cyril. I don't quite see yet how this leads us to Connie.' Beatrice was baffled.

'I've been in touch with Louis – don't ask how. I thought he'd be bound to know something about Connie if anyone did.'

Both Beatrice and Evangeline nodded.

'I don't really want to know what his game is. Let's just say that his business hasn't suffered under the Occupation. Louis remains on friendly terms with that fellow at Lanvin. Or was it Lucien Lelong? Doesn't matter. Both places are prospering.

'Louis went to see Renée and Daphne one night recently at La Gamine – that's the name of their club, you know. Before the second cabaret, after supper, Connie arrived on the arm of a distressingly handsome German officer. She looked sensational. More beautiful than ever and glowing, shimmering like a pearl. He recognized the dress as being from that House I mentioned but it was her skin and hair that struck him. You notice that when most women you see these days, however attractive, have lost their shine: dull hair, blank eyes, felty cloth. You know what I mean? Bad food can't help.' Beatrice and Evangeline nodded again.

'Anyway, Connie's officer – Louis says those Nazis are very well tailored indeed – left her for a minute and he snatched the moment to speak to her.

'What happened next?' asked Evangeline.

'They had a quick lunch the next day in one of the cafés in the Seventh. She explained about her relationship with the officer. About how she still modelled for Louis's friend at Lanvin or Lelong or wherever, although she hated most of the clothes that the Germans want to buy for their wives and send home.'

'And what is her relationship with this German?' Beatrice had been longing to ask for several minutes.

Cyril drew yet again on his brandy glass. He paused. 'She is his mistress . . . The relationship must be complex. On one level she despises him, surely. She is a Jewess, after all. He cannot know this. Did you?'

'Yes, we did.' Beatrice and Evangeline spoke at once. They explained that they had only recently learned of this and that now they felt desperately responsible for Connie.

Cyril continued, 'She is in terrible danger, however cleverly she passes herself off as French. We must try to get her home.'

Evangeline was trembling, voicing agreement, and Beatrice laid a palm on her sister's wrist. 'Cyril, we can't thank you enough. Connie's father will be so relieved to hear that she is alive and in some respects well. But you and Evie are right. We must get her home. I hesitate to ask for more help since you have already given us so much, but do you have any ideas?'

Cyril reached again for the brandy bottle. 'You must remember, Beatrice and Evangeline, that we are not talking of Connie Taylor any more but of Constance Travis. What has she to come back to? A blasted city, a past which she has tried effectively to hide, a class system which marks her the moment she opens her mouth, as I understand only too well. In Paris she has re-created herself . . .'

'But in London she has a father. And us,' insisted Evangeline.

'In Paris, Evangeline, Connie is not merely a mistress and a mannequin. As I understand it, reading between the lines of what Louis said, her officer tends to talk once his boots have been pulled off and to talk again in his sleep. Connie would be the last person to suggest that she is privy to vital secrets but now and again she hears a little indiscretion, a detail here or a name there which is of interest to the consulate in Biarritz. She can sometimes get a message through.'

'You mean she's a spy?'

'Not really, no. She does what she can, that's all.'

'Even though she is Jewish and could be . . .' Both Evangeline and Beatrice were shocked and unable, quite, to absorb all of Cyril's implications.

'It must be your decision, having discussed it with Connie's father, of course. She seemed to me to have no wish to come back to London. She wants to continue her work in Paris.'

'But does she understand the danger she's in?' Evangeline was still breathless and bewildered.

'Oh, yes,' said Cyril. 'But I believe Connie has developed an appetite for danger. And there's another thing. Louis thinks she quite likes her German. Until and unless he discovers her background, Connie maintains that she is probably perfectly safe. She is generally assumed to be French and, in any case, is, as a civilian, under Red Cross protection, although I'm not sure just how effective that would be in Connie's case. And her officer is certainly in love with her.' Cyril lit a cigarette. 'Apparently it's evident in the way he stares at her when she's looking somewhere else, the way he lights her cigarette or touches her shoulder. Great love seems to be expressed in every tiny gesture, whenever he has the opportunity.' Cyril drew again on his cigarette. 'Isn't it strange how love, or the approximation of love at any rate, isn't necessarily affected by official hostilities or rules? Why else would men fall in love with other men's wives, cabinet ministers with butcher's boys? Enemy with victim? They say that love conquers all. I say that love, if you're unlucky enough to fall into that particular cess pit, poisons all.' His voice trailed off into a quiet reflective murmur and his eyes dampened. Neither sister felt strong enough to ask Cyril if he cared to elaborate personally.

Beatrice looked up slowly and met Evangeline's eyes. 'We were in touch with Louis too. That letter you wrote to him, all those months ago when Connie's father came here. Did you send it?' Evangeline nodded. 'Did you mention that Connie was Jewish?'

'I've been trying to remember that myself. I hope to God I didn't but it didn't occur to me then that Louis might not be entirely trustworthy. He didn't reply so I wrote again in case the letter had gone missing. I was less hurried with the second letter and I'm certain I was careful then not to specify the danger that Connie might be in.'

'I told you this would be difficult.' Cyril dabbed his eyes just before the sirens went. 'Whatever she says Connie's danger is very real and it would be all too easy to deepen it even as we strove to help her and even if she wishes to be helped.' When the warning rang out they all ran upstairs for the children and met Molly on the landing. The rest of the night was spent in the cellar with the ever-ready Thermos, the blankets, the torches and fearful thoughts that grew darker even as the sky lightened outside and the sound of the 'all clear' made Clare and Edmund stir.

'You know what?' asked Beryl, in the certainty that she was in unique possession of information concerning the announcement she was about to make. Heads looked up and treadles slowed down. Beryl was still a mistress of timing and all the other girls in the bee-hive knew by now that if Beryl prefaced an announcement in this way – just before the morning tea-break, which would give them all fifteen minutes to chatter – some particularly choice gossip was in the offing. Beryl waited, dramatically.

'Come on, then, Beryl. Spit it out.' Doris was impatient.

Beryl savoured the moment. 'Number one. I think Connie might be coming back.' There were gasps and claps of delight. Beryl span out her revelations, sipping her tea and examining her fingernails. 'Number two. I think Miss Evie's expecting.' She enjoyed the glassy silence of some of the girls as much as the calls and cries of the rest of the women.

'I don't b-b-b-believe it,' said Coral. 'You've been looking at the things on her desk again, haven't you? Been snooping.'

'What if I have?' replied Beryl.

'But how do you know of these matters?' asked Ánya and Ruth in unison.

Beryl gave a sly look from under her lids. 'She don't drink coffee any more, always tea, it is, these past few weeks in case you hadn't noticed. And I saw all these drawings for baby dresses on her desk.'

Doris was not impressed. 'The baby clothes could be for anyone. Remember how we had to make up little girl's frocks for that sweet film kiddie when she sent the sketches back here from Hollywood? And as for the coffee – they say they make it with ground-up acorns now, so I'm not surprised she can't stomach it. Honestly, Beryl, you do jump to conclusions.' There was a slightly disappointed murmur of general agreement with Doris.

Only briefly deflated, Beryl shrugged. 'Well, we'll just have to see, won't we? And I'm certain about Connie. I held up Miss Evie's blotter to the big mirror, see? That way you can often read nearly all of the letter. I couldn't make out all of it but I caught the words, 'Connie something something working something back here something something friend something quickly something something something important.' The rest was too faint to read.'

'Who was it to?'

'There was an envelope, sealed and stamped and addressed to Connie's dad on Miss Evie's desk. That's all I know. Wait and see, eh, girls?'

CHAPTER THIRTEEN

B y the late winter of 1944 both nothing and everything
had changed. The dining room in Gower Street had
always been sombre and kept deliberately so, even
before the black-out, with its curtains in deep, heavy folds,
low lights in corners, rugs and paintwork chosen to blend
with the mahogany and the dark spines of sagging shelves of
books. But before the wood had gleamed, scenting the room
along with the abundant flowers Penelope arranged and it
had always been warm. No fire had leapt in that grate since
Christmas; Penelope had only recently made herself throw
away her dry arrangement of holly and winter twigs and
there was a patina of dust everywhere but on the dining table
itself.

We look the same, and yet we, too, are all changed,
thought Beatrice as she glanced around the table. Penelope
was thinner than ever. She had taken on a pinched look and
to wearing a mishapen felt hat indoors, constantly tucking
back strands of her now white hair. Leonard seldom smiled
these days, far less laughed. He sat muffled in a scarf and
with fingerless gloves trying to light the half cigar he still
allowed himself each evening. Beatrice shivered and cast a
surreptitious look at Jack.

He had aged considerably since making the North Atlantic film, or maybe, Beatrice thought, because of it and during

it. All those weeks he had spent in the Arctic on supply ships with the merchant navy and on one of the frigates that accompanied and protected the supply line had been more harrowing for him than any work he had yet done, or any conditions he had yet seen on dry land in this war – Jack tended to compare everything he saw with the forces now with his memory of trench warfare in 1916. Beatrice, too, had been most worried when he was at sea, taking trip after trip back and forth to Canada and Newfoundland. The German U-boats were getting very skilled and twice ships in his convoys had been sunk. She prayed that she might be able to dissuade him from completing his proposed Forces Trilogy. He was talking about attaching his film unit to the RAF and accompanying them on operations next. Beatrice took another glance. Even in this weak light Jack was very grey, lined and tired. She frowned.

'What's up, Bea? Have I got spinach on my teeth or something?'

She smiled wanly. 'Chance would be a fine thing, wouldn't it? Why is it that we only seem to be able to buy carrots and potatoes and those revolting swedes and turnips? Fine, if you happen to like root vegetables, I suppose, but so dreary if you long for some of the others. They haven't rationed green vegetables yet, have they?'

'Take up too much soil and space to cultivate. Root vegetables are much more productive, and they grow all the year round,' said Penelope briskly.

'You're right, I know. Even my unofficial country "suppliers" barely have anything else these days. After her son was killed last year even Maudie Carstairs gave in and abandoned the old asparagus bed for kale.' We talk of food all the time, thought Beatrice, we reminisce about meals we had in the past and daydream about what we will eat again in the future. 'Still, at least we don't go hungry, even if delicious things are hard to come by. Even the restaurants are struggling now or charging positively immoral prices. I just can't bring myself to have a soufflé at Le Caprice any more, even though I could still, I suppose, afford it. It takes up the average person's egg and cheese ration for weeks.'

'If you're so high-minded, these days, Beatrice, I should have suggested that you finished your snoek earlier tonight. Fishermen went out to catch that in very dangerous circumstances to get it on your plate and others got seasick and shot at to land it.' There was humour but also an edge of irritation in Jack's voice.

For all the talk of the war making people at home co-operative and tolerant, Beatrice thought, it also makes us tense and cold and snippy and fractious. She decided to take Jack's remarks lightly.

'I know, Jack, I know. But whalemeat tastes disgusting, you have to admit. They'll be asking us to eat mackerel next.'

'Now there even I would draw the line, especially now,' said Jack darkly.

Leonard looked up. 'And why is that, my dear chap? I always thought mackerel rather tasty when I ate it in France before the war.' It was his first attempt, that evening, at conversational banter.

Penelope answered for Jack. 'Scavengers, Leo. Eat anything. Like nothing better than nibbling at dead bodies, especially those of drowned sailors. Why do you think I never bought it, even before all this? Come from a naval family, remember, Jack and I. Fat lot you land-locked Austrians know about these things, and as for the French,

I've always had my doubts about some of their national delicacies.' She had been aware of her husband's bleak, distracted face all evening and she attempted to defuse the tension. 'Coffee, anyone? Only acorn, I'm afraid.'

Beatrice remembered that her sister had handed her a tin of American condensed milk to give to Penelope. She delved in her bag and passed it across. 'Evie didn't drink acorn coffee for ages but she now says it's tolerable if you stir some of this in. Sweetens it, too, so it saves on the sugar.'

'And how is Evangeline? Dining with some handsome young officer tonight?' With an almost visible effort Leonard attempted again to dispel the horrific images and fears that haunted him most of the time. Fears for the safety of the remaining members of his family and, indeed, for the future of whole communities, his entire race, had darkened and deepened in Leonard's heart ever since he had heard the news about the work camp at Belsen. A niece of his, Basia, had died there, he'd heard from someone who had miraculously managed to escape from Poland, burdened with a series of tragic, remembered messages more than by their small and battered suitcase.

'Evie? No, she's working at the canteen in Waterloo.'

'I thought she went there on Fridays.'

'She does, yes, but Sundays and Wednesdays as well, these days.'

'Does she hear from Hugo?'

'Not since Singapore. She's terribly worried, of course. We all are.' Beatrice sighed. 'She still dines out, meets friends when she can. She hasn't become a complete do-gooder, or a social dormouse by any means. But she's driven in a different way these days. She needs to be busy but in a rather detached, untouchable way. Even with me, I'm afraid.

Emotionally she's been in suspended animation – has been since she fell ill just after Hugo left. Remember when I had to pack her off to those friends in Shropshire for a good few weeks?'

Leonard nodded. There I go again, thought Beatrice. Everything is the same, but different.

It was Tuesday evening, nearly a week later. Jack had been having discussions with someone from the Air Ministry for the past several days and had driven up to Suffolk after lunch, having been given a special docket for extra petrol. This alone gripped Beatrice's heart with fear: it smacked of official business and the increasing likelihood that nothing she or anyone else said could deter Jack from making his film with an RAF unit. She and Evangeline had sat quietly over supper, talking little. It had been Evangeline's turn to cook as it was Molly's night off, and at least the food was wholesome. Molly had queued that morning, reaching the fishmonger early, to buy enough cod for two meals for everyone if they were careful and, since the fish wasn't rationed and she had also been able to coax the butcher into giving her a ham bone which would make a lovely stock for soup later in the week, Molly had felt justified in using a little of the household's precious butter ration so that the fish could be sautéed instead of boiled. The fishmonger had even given her a handful of parsley. Molly was an expert wartime shopper.

'Wasted,' said Beatrice.

'What is?'

'Molly is. She should be taking care of her own house, her own children. Not our house, my children.'

Evangeline answered slowly, 'I don't think Molly feels like that. It's her house, too. She's family, isn't she, after all these years? If she hasn't settled down with someone it's not for want of admirers. I think that perhaps we haven't set her a very inspiring example.' It was the longest speech Evangeline had made all evening.

'I don't know what you mean.'

'Molly doesn't miss much. Here am I, a spinster in the mid-thirties, emotionally paralysed and dead from the neck downwards, constantly on the brink of tears when I allow myself to dwell on what might be happening to Hugo. You — well — anyone can see that things are sometimes difficult with Jack . . .' she faltered.

'But he's here. I've got him.'

'Is he? Have you?' Evangeline spoke sadly, not with bitterness, and searched her sister's face.

Beatrice stared back and astonished herself with the utter confidence and certainty with which she answered. 'Yes, he is. He's always here. I know that. He always will be.' To Beatrice's horror, Evangeline began to cry, brushing tears away with the back of her hand, of which Beatrice took hold. 'It's my turn to do the dishes but tonight you can help me in the kitchen. Remember how we always used to talk in the kitchen when we were little? I always thought I was so grown-up compared to you, settling you on a stool in front of the sink so that you could "help" me while I washed up or whatever on Molly's nights off. Wasn't Father mean? He could easily have paid for a full-time skivvy, not just that poor girl who came in for a few hours every morning.' She paused, and handed Evangeline her handkerchief. 'Kitchens are good places to talk. Come on.' She led her sister through.

Beatrice did not want to waste this opportunity if Evangeline felt ready to confide at last.

They stacked the dishes but did not wash them until much later. Evangeline watched as Beatrice poured each of them a brandy and then she began to speak again. 'You must forgive me, Bea, for what I just said. It's just that sometimes I feel painfully jealous of you. I love Clare and Ned so much but sometimes I can hardly bear to play with them or read to them. My life feels empty.' She choked.

'Go on, Evie. It's been a very long time since we talked like this.' Beatrice took her sister's hand again. 'Don't imagine that I haven't seen that pain behind your eyes sometimes. You usually disguise it awfully well, though.'

Evangeline spoke into a space just above Beatrice's right shoulder. 'The longer Hugo's away the more I miss him and the more I worry about him. But then I find I'll have forgotten his parents' telephone number and home address, or the name of his business partner, Patrick, that cousin of his – things I used to have committed to memory.' She tilted her face to meet Bea's eyes. 'And then I worry that clinging to the idea of Hugo is hopeless. Perhaps these memory lapses are a sort of preparation, a means of accepting that something is over. So maybe it's a good thing if I've lost some vital emotional widget . . .'

'I don't think so. It's just a defence. And I don't think you've lost that widget or grommet or whatever . . . It's just in cold storage. Besides, you'd go completely potty if there weren't times when you couldn't switch away to other things.'

'I suppose you're right, Bea.' Evie set her glass down. 'But one of the worst things is that I can't even remember what it was like to make love with Hugo. Oh, I remember that it was wonderful and I know that I long for it again. I just can't picture it.'

'How could you? If you had a clear memory of things you said to each other, how you touched each other, how you moved, how you breathed, you wouldn't have been fully engaged in it at the time. You were there. You weren't watching something in the theatre. You weren't observing and considering it all as you went along, either of you, so why should you expect to retain some kind of precise mental record?'

'That's true, of course, but because I can't recall detail it's hard to believe it'll ever happen again. And then I think about Shropshire, you know.'

Beatrice had been expecting this. 'That wasn't your fault, Evie. You did all you could to save it. Rest, calm, absence from the raids and stress down here, the lot.' Beatrice waited until Evangeline could look at her again. 'I'm so sorry, darling. I think I can try to imagine how you feel, but there's lots of time – think of me having Ned when I did. I was nearly forty, after all – and when Hugo's back—'

'But at this rate I just can't imagine how any of that will ever be possible.' She slammed her hand on the kitchen table. 'Sometimes this seems to me to be like the Thirty Years War all over again.' She remembered her schoolroom history lessons.

Beatrice, by association, thought back to 1914, when she had still been a child. 'Yes, Evie, I don't blame you for looking at it in that way. And now', she rolled up her sleeves and tested the copper for hot water, 'I'll wash, you dry.' She looked at her sister with a tilt of her chin as they finished the plates and pans. She seemed deep in her own thoughts again.

'Evie, would you like to take a few days off? Really rest, regenerate somewhere? Jack's parents would love to spoil you in Henley. I can manage for a few days, you know.'

'No. Thanks, Bea, but I'm fine now, or much better, anyway. Needed to unload a bit, I guess.' She hugged Beatrice, then released her and said, her voice a little unsteady, 'Actually, what I was thinking just then was what ghastly cooking-smells fish and cabbage leave behind. I don't think I want to eat either of them ever again. And the pongs reminded me', Evangeline's eyes narrowed, 'that I've had a couple of ideas which seemed too fanciful to mention to you until now. Shall we take the brandy upstairs and have a quick talk before turning in?'

Women were running out of curtains, bedspreads, table-cloths and linen to have made into dresses. There was a limit to the number of times a garment could be remodelled and the supply of good men's suiting stuff ready and waiting to be made into coats for ladies was running low. Clothing coupons, moreover, meant that even if beautiful new cloth was available it was difficult for an individual to buy it, quite apart from it being deemed by many to be unpatriotic to look ostentatiously smart these days. The style of the English countrywoman was becoming rather chic. Evangeline became almost hectic as she prefaced her ideas to her sister.

'But have you noticed, Bea,' asked Evangeline, sipping her brandy, 'how even if some of our shires ladies now wear ankle socks with their brogues in town, turbans made from dusters and knit their own lumpy woollies from yarn unravelled from an old one, they always smell nice? A dab of Yardley's this, or lavender, or cologne.'

'Get to the point, Evie.'

'I've made the point. I don't believe scent is rationed and

I can't believe it will be. Couldn't we go into partnership with someone and produce a small range of British and patriotic scents? That way our customers could have their little treat – in fact, we'd probably gain a few new ones because a bottle of scent can't possibly cost as much as a new hat and it would be a discreet way of wearing something personal and secret and feminine. Like silk knickers in the old days. Besides, it's awfully hard to get hold of decent French stuff these days unless you're on good terms with a black marketeer or exceptionally friendly with a liaison officer.'

Beatrice was thoughtful. 'It's not such a crazy idea, Evie, although there would be lots of practicalities to look into. Exactly how much thought have you been giving to this scheme?'

'Not all that much. Sketched a few bottle shapes, come up with some names, that's all.'

'What names?'

'Well, two themes, really, day and night, and I thought two scents for each. 'Smoke' and 'Cab' for the nocturnal ones.' She registered Beatrice's puzzled expression. 'Don't look like that, Bea. Aren't they two divinely evocative and sexy words? Or don't you remember, you clot?' Beatrice laughed as Evangeline continued. 'And for the daytime I'd toyed with "Cambric" – all pure and crisp and clean and nostalgic – and "Bee", which is our pun for a start and a bee can remind people of gardens and honey and summers and the odd little sting too, if you like. The other one I liked was "Elle est Haute" – our name, again.'

Partly to encourage and humour Evangeline, to help to sustain her brighter mood, Beatrice expressed slightly more enthusiasm than she felt. But she agreed that there was the germ of a good idea here. 'We'll need to research, to take advice. I think you'd better telephone Priscilla in the morning, don't you?'

Only as she undressed did Beatrice realize that there had been no raids tonight – no raids, in fact, since the weekend. She dared not even hope that some tide was turning but thought how sad it would have been if her evening and conversation with Evangeline had been so disrupted and then, after checking on Clare and Ned this spring night in 1944, she thought a prayer for Jack in Suffolk before drifting into sleep.

Beryl had been wrong about Connie and no one at the House of Eliott now expected her to return to London. Cyril had tried to get a message through to her, offering to arrange a passage via Lisbon through some contacts he had in Bordeaux, but it seemed she had refused point blank. He had been told that she felt Parisienne through and through— after all, her mother's family had originally come from Paris. She saw no reason to leave.

Sometimes when Cyril visited Beatrice and Evangeline, on leave, he had a fragment of news: a year ago, he had heard that she no longer modelled. He was worried. 'It's all very well for her to enjoy the "protection" of working for a collaborating House but that position makes her vulnerable if her true background should ever be discovered. Now that things are shifting, that the Allies are clearly, now, going to beat the Nazis, it's merely a matter of time, which puts her in double jeopardy – firstly as a Jew and secondly as a perceived collaborator. I'm sure she can't understand this – or simply doesn't want to. Apparently she had begun to find modelling tiresome but I think her officer must have taken exception to the numbers of admirers she attracted. It would be ironic, wouldn't it, if it should have been he who made her give it up?'

'I wonder how we'll explain to her father,' mused Evangeline.

Late winter turned into early spring and by May London's population seemed to have doubled with the influx of American soldiers. Tilly's lieutenant, Brad, the friend about whom she had confided to Anya and Ruth, had a staff sergeant friend in the air force and Beryl was desperate to be introduced to him. 'Ask her, Beryl. Tilly's got no side, she's still one of us, really. Go on, she'll fix you up.' Elsie was recently engaged to a corporal in signals and she wanted everyone else to be paired off, too. 'None of the Yanks have any side either, do they? You'd never find an English officer going about with one of the men like they do.'

Tilly arranged a foursome for tea at Lyons. Beryl's hair was now long enough to catch in a snood and she had rolled her fringe back over horse-hair sausages at the front, her elegant entrance only slightly spoilt by an unsteady gait – the new platformed cork-soled shoes took some getting used to. Brad and Tilly left the younger couple ordering another pot of tea as they hastened to the cinema in the Haymarket. There was definitely something in the air by the beginning of June.

CHAPTER FOURTEEN

'Do you ever wonder what happened to the Crawleys?' Beatrice laid her cup down and had to remind
her sister of the loathsome 'paying guests' that had
been friends of their late Aunt Lydia. The couple had been
'billeted' upon the sisters just after their father's death when
– desperate for any respectable form of income – they had
briefly tolerated the Crawleys' pretentious airs and greed. Old
Major Crawley had even tried to molest young Evangeline,
and that was when Beatrice sent the couple packing.

'Only about once every twenty years. Why ever do you
ask?' Evangeline looked up from her work, pencil end in
mouth. She was trying to work out if a supper dress could
be cut from pieces of silk, both the large ones and the
fragments salvaged from Jennifer Marston-Strong's exquisite
but ancient and often damaged collection of scarves. A
patchwork effect seemed unavoidable and, besides, to hark
back too much to the handkerchief point dresses of the
twenties. But it would be a crime to dye the cloth a uniform
shade and much of it was too fragile, anyway, to survive the
process. After a few seconds she looked up. 'Bea, you're
dreaming. What made you think of that pair of old monsters
after all this time?'

'I've thought about them quite a lot lately. In fact, they've
been on my conscience.'

'On your *what*?' After what they did to us? Are you mad?'

'Possibly.' Beatrice walked to the window and turned. 'You see, Evie, years ago they wrote to me from Singapore.' She saw her sister's eyes widen. 'I could scarcely bear to hold the writing paper so I didn't read it properly for weeks. They were in horribly greasy mode, saying how wonderful life was out there, how much money there was to be made, how many servants and gardeners they had. She made out that invitations to her little "evenings" were prized, that anyone who was anyone, especially poor, bemused ex-pats simply loved to call. The letter closed with a few remarks about them thinking of planning a trip back to the "old country", and could I recommend a good, reasonably priced hotel. I had to laugh then. Up to their old tricks as well as their old airs and graces.'

'So what did you do?'

'I'm afraid I threw the letter away and forgot all about it. I certainly didn't reply. And then, after quite a while, the other letters started to arrive, increasingly supplicating. Beseeching, really.' Beatrice sighed. 'They were begging for our help. Obviously don't know anyone else in England or they wouldn't resort to writing to us. But you know how it is, Evie, when you delay an unpleasant duty? The longer you wait the harder it becomes.'

'I don't see why we should feel any sense of duty towards the Crawleys. But you'd better tell me why they're in such dire straits.' Evangeline thought. 'Singapore, eh? That's supposed to be a tightly-knit British community. They might know something about Hugo . . .'

'Well, from what Vera Crawley wrote in the first letter — maddening that I can't remember many of the details —

they'd travelled a lot. Kenya, I think she said, and then Ceylon. No doubt Major Crawley tried to pass himself as some sort of planter wallah . . .'

'And made a little too free with the dusky maidens for Vera's liking.' Evangeline giggled.

'And made such a hash of his work that they had to keep moving on,' Beatrice finished. 'Anyway, it sounded as if they'd settled at last in what Vera was pleased to call "Singers". Seems the Major got some high-up managerial position with a local shipping firm. I expect he lied about where he went to school and his regiment but obviously no one found him out.'

'Then why that first letter, do you think?'

'She may have been an evil woman and a silly one, but Vera had a combination, as we know all too well, of middle-class shrewdness and peasant cunning. Certain instincts. It's obvious to me now that they had somehow got wind of things to come and wanted to get out before the rush. For people like the Crawleys the threat of being under a German thumb would be far less abhorrent than having to kowtow to Johnny Jap, as the Major would doubtless have described them. Evie,' Beatrice laughed briefly, 'can't you just hear him saying, "Me and Fritz, we speak the same language, you know," as he knuckled under the status quo?' Evangeline nodded and Beatrice continued. 'Anyway, they obviously didn't get out and are living under increasingly desperate conditions. First it was curfew and deprivations and various other indignities. Now they seem to think all the remaining "enemy" Europeans are to be rounded up and sent to prison camps. I can't help feeling guilty about not taking any notice of the pleas.'

'That's jolly bad luck for them, but I don't see what we

could have done for them in the first place. They were perfectly capable of finding a hotel. What Vera really wanted was social entrées. And now there is absolutely nothing we can do.' Evangeline was adamant. 'If you'd told me they'd run into some English architect chappie and wasn't it a dinky coincidence but he seemed to know us, then I'd rack my brains. But only if.'

'There is something we could do, Evie, or attempt. It wouldn't get us saddled with responsibility for the Crawleys, but it might be to everyone's advantage. Do you remember Mr Lee?'

'The silk merchant? Of course. But he was from Hong Kong.'

'But I'm sure I remember him saying that he had cousins in Singapore. He was always talking about his family, showing me photographs and boasting about his children. I can't imagine why I didn't think of contacting him before.'

'I can. We parted on such very bad terms, with him owing us all that lolly, that you decided to excise him and the whole business from your mind. But I'm still not quite sure where Mr Lee fits in. How could he help us, anyway?'

'I'm not sure that he can, Evie, but it's worth a try. He knows he's in our debt, he must still remember that. We all know about that Chinese "face" business. You know, the way that it is a matter of honour there not to actually admit to error or failure. Supposing we sent a wire suggesting that we were in urgent need of thin silk for parachutes – he'd simply imagine that we'd turned the workroom over to the war effort – and would like him to tender. Supposing we suggested that we would look favourably on his estimate and, moreover, let bygones be bygones, if he could help us with a little family matter out East? The very fact that he spoke of his own enormous family as he did makes me think he'll rather like the idea of helping us help ours.'

'The Crawleys aren't family. Neither's Hugo.'

'Mr Lee isn't to know that. Oh, Evie, I know it's a shot in the dark, but it's the best shot I've got.'

'I agree, Bea, we should try, but I still don't quite see why you care about what happens to them. Unless Mr Lee can somehow come up with Chinese whispers and news about Hugo I don't much care if the Crawleys live or die.'

'Sometimes, Evangeline, the difference in our ages is as great as it was when I was ten and you were a baby and our mother died. Don't you see? I only met Jack and had my children because of their indirect, admittedly malevolent, influence. Doubt if I would have been desperate enough to go to work for him in the first place if I hadn't been determined to be independent of the Crawleys. And it was as a consequence of that meeting that you met Hugo later. They were pigs, both of them, ignorant, greedy, self-deluding and second-rate. But they led each of us, unwittingly, to the source of our greatest happiness. That's why I feel we should at least try to help them. Who knows? If we set them off on some new, silly and selfish course they may yet again accidentally bring about marvellous things for some other astonished but fortunate people.'

'Watch out, Bea. You'll have them canonized next.' Evangeline pulled a black look but laughed at the same time.

The phone did not stop ringing. Each time Jack replaced the receiver and met Beatrice's enquiring glance he said the same thing. 'I wish I could tell you, darling, but I can't. All I can say is that it matters a lot and that you'll have to try to understand. You'll know soon enough.' A small case was packed and ready at the foot of their bed and Jack had been transferring other items to the small office he worked from at the Ministry of Information.

The streets of the West End had mysteriously all but emptied of American soldiers and airmen. A tearful Beryl fumed about how she had been stood up by Arnie, her staff sergeant, the evening before. 'I've heard about "over-sexed, over-paid and over here" and that's all fine by me. He gave me some nylons only the other day. But I can't be doing with "over and done with". The least he could have done was to tell me, if that's how he feels.' She sniffed. 'At least you know good and proper when you've been chucked by a London bloke.'

'Usually, yes, but not always.' Doris spoke from ancient bitter experience. 'And, Beryl, you mustn't judge him too fast. Maybe there was an emergency and he couldn't tell you. Ask Tilly, she might know if something's up.'

Tilly couldn't help. 'I do think something's going on, Beryl, because Brad had his leave cancelled. But I don't know what it is. Bit bad that Arnie didn't let you know, I agree, but give him the benefit, eh?'

That night the phone rang again a few minutes before midnight. Jack and Beatrice had only just slipped into sleep. After making a few monosyllabic responses Jack replaced the receiver.

Beatrice turned over. 'What is it, Jack?'

He kissed her cheek. 'You'll know in the morning. I have to go, Bea darling. And I'll call as soon as I can.' Still befuddled, Beatrice watched Jack pull on his clothes and grab his things. 'Tell Clare and Ned that I love them very much,' he called from the bedroom door before running back to her and holding her as if it was the first and last time. 'And I love you more than anything, Beatrice,' he whispered into her hair. He was gone. Beatrice looked at the clock and then reminded herself of the date. As the hands met at midnight she registered 6 June 1944.

Two weeks later Jack was back with footage that would come to be regarded as the classic, definitive filmic record of the invasion. At first some of it was screened in every cinema throughout the Empire and later, with judicious cutting, music, commentary and supplementary footage from American film-makers it was wrought into a documentary film of such power that Hollywood and Pinewood both replicated certain passages with dog-like fidelity when, in later years, D-Day was filmed for a different type of public entertainment. All the glory of the beach heads and all the horrors were captured by Jack Maddox and his tiny unit. The Allies' flower-strewn progress through Normandy and the little towns that lined the route to Paris were frozen for ever – all the triumphs and all the shame. The flight of collaborators, and the misery of young girls on bicycles avoiding the camera's eye as they tried to pull their scarves and hats over their shorn, tarred and feathered heads. The bellicose pride of small-town mayors. The tragic devastation of farmland, villages, animals and the bewilderment of some was captured just as surely as the exultant relief of others. Above all, Jack had managed to express both the weariness of the soldiers and their joy as they entered Paris.

'What do you think, Bea?' Jack had asked Beatrice to watch some early rushes. 'Bea?'

'I can't speak.' She took his hand. 'It's a work of great horror, Jack, and great, great beauty. I'm so proud of you.' Beatrice reached for his other hand and clasped them within her own. 'Is it over, then?' Is it really?'

'Nearly, Bea. Nearly, but not quite.'

Cyril rang a day or two later. He, too, was back in London. At first Beatrice couldn't interpret the noises he was making. 'Speak in English, for heaven's sake. Or come round for lunch – we've got some Bolly left.'

'Not a champagne day, Bea dear. At least not for me.'

'What is it?' Beatrice's heart froze with a rapid and terrible certainty. 'Connie?'

Cyril came to the Mayfair house and tried valiantly at first to be bright. He had presents, tales of his own delirious adventures in Paris after the D-Day landings and waspish stories about competitive generals. But he sipped his champagne slowly and finally set down his glass before addressing Beatrice, Jack and Evangeline. 'I must come to the point now. As you may have feared or guessed, Connie is dead. Her lover was informed of both her race and her work by Louis, just before the invasion. Louis had known that Connie was Jewish.' Evangeline gasped and remembered her letters. Cyril continued, 'But he had chosen to remain silent for a long time. As for the espionage aspect, I truly believe Louis was simply guessing, but then in Paris, a great many people were desperate to save their skins and unsure which way to jump.

'Everyone knew that the end of the occupation was imminent. It was in the air. They just didn't know whether it would be this week or next. Connie told a friend, Jean-Luc, on the evening that she died that she had always understood the dangers and that she knew what would happen but that she didn't care. She'd had her life. She simply wanted to send love and thanks to a few people.' Cyril lifted his head and met the eyes of the sisters. 'Then she met her German at a restaurant. They had dinner at some place near St-Sulpice, walked back to her apartment and, I suppose, made love. One can only suppose what happened next. He probably shot her as soon as she had fallen asleep. Then he blew his brains out. At any rate the gun was in his hand and the experts seem to think that she died slightly earlier than he did.' Cyril waited for a moment, dabbing at his eyes. 'You know, I'll always believe that Connie was at least partly responsible for the Germans being fooled by those false documents they found in the pockets of a drowned English naval officer – you know, the ones that made the Germans wonder if the invasion would be launched in southern Brittany. At the very least it made them dispatch a few divisions there, just in case.'

After the long silence Evangeline filled all their glasses with the last of the champagne. 'To Connie,' she said quietly. 'No, to Constance Travis.'

Cyril was still shaking. There was a long silence. Evangeline gulped and eventually Beatrice grasped her hand. She knew that her sister was, once again, assuming blame.

Jack tried to break the mood and turned to Cyril. 'What now, old man?'

'Me? I'm back to Paris, soon as possible. You see I met someone there and I want to find out if the heady atmosphere of the liberation can survive a three-week absence. Nothing else really matters to me any more.' Cyril raised his glass. 'Present company excepted, of course.'

'Is it all going to seem like something of an anticlimax to you now, Jack? Now that it's all over? What will you do next?' Jack and Beatrice had retired soon after Cyril left. 'It's certainly going to be very different here. I expect Evie will go back to the mews soon now that most of the danger has passed.'

'Yes, Bea, it will be different. Nothing can ever be the same.' Jack sighed. 'But it's not over yet. We've taken back Paris but there's still a long way to go. Japan, Italy to finish off . . . Even though the Italians surrendered some time ago the Germans are still there and disinclined to wave the white flag just yet. I'm sure, now, that the Allies will triumph but don't be mistaken. It'll be a while yet. And Evie should stay with us until it really is finished.' He turned to his wife. 'As for what next, I haven't the faintest idea.' Jack hooked his arm around Beatrice's shoulders. 'It's the nature of the beast, isn't it? All climaxes are anticlimaxes, really. There's a part of you that wants the drama to stretch out, for the play to have another act. Don't only unimaginative human beings long for neat resolutions? And aren't those people usually rather stupid? There may be happy endings but in the real world there are seldom tidy ones.'

Beatrice was sliding in and out of consciousness. She was only able to mumble a few words into the crook of Jack's shoulder. 'I don't think I could bear another five years like this. Wherever you have to go, Jack, and for however long, don't leave us. Don't leave us again. You know what I mean?'

'Yes, I do.' He kissed her shoulder. 'Never. Never again.'

Tilly's demeanour exemplified an unusual but triumphant combination of delight and regret. 'You do understand? I feel terrible but, as they say, I have my own life. Bit of a turn up, isn't it? Fancy. Me going to America and running a ranch house. I really am going to be the oldest GI bride, aren't I?'

'And the best ever. Will Brad meet you from the boat?'

'No, Miss Evie. Kansas is a long way from New York – you should look at the map. And, in any case, he's being kept in hospital for a few more weeks. No, Brad's written it all out for me.' Tilly produced a much-creased map from her pocket. 'I get the bus from this place here,' she pointed with her finger, 'to this huge station on 32nd Street. Penn, it's called. When I get there I ask for the D-track and then I'll get to Kansas City. Takes more than a day but they say those trains are very comfortable, with waiters and that. Then I'll change trains for Excelsior. Lovely name, that, isn't it? Brad's mother and his sisters will be waiting for me there. We're going to be married in his family chapel. Funny, isn't it? Still, I suppose I haven't got any parents to go with me. I don't mind. It's a new life.' Tilly smiled widely.

Beatrice and Evangeline exchanged glances. Evie spoke first. 'Tilly, you may only be allowed to take one little case on the boat but we'd like to help you to fill it beautifully. Would you let us?' She turned to Beatrice. 'Bea, we could make Tilly some lovely nightdresses and travelling coats and blouses and even a dress or two from material in stock, couldn't we?'

'Yes, we could. And we will, Tilly. You'll be a sort of ambassadress for the House of Eliott. It's essential that you look quite marvellous. And I think your wedding dress, this time, might be made from that bolt of lilac silk that Helen Urquhart forgot to collect after we fell out, don't you, Evie? Tell us what you have in mind, Tilly,' Beatrice smiled, 'and we'll try to do our best. You might need to smuggle it in another little bag, but you only get married once.'

'Twice, in my case,' laughed Tilly.

Once, if you're lucky, thought Evangeline.

'Did you ever hear back from Mr Lee?' Evangeline was drawing idly, little hats and shoes. A waste of time, she realized.

Beatrice looked up. 'Mr Lee? Sorry, Evie, I was miles away. About sixty miles, actually. Cheam is going to be relocated in Hampshire. Shame in a way, but we'll still go whenever we can and I'm sure the air is healthier than in South London.' She smiled. 'I have to take Ned there this afternoon. Apparently it's my audition as much as his. Poor little chap, I'm sure he'd prefer to go with his father but needs must.'

'And I suppose he'll go to School after that?'

'All being well, yes. Hate even to think of it, but I know it's for the best.' Beatrice patted her hair. 'Will I do?'

'You look lovely, Bea. Now, will you answer my question?'

Beatrice thought and remembered. 'I'm so sorry, Evie. Mr Lee. Yes. Mr Lee wired me. He said that one of his nephews knew about the Crawleys through some other relative who worked in customs. He thought that the Major had remained safe for some time after Singapore fell because he was "helpful" to the Japanese and that Madame Crawley was thus safe and well, if not quite maintaining her former standards. Now, it seems, the Crawleys' usefulness is over. They've both been interned in a place called Changi. I looked at the map but I couldn't find it. Beyond our help now – we don't even know where it is. But war in the Pacific could be over soon and we might be able to help them with their passage back. If that's still what they want. I doubt it, somehow.' Beatrice averted her gaze.

'Why didn't you tell me this before? What about Hugo?' Evangeline was almost shouting.

'I didn't know when the right moment could possibly be.' Beatrice tipped her chin forward. 'Amid his enquiries about the parachute silk Mr Lee did mention that he knew someone like Hugo. He remembered the name, thought it extraordinary. Says that everyone laughed at him with his pencils and graph paper and compasses and elevations. He said that Chinese engineers have no use for Greek geometry. He says—'

'What did he learn about Hugo?' Are we talking about the same man? I can barely remember his face. Thank God for photographs. Why am I desperate for this sort of hearsay news? Evangeline knew that her brain was frizzled into pieces like a jigsaw, that they would be unlikely to fit together again, and yet she was compelled. 'I'm not interested in Mr Lee's views about classical geometry and mathematics. Tell me, Bea. Does he have news?'

'Yes, he does.' Beatrice tightened her grip on Evangeline. 'Hugo was taken to the same internment camp nearly three years ago. I'm sorry, Evie. That's all I can tell you. I wish I had better news. Now we must wait.'

Evangeline cried, howled like a hound. Over her sister's tangled head, raked with fingernails and crashed against the arm of her chair, Beatrice motioned for Clare and Ned to go back upstairs. The children, awakened by the cries, seemed far more alarmed by the sight and sound of their aunt's anguish than they had ever been by the sirens. Beatrice stroked Evangeline's hair. 'This is terrible pain, Evie, and I wish you didn't have to endure it. But it makes a bit of a nonsense of some of the things you said earlier.' She tried to become crisp and brisk. 'Do you remember when I read you stories? You were just a little girl.' Evangeline nodded. 'Do you remember your favourite?' Another nod. 'It was *The Count of Monte Cristo*, wasn't it? And do you remember the hero's motto when he was incarcerated in the Château d'If?' Evangeline's head dipped, only slightly.

'Wait and hope,' she whispered. 'Wait and hope.'

CHAPTER FIFTEEN

The euphoria that followed the success of the D-Day landings did not last. News from the Russian front was appalling and the final stages of the Allies' progress up through Italy were slow and bloody. Terrible stories and rumours were circulating about conditions in the Japanese internment camps. Evangeline felt physical pain herself whenever she heard them and had begun sometimes to shun company and conversation, scared to place herself at risk while sometimes courting it, hungry for news, however bad, which could help her to picture Hugo.

Jack was away, making a film about the Italian campaign, and had, it seemed to Beatrice, been stuck at a place called Monte Cassino for months. There seemed to be more wounded soldiers than ever on the streets of London. It was hard to decide which were the most pathetic – the older ones only conscripted in desperation as the war wore on, or young ones, boys who barely needed to shave and who, none the less, bore their injuries with an ersatz manly pride. Jack had told her how these boys invariably sobbed and cried out for their mothers when wounded or in a military hospital. She blinked, remembering Tom. She dared to hope, could not believe, that Edmund would ever have to serve his country but in a very few years Tom would have joined up. With his eyesight he would have been turned down by the RAF, she knew, and would probably have succumbed to pressure from Jack to join the navy. She blinked again. Tom, at least, was safe now . . .

Outrage hung in the air everywhere, an indignation not caused solely by the illogical bafflement about the war's continuation or by shortages which were, if anything, worse. German scientists and engineers had perfected a new kind of bomb, one that did not need a pilot or a plane. These weapons were aimed with astonishing accuracy at specific locations in southern England and powered by an engine that cut out when its carefully calculated fuel supply was spent. Then the bomb would fall. People were calling them 'doodlebugs'. Beatrice found this slang alarming – even though the nursery-like term was coined and used to lessen the threat somehow of the weapon, she felt the word trivialized its devastating effects.

'A lot of people I know say it's more frightening than the Blitz,' said Doris. 'Some neighbours of ours just had time to get to the tube station before their street went and that was only because her old auntie had one of her psychic turns. This friend of mine said you can't concentrate on anything while you're listening out for the motor. If it stops just above you, you run. Awful, makes people hope it'll carry on and the houses a few streets away will get it. Makes it worse that Jerry doesn't even have the guts to risk any of their people to fly them. Don't know why but if I'm going to catch it I'd rather there was some human being doing the business. Easier to get a good hate on then. Can't hate a machine, can you? Cowardly, isn't it? Like . . .' Doris thought, 'like sending poison pen-letters, but more horrible.'

'It's funny, but I feel safe here,' said Elsie. 'Sometimes I don't want to go home.' The others looked askance. 'Well, we live near the docks, but our little row of streets hasn't had it yet, not after all these years. I reckon we're due. But here,' Elsie looked upwards, 'they got it right at the start, or almost, didn't they? So it can't happen again, can it?' Elsie had barely finished before Beryl had leaped up and pulled her to her feet. 'What y'doing? Leave off, Beryl, do.'

Beryl had her by the shoulders and was twisting her around. 'That's bad luck. Bad luck that is, talking that way. Tempting fate.' Elsie giggled. 'And don't laugh. You've got to hit your right ankle with your left foot three times now and we should be all right.'

'We didn't realize you were superstitious, Beryl.' Anya and Ruth were smiling behind their palms. 'But it can do no harm.' They both fell silent, offering their own entreaties. 'God will protect the just,' said Ruth quietly.

Beatrice had been watching and listening from the top of the stairs for the past few minutes. She had planned to check on the progress of a coat for Lady Wentworth made from coarse brown cloth brought back by her husband from Normandy. It was woven from an amalgam of horse-hair and wood-shavings and Lady Wentworth intended to wear it with pride. The only way it could be redeemed was by lining it with a patchwork of irregularly shaped pieces of rabbit fur, fragments cut and stitched together from the pelts of animals Lady Wentworth had shot herself before using the rabbit meat in stews and pâtés. But now she had no heart to see how the coat was shaping up and she turned to walk upstairs again, tears once again behind her eyes. God will protect the just, Ruth had said. How could those girls be so unvengeful? How could they, of all people, retain such faith and trust? She made a mental note to tell Evangeline about it later.

The doorbell rang and Beatrice answered it herself as she sometimes had to these days. Marjorie was busy in the fitting room and Evangeline was out somewhere. After all this time, Beatrice still did so with dread. A telegram could contain good news, of course, but Beatrice always feared the worst and could not remember an appointment due now. She clenched the handkerchief in her palm and almost hugged Priscilla Dawlish when she saw her on the doorstep.

'You've been crying, Beatrice. Never mind, I'm taking you to lunch. Get your coat. If this isn't going to be ten bob well spent, I don't know what will be.' Priscilla hailed a taxi and they headed for Sheekey's where Priscilla had heard that sole was on the set-price menu today. 'I can't wait! I've been living on sandwiches and greasy mince for weeks. There just aren't any presentable men to go to restaurants with these days, are there?'

'Hardly any men around full stop,' Beatrice replied wryly. But she was amused. 'So I'm a sort of last resort, am I, Priscilla? Were you stood up or something and didn't want to waste the booking?'

'Not at all,' Priscilla replied crossly. 'I've got a plan and I want to air it to you. In my business there are a lot of very silly women, Beatrice, and I want to speak to someone with a brain. Specifically a woman with a brain,' she added, lest Beatrice misunderstand. There was a wait at some lights. 'Evangeline was right about "Cab" and "Smoke", you know.' "Elle est Haute", too. Not so sure about the summer ones – there are enough rosewaters and gardenia colognes available already – but spot on about those others, particularly as it's so difficult to get hold of Tabu or Shalimar or whatever at the moment. Even if you're by yourself there's something heady about being in the back of a black cab. A sense of anticipation as well as the darkness, privacy . . .'

Beatrice looked across sharply. 'Goodness, Priscilla. What's got into you? You can't be in love, given what you said earlier about the dearth of presentable men these days. Do tell.' The cab jumped across another set of lights, turned a corner and pulled up close to the front of the reassuringly familiar windows of the oldest fish restaurant in London.

'This plan,' said Priscilla, after they had ordered, 'concerns the launch of a completely new kind of magazine for women. At the moment there are *Mode*, *Tatler*, and *Harper's* and the like and we have *Woman* and *Woman's Weekly* but nothing in between. You mark my words, Beatrice, when the war is finally over there are going to be thousands of women for whom neither the higher nor the lower ground will be appropriate. Lots of women will be too busy working or otherwise disinclined either to leaf longingly through my magazine or buy the cheaper ones for their recipes and knitting patterns. I'm sure there's a vast middle-ground readership to satisfy. It was Evangeline's ideas for scent that got me thinking, actually. Working girls, working women, could wear a touch of *haute couture* behind their ears and on their wrists – they'd be earning enough to pay for that – while they're working in offices, shops, even. Makes even more sense if they have to wear horribly unfeminine overalls – or uniform. That philosophy would underpin the whole enterprise.' Their first course arrived: it was vichysoisse. 'Rather inappropriate just now, wouldn't you say, after the fall of *that* government? I'm surprised they don't just call it leek and potato for the time being.' She took a sip. 'But delicious, is it not?'

Beatrice nodded, pensive.

'You haven't told me what you think. I'm not completely barking, am I?'

'I don't think so, Priscilla. In fact I'm surprised no one has thought of it before. But wouldn't you have to give up the editorship of *Mode*? And how would you find the financial backing? These ventures cost an awful lot of money to launch, don't they?'

'Indeed they do. But I don't see why I shouldn't carry on at *Mode* and be called something like editor-in-chief of the new magazine with a proper editor dealing with the week-to-week business. I'm going to talk to my American bosses about it. If I can convince them that it's a sound financial proposition, they can back me, easily.' Priscilla put down her spoon. 'And that is where you and Evangeline might be able to help me.'

'Go on.'

'What I intend is to have a number of consultant editors – non-executive, of course – to advise on all the main sections of the magazine. Ideally I would ask Guy Birdsey to comment on house and home, someone like Marguerite Patten or Theodora Fitzgibbon to be on call for cookery and it would be wonderful, Beatrice, if the House of Eliott could be our fashion consultant. If I could tell my Americans that things like that had been provisionally agreed it would make such a difference. All concerned would be paid a substantial fee . . .' Priscilla's voice trailed off and she looked up with uncharacteristic timidity.

'I'll have to speak to Evie about this, of course. We'll think about it, Priscilla. We'll think really hard. And thank you for asking us.' Beatrice looked up. 'Oh, look! Our sole is about to arrive. May I?' She poured them both some cider and chinked her glass against Priscilla's. 'Whatever happens – and you'll understand that I can't give any kind of commitment so soon – I drink to you, Priscilla, for your bravery and optimism. To the future.'

'And I drink to us all, for our survival.'

Beatrice arrived just in time for Lady Wentworth's fitting. The elderly eccentric was delighted with her coat. 'My dear, it will be perfect for the country. So cold in church these days. Not exactly tropical in the house, either, now that we're not supposed to go wooding.'

'Why on earth not?'

'Some silly nonsense about all our wood being needed for the factory furnaces in Bristol. Saves coal for the ship-yards, they say. My guess is that it goes straight into the officers' mess. Still,' she winked, 'we do manage to save just a little for ourselves.'

'Sounds a bit like the saucepans and iron railings to me,' said Beatrice amused, 'when they asked us to hand over all but our most essential pans and pulled up all the lovely old railings here in London. Said the metal would be melted down and turned into battleships or some such. I always had my doubts about that. I think it was simply an exercise to make people here at home think they were doing their bit. I sometimes wonder what really happened to all those old pots and pans. At least your wood will probably be warming someone's toes.'

'You have become cynical, haven't you, Beatrice dear?' Lady Wentworth patted her hand. 'And I don't blame you one bit. The war has made cheats, liars and black marketeers of all of us at times.' She sniffed. 'What's that scent you're wearing? It's delicious.'

'Oh, it's not really a scent yet, not officially. Evangeline, my sister, has gone pell-mell for an interesting new scheme. You know what she's like. She asked a young chemist friend of hers to mix up a sort of potion. I suppose I'm a guinea-pig. I dabbed some on just now.' Beatrice sniffed her wrist. 'It is rather nice, I agree.'

'What's it called?'

'Cab, I think.'

'Splendid. Puts me in mind of my younger days. Nothing like it, canoodling a bit on the back seat. Ask Evangeline to have some made up for me. Beats all that mimsy-pimsy lavender water and ruddy violet stuff that people seem to imagine I want to use these days. Next thing you know I'll be wearing me coat inside out and putting feathers in me hair again.' Then, handing the tissue-lined cardboard box containing her coat to her maid, Lady Wentworth swept out.

Evangeline returned home that evening with a face like thunder.

'Evie, whatever's wrong?' Beatrice had been looking forward to telling her sister of Priscilla's plans over a light supper. 'For heaven's sake, tell me.'

'Viola. Viola is what's the matter, Bea. What a snake, what a bitch, what a cat, what a bloody actress!' Evangeline spat out the last word as if it was venom.

'Calm down, Evie. What's happened? What would you like?' Beatrice looked to the drinks tray. 'We've got some sherry left, no gin, I'm afraid, that bottle of rather nasty sweet red vermouth that Pamela gave us and some Scotch.'

'Whisky, please.' Beatrice poured her sister a large measure and another, smaller one, for herself. It was the only household commodity that Jack was the least bit possessive of, but this looked like an emergency. She handed Evangeline a heavy-based tumbler. She waited.

Evangeline's breath came in short, deep gasps. 'Viola stood me up for lunch today but suggested that we meet instead for tea. I was a little irritated as you can imagine as I'd awarded myself a day off, but I agreed and started to wonder whom I could ring to take me out to lunch instead and cheer me up. Everyone seemed to be out or busy. In the end I found Patrick's number – do you remember Patrick Mortimer, Hugo's cousin and his old partner? I felt a bit sheepish because I hadn't spoken to him for ages – and suggested we met. He seemed delighted, surprised but delighted, and he booked us into Luigi's.

'When I arrived it was all chatty and tickety-boo and then he asked why it had taken me so long to get in touch. I didn't know what he was talking about. It seems that just before Hugo was interned he managed to get a letter to me out of Singapore but it had to be sent care of Patrick because of some complicated business involving mail to families only. The parents were in Kenya at the time, no one quite knew where. Patrick couldn't reach me and he was going to Iceland. I gather he lived in a Nissen hut there for about two years. Boring as hell, he said, but not the least bit dangerous. Anyway, he happened to see Viola on his last night and entrusted the letter to her. He knew we were friends and assumed I got it right away.'

'But you didn't, did you?'

'I did not. And when I asked Viola about it later on today first of all she feigned to know nothing. Then she "just remembered" that she might have packed it in her things for the States by mistake. She reminded me that she went back in 1942 for some months. And she thought she must have left it there. Anyway, she said to me, it might have been bad news. I asked her what she was talking about and she went all coy and blushed and said that when she'd been doing some sort of troop morale-raising tour with ENSA in the early forties she'd met Hugo in Singapore and they'd had a couple of "heavenly evenings".'

'You don't believe this horrible, bitchy mischief, do you, Evie?'

'No, I don't, Bea. I don't believe it, I mustn't. But, of course, I can't help wondering. The first news I get for nearly four years is simply horrid. I don't have that letter and I know I never will. Hugo always used to say how pretty Viola was . . . I didn't give it a thought.'

'You must try not to think about it now. I didn't say anything at the time because you were such friends, but I don't think Viola ever truly forgave you for her costumes receiving better reviews than she did in *The Scarlet Pimpernel*.' Bea emptied the whisky bottle into both their tumblers. 'I know you're distracted, Evie, beside yourself. I would be, too. But try and listen to me for a little while. I saw Priscilla today . . .'

Lady Carstairs had telephoned ahead to say that she would be late. When the doorbell rang just after eleven Beatrice patted her hair and stepped downstairs to welcome her. She was handed a telegram by a boy who looked about fourteen, his cheeks pinkened by the December chill. 'Thank you.' She remembered to dig for a sixpence in the jar they kept by the door for special deliveries.

She closed the door and leaned back against it. Her fingers shook as she opened the small blue and white envelope.

REGRET TO INFORM MR JOHN MADDOX WOUNDED
MONTE CASSINO TUESDAY LAST STOP REASONABLY
COMFORTABLE IN FIELD HOSPITAL STOP TRANS-
PORT TO LONDON ARRANGEMENTS WILL BE MADE
IF POSSIBLE STOP

If possible? If possible! It was signed by the Colonel of an American regiment whose name Beatrice did not recognize. She gave a small cry before she fainted and was helped upstairs by Molly and Evangeline, the wire still gripped in her hand.

'Funny here without Tilly, isn't it? I still can't get used to it.' Elsie knotted the final thread of the bee inside Lady Pamela's neck facing and laid the dress down with satisfaction. 'Lovely, this is. She'll look a picture at the christening.'

'It's Anya and Ruth that I miss. Got used to T-T-T-T-Tilly not being around. Anyway, she writes, doesn't she, though by the sound of her letters America's not all it's cracked up to be,' said Coral. 'Still, everyone has to have a mother-in-law, I suppose.' She resumed machining.

'Anya and Ruth, eh? Found their Polish airmen after all, twins too. Pity they had to leave. Quite unnecessary in my view,' muttered Doris.

Elsie looked up again. 'But they couldn't very well come down from East Anglia every day, could they? And when they were staying with their old mother-in-law in South Kensington she made their lives hell. Anya said she told them she only had room for one of them and the other would have to find lodgings. Well, with those two. She was on a hiding to nothing, wasn't she? What else were they to do, I ask you? Anyway, if you get married you want to be with your husband, I should think. When I get married—'

'Shut up, Elsie,' Beryl interrupted. 'Shut up, everyone. Stop that treadle, Coral.' In the silence that followed they all looked upwards and heard the noise of the engine above, slow and rhythmic. It spluttered. 'What are we going to do?' whispered Doris. Beryl had already grabbed her bag. 'You all do what you like. Up to you. I'm going for the park.' She was half-way up the stairs already. The others were frozen, petrified. Seconds later the sky was quiet.

CHAPTER SIXTEEN

The war in Europe was over. It had been over for several weeks but it wasn't until June 1945 that the House of Eliott felt strong enough, or willing, to celebrate in any way.

The flying bomb had missed the House's offices and workroom by a crucial few hundred yards, thanks to the stiff winter winds. The House was undamaged this time, but Beryl had been killed. Ironically, her frenzied dash to the park across the road, unhindered now by railings to be scaled, had brought about her death.

A few days later the others sat numbly in the workroom, still stunned. 'We couldn't move, you see,' Coral explained to Anya and Ruth, who had visited to offer condolences and large Thermoses of chicken soup. 'We were saved by our fear. Funny that, isn't it?'

'No,' said Anya firmly. 'You were saved by your faith. Elsie was right. Do you remember? God does protect the just. It would have indeed been unjust if this house had been struck a second time.'

Elsie began to cry again. 'Be quiet, Elsie, and have some chicken soup.' Ruth handed her a cup.

The war was over but Evangeline felt as if her life was over, too. There was still no word of or from Hugo.

The war was over and Beatrice felt that something of her

marriage had perished with it. Jack was home, but he might as well have been a spirit. He was attentive, affectionate and gathered physical strength daily but he was distracted, almost absent. To Beatrice he no longer seemed to be the man she loved but a bloodless replica.

'We should make an effort, you know, Evie. Have a party of some kind. I mean we're still alive – most of us, anyway.' Beatrice tried to turn a sniff into a bright smile. 'We must be the only people we know who haven't had some sort of thanksgiving.'

'I know you're right, Bea, but I can only try to make myself feel grateful. I can't feel gratitude in my heart, only a void, except when I feel pain and rage. Quite apart from the main things – the most important things – I don't notice any lessening of restrictions. Rationing is even worse. Even bread is on the coupons now. But now that the war is over I don't feel so motivated to grin and bear it, do you?'

'In some ways not. But we must. We are still very privileged, you know.'

Evangeline bit back a bitter retort and she, too, approximated a brief smile. 'Then, yes, a party it is. Who shall we invite, and when? And we'd better be sure to do something for the girls downstairs. They deserve it. When you think about it, they've been amazingly patient and loyal, haven't they? What do you think they'd enjoy the most – a night out somewhere, husbands and boyfriends included?'

'I think not, Evie. That would make Coral feel awful. Doris, too.' Coral's fiancé had been killed at Arnhem, shot dead by enemy fire when his parachute had caught in a tree. Doris's husband had just been released from a POW camp, sound in body but severely damaged in mind. It would be some time before he was able to socialize much, if at all. 'Best if we give them all an afternoon off, book a table somewhere that they'd like to go and ask the restaurant to send the bill to us, don't you think?'

'And our party?'

'A small dinner at home, I think. Us, Jack – Clare and Ned can stay up for a little while – Cyril, Priscilla, Leonard and Penelope. That's enough, isn't it?'

'Not really, but it will do.'

The girls downstairs were respectful and appreciative but, collectively, they shared the mood of the sisters. Each had already participated in street parties, helped hang the bunting, cut sandwiches and made jellies but few felt much jubilation. Relief, certainly, but triumph – very little.

'I preferred it when we were at war. Does that sound awful?' asked Elsie. 'I didn't mind the bus queues and sleeping on the platform of the tube during the raids, and the ding-dongs we sometimes had when a whole crowd pooled their rations. I never expected it to get worse when we won. We don't have air-raids any more, so we don't even have that excitement. Why is peace less fun than war?'

'Why don't you get on with your work?' replied Doris.

'I heard that Mr Attlee on the wireless,' said Coral. 'He's t-t-t-talking about a programme of National Recovery. Said that there'll be free doctors and hospitals for everyone, proper schooling for all the kids. Said that if his party gets in he'll make sure that all the b-b-b-bomb sites are turned over for new houses for ordinary people like us. Houses with bathrooms and little gardens. Sounds OK to me. He said that if his party kicks Mr Churchill out there'll be no more strikes or anything because the working people will live decently, like the t-t-t-toffs, whether they are sick or well, employed or not.'

'Politicians talk a lot of rot,' said Doris, darkly, 'all of them. And how could we kick Mr Churchill out? He won the war.'

'No, he didn't, we did. People like us. The King didn't win the war either, or the Queen, for all their deigning to look at the rubble in the East End once or twice when the press boys were around. It was the ARP men, and the shopkeepers and the people like us who just kept going who won it. That's why I can't understand why it's worse now, not better.' Elsie would not be silenced. 'This party which Miss Bea and Miss Evie want to give for us. Well, it's very kind of them and I suppose I'll go. But I'd much rather be able to get home in forty minutes, like I could before the war, and buy a packet of bacon from the corner shop if I was flush on a Saturday morning. Don't expect Miss Bea and Miss Evie go without, these days.'

'I wouldn't be so sure of that. Everyone's still on the coupons, even the toffs.' Doris sighed. 'But I don't blame you for moaning, Elsie. We all feel the same, I'm sure. Thing is, we've got used to having an enemy, someone to fight against. I suppose it united us all in a way. Now we just want to fight each other instead.' She paused for a moment. 'And I suppose that's what your Mr Attlee realizes. He wants us all to be equal so that we don't fight each other.'

'You've got to admit, Bea, that it's a bit of an anticlimax.'

'Peace?'

'Yes. There used to be a point and a reason. Now all the dreariness seems like punishment, not motivation. Where are the victors' spoils? Where's our reward for gritting it through?'

'The very fact that we're speaking like this. You wouldn't want to go back to war-time, would you Evie?'

'No, of course not. But at least while we were at war one kept hope in the breast, hope that it would end. Now that it has ended we've been deprived even of hope.'

'Brace yourself, Evangeline.' Beatrice was wearied by her sister's negativity and privately hoped that she would soon return to live in the Knightsbridge mews. 'At least try to be cheerful this evening. Molly has worked wonders with her tradesmen – God knows how and I dare not ask. Just enough salmon trout to get us started, we've got the mushrooms and runners which Lady Wentworth sent up, a beautiful leg of spring lamb from Maudie Carstairs, Scottish raspberries from Pamela Inverness but Molly has found us the eggs for the mayonnaise, the new potatoes, some Stilton and, can you imagine, some cream!' Beatrice counted items on her fingers. 'And Jack informs me that tonight he will open his VC.'

'His VC? Victoria Cross?'

'No, silly. Victory case. Some 1937 claret he put down before the war.' Beatrice looked at her sister both worriedly and sharply. 'I know, Evie, that you don't feel very festive. Neither do I, as a matter of fact. I feel as if my elastic could snap at any moment, what with Jack being so distant and the children so fractious. But tonight we've got to pretend. We must do our best and try to be happy.'

'I promise you, Bea, that I'll try. But I know that I'll never be happy again. You won't mind, will you, if I start packing up over the weekend? Much better for all concerned if I take myself back to Knightsbridge.'

Beneath the hectic gaiety later there was a deep, shared sadness. Every raised glass seemed to toast an absent friend rather than to celebrate peace and survival. No one spoke of Connie, of little Tom or Hugo. Reference to the doodlebug that had claimed Beryl was avoided. Even Tilly's happiness in Kansas, as it was chinked and wished for, was under-pinned by a silent sadness that she, too, was missing. Despite the many loud exclamations about the excellence of the food and wine, and optimistic statements about the future, this was a party with a hollow heart.

Cyril Hunter was returning to Paris the following day. He was probably the only truly happy person at the table. 'I'll see you lots, darlings. Paris is only a few hours away, after all. Next time I'm in England I'll bring Jean-Luc with me. I know you'll love him as much as I do. And he's got the backing to make films, Jack, so you two will have masses to talk about.'

'Good.' It was Jack's fourth monosyllabic contribution to the evening's conversation. Beatrice looked at him again, concern darkening her eyes. He met them and took her hand beneath the table, muttering, 'Sorry, Bea. Best I can do,' as he did so. She squeezed his hand, very tightly.

'And, Priss, you mustn't be disheartened.' Cyril was, at this point, tactless and unstoppable. 'Just because those foolish Americans won't back your idea, it doesn't mean that more enlightened people won't. I think you were brave but also sensible to resign from *Mode*. That's the past. We've all got to look towards the future. It's there to be grasped.' Cyril looked round the table and seemed to register for the first time the strained faces and forced smiles. 'Well, forgive me, do. I didn't mean to offend anyone by being cheerful. There must be some mistake. It's a funny thing, but I thought this evening was supposed to be something of a celebration. Perhaps I should leave.' He sobered and silenced himself instantly, shamed by his remarks. 'Sorry,' he muttered, 'sorry, everyone. I really had better go.'

Evangeline leaned across and took his hand. 'Please don't, Cyril. Thank God that someone's happy tonight, and God bless you, too. You deserve it. It's just that the rest of us are all . . .,' she hesitated, 'adjusting, I suppose you could say. And it's hard to have a party, or to enjoy it to the full, at any rate, if the occasion reminds you of the absentees.' She forced herself to be bright. 'At least one of our absentees is happy tonight.' Molly, she reminded everyone, was with her family in County Kerry for the first time since 1938, having caught the night boat the previous evening. 'I could understand our being at war with Germany but it always seemed senseless that Ireland was out of bounds. She'll be back in two weeks and we'll have to struggle on till then. Now that the meat ration has gone down to eightpence a week we've no chance of a lamb chop or a little extra mince until she comes back and flirts with the butcher.' Evangeline had hoped her remarks would be leavening but Jack fixed her with a cold stare.

'Can't you ever think about anything serious, Evie? Does life come down to lamb chops and silk petticoats? Does it really?'

'Is there any more champagne left?' asked Beatrice nervously.

'It's late, Beatrice. I don't think Penelope or I want to

drink any more champagne, thank you.' Leonard Golder turned to his wife, who nodded. 'We'll fetch our own coats. Please don't get up. And it will be our pleasure to walk home tonight in peace.' Both Beatrice and Evangeline knew that nothing they had said in the prattling, silence-filling chatter during dinner had offended Leonard. His sadness was too deep to be tempered by even the merriest of evenings and his pain about lost family and friends was certainly not to be eased by a tense one like this. 'Forgive me, Beatrice. Forgive us. You were dear and kind to ask us to the party tonight. I fear we have not made much of a contribution. You must give me time.'

'Of course, Leonard. Safe home.' Leonard's eyes filled with tears and he cupped Beatrice's face with his palms, then Evangeline's. 'You are dear girls, both of you. You have always been brave, haven't you? You can remain so.'

Shortly afterwards, declining coffee, Cyril and Priscilla also left, and walked to the cab rank.

Jack helped clear the plates and glasses from the table, stumbling once or twice, as he no longer believed he needed his stick indoors, and then limped, wordlessly, towards his study. Beatrice and Evangeline took their coffee and the brandy into the drawing room where they both stared glassily at the walls before heavy tears began to run down their cheeks.

'Why do we feel so bereft, Bea?' Evangeline was the first to speak. 'How can we rebuild, when the foundations are all slipping? There may be a sort of peace now, but there is no peace of mind. I feel as lost and betrayed and abandoned as I did when I was a child. When you were the only person I trusted. Are we really back there again?'

Beatrice gulped. 'I don't think so, Evie. I will always be

here for you but I know you need something else now, something more. And I believe you will find it, just as I believe that I will retrieve it for myself. Leonard said, "Give me time," earlier tonight. We all need time. You, me, Jack, Leo and Pen, Priscilla, all of us. Not Cyril,' she forced a smile, 'he just needs luck. And knowing him, he'll find it.' There was silence again and the sisters sipped their brandy. The light in the room was curious – half day, half dawn and yet, still, night light, the yellow-edged night light of a city that never slumbers completely. Everyone, these days, kept their curtains pulled open at night as a celebration of the end of the blackout. 'Do you remember that time when we spoke of the nature of climaxes?' Evangeline nodded. 'All climaxes are anticlimactic. They must be, because once you have reached the peak you can only start coming down.' Beatrice sighed.

'And peace is the greatest anticlimax of them all,' said Evangeline. Her sister shrugged and nodded. 'But I'll settle for an anticlimax if Hugo comes home. However mundane peace may be, I'll embrace it with him,' continued Evangeline. 'Until then, I'm still at war.' She smiled widely and wildly for the first time in weeks.

Beatrice set the tea-tray on the floor and climbed back into bed. She stroked Jack's hair away from his brow. He looked in sleep like a little boy. It was always in the morning that he slept most peacefully these days, no longer calling, no longer twisting and shifting, no longer scratching at the sheet as if trying to get to the itch beneath the plaster that had been lifted off weeks ago. She looked at his left arm. It was withered and weak. Despite the reassuring words of the doctors Beatrice found it hard to believe that it would ever be strong again. His left hand, oddly, was as beautifully shaped and firm as ever. The stitches in his shoulder had been removed and, although a deep scar would always remain, Beatrice – and Jack, too – knew that, although heavy luggage-heaving was out of the question for ever now, there was no serious damage. He had no wish to be a coal-man, so what did it matter? She stroked his brow again. That was where the damage lay.

'Jack fell down and broke his crown and Jill came tumbling after.' She kept stroking as she whispered, 'And you did break your crown, didn't you, my darling? Something has happened to your head and your heart. When will you talk to me?'

Jack stirred. When his eyes opened a moment later Beatrice's heart leapt. It was, just for a time, the old hazel gaze she knew, not the blank stare that she had met every morning during the months since he had come home. 'Beatrice, what has been happening to me?'

'You tell me, Jack darling.'

'Not all at once. But I think that now I can start.' He reached down to the tray, lifted a cup and saucer with his good arm and passed it to Beatrice before taking the other one. 'I knew we had won, you see. It was only a matter of time. That's what made it so pointless. Last time when I saw such misery, mutilation and pain there seemed to be a purpose. We struggled to regain every inch of terrain. In Italy it was different. The real war was between Montgomery and Patten by then. It was a generals' competition. The enemy were making a magnificent final stand and it went on for a long, unnecessary time. Everyone knew what the outcome would be, both sides, I think. It was over. There should have been white flags and football matches. I became heartsick and headsick watching it, recording it. I was disgusted by what I saw. I didn't care about being injured. I was actually pleased. It made me feel justified – at least I had suffered like some of the others. At last I was a participant, not just an observer.' His eyes filled with tears and Beatrice cradled his head. 'I've been rotten to you, haven't I, Bea? So sorry, my darling.'

'No apologies. But permission to speak, sir.' Jack's eyes lightened a little and Beatrice went on. 'Do you promise me that you'll not go away again? You promised me once before but you went, didn't you?'

'Yes, I did. So, no. I cannot promise that, Bea. But I am wearied of observing war and I'll never participate in one that I believe to be pointless. These last few years I've been paid to glorify destruction and to record misery, although I've tried hard to sneak objectivity through. I've been somewhat strapped by the ropes of propaganda at the Ministry. I don't say that some of it wasn't worthwhile, but in future I'll try to make truthful films about enterprise and hope. I won't be restricted politically. God knows where I'll find the backing. Perhaps Cyril's Jean-Luc will give me a few tips.' He managed a narrow smile. 'There will be struggles, of course, and they must be recorded honestly. But after all this despair and misery, our Tom's death and all,' Jack stopped briefly, 'I want to address hope. Hope and faith.'

CHAPTER SEVENTEEN

Molly ran to answer the door when the bell rang in the kitchen. The tea was already brewing and she had saved some of the gingerbread of which the butcher's delivery boy was so fond. He was an over-familiar youth and apt to amuse himself – though not Molly – by lapsing into an Oirish accent when he spoke to her, but smiling thinly was a small enough price to pay for the kidneys, extra meatbones or string of sausages that invariably found their way into her order. Now that the children were older and the cook had been disinclined to return to her old job after the war, Molly was back in charge of the kitchen. She didn't mind in the least: it was her empire. The bell clanged again. 'Coming, coming,' she called as she scrabbled with the lock. A small, exhausted and defeated figure stood hunched outside, resting a battered case on the step.

'*Tilly!* Tilly, what are you doing here? I thought, we thought . . .' She saw Tilly's face begin to crumple and took the case. 'Now, you come right inside, my sweetheart. Tea's ready.' She took Tilly's coat from her shoulders, poured tea and sliced the gingerbread, pushing a plate towards Tilly. As Molly waited for her to speak the bell rang again and Tilly looked up. 'Am I in your way? You must be busy.'

Molly was already on her feet and rumpled Tilly's hair

as she rushed to the door. 'Don't be so silly. I'll only be a minute.' She took the butcher-boy's basket and handed him the empty one for next time. 'I'm sorry, Charlie. Can't ask you to stop for a slice of cake today but we'll make up for that next time, eh?' The boy tried to peer over Molly's shoulder but could see nothing except the usual kitchen things and a woman in a dark blue dress sitting hunched at the table. 'Tuesday, then?' Molly enquired. 'Same time?' He nodded. 'We'll be needing a boiling fowl, if you have one, a nice piece of belly pork and a couple of pounds of your best mince. That'll do us all for next week unless', she gave the lad a sly look, 'you've any more of that good Oirish bacon.' She winked at him. 'Be off with you now. I'm baking again on Tuesday morning.'

Molly returned to the table and waited for Tilly to speak. She was rolling gingerbread crumbs between shaking fingers. 'I'm sorry, Molly. I didn't know where to come. Thought about going to the House but I couldn't face Miss Bea and Miss Evie right away, not like this. I hope you don't mind me coming here.' Tilly looked up. 'I'm straight off the boat, me, and I feel so dirty and grubby.'

'We'll get you bathed and your clothes pressed. You can use the nursery bathroom like I do. But where're you going to stay, Tilly?'

'My sister's, I suppose, until I get something sorted out for myself. But I didn't want to go straight there either, without tidying myself up a bit first. She wouldn't understand. Or rather she would. She'd be pleased to see me like this. Very free she was with her remarks about me going off to America and getting grand ideas about myself. What a laugh.' Tilly gulped her tea and looked up. 'Lovely,' she said and grinned. Then she began to cry quietly.

Molly kept pouring and waited until Tilly was calmer and ready to speak.

'You see, Molly, these Americans, they all seem to have the idea that English girls are always posh, ladies. And Brad had written to his family that I was very high up in some hoity-toity fashion house, so they were expecting me to be some sort of toff. And he'd given me to understand that his folks, as he put it, were ranchers with acres and acres of farmland. He was an officer, after all, and he'd shown me pictures of the house.'

'I remember those. You showed them to me, remember? Didn't it exist?'

'It existed, all right. But it wasn't his family's place.' Tilly wiped her eyes. 'I really don't think I misled Brad, Molly. I always did try to explain that I was an ordinary working girl but he obviously didn't believe me. I think he made up things about his own background to try and impress me. It was a terrible, terrible mistake. It might have worked out, we might have been happy, if there hadn't been all the deceit and disappointment.'

'Tell me about it.'

'Well, Moll, I knew it was going to be hard as soon as I arrived in Kansas. His mother and sisters were waiting for me at the station. Excelsior, that was the name of their nearest town. I was worn out and Brad was still in hospital. I'd been expecting that we'd drive to that lovely big white house with pillars and a porch upstairs but we drove in a sort of motor wagon down these bumpy dirt roads to a little house by a creek. It was mostly made from corrugated iron. Tiny, it was, with chickens running around everywhere and no bathroom. Only a pump outside. I was that tired, I just wanted to wash and sleep. They'd made up a bed for me in the corner of the sisters' bedroom, just a curtain separating me from their bit. I wasn't allowed to sleep in Brad's Holy of Holies until he came home.

'When I woke up I peeped through the screen and saw that they'd opened my case. They were fingering all the lovely things which Miss Bea and Miss Evie had had made up for me. The elder sister, May-Beth, had put on that lovely pale yellow peignoir over her farm dress. She was twirling about in it – she'd even crammed her great plates into those dear little satin slippers that the girls collected for.' Tilly's voice rose in remembrance of this particular outrage. 'I ran out and almost tore it off her. I was angry and bewildered. "Oh, excuse me, Your Ladyship. I know this isn't what you're used to, ma'am," she said, and did a little mocking curtsy. It just went on like that, bad to worse.'

By now Molly had put some eggs on to boil and had cut slices of bread for soldiers. She decided to use the last smear of butter on them. It wouldn't be the first time that the evening meal for the family would be cooked with a dab of lard. 'What happened next, then?'

Tilly explained that by the time Brad came home from hospital some sort of understanding had been reached. She had made it clear to his mother and sisters that she was quite willing to work in the house and on the tiny smallholding from which the family scratched a living, and they seemed to have overcome their disappointment that she was not some sort of monied débutante. 'I used to talk about how things would be when Brad and I got our own place. His mother used to give me these odd looks. "Dream on," she'd say. May-Beth and Sissie left me alone, mostly. I didn't mind that except when they wore my clothes without asking.'

'What happened when Brad came home?'

'I was expecting him to be pleased to be back, of course, to be attentive to his mother and sisters and all, but I kept asking him when we were going to have our own place. We were sleeping in his old room – tiny, it was, and right next to his mother's, if you get my meaning.' Molly nodded. 'I worked in the yard, didn't mind that. I did all the sewing, even cooked sometimes. But it was always for the whole family. We never had time to ourselves. In the end I gave him an ultimatum. He had to find a separate place for us or I'd leave.'

'He just said that the farm – he called it a farm – was his, it had been his daddy's before that and that he was staying there. Got kind of nasty, as if I'd been the one who'd made things up about themselves.' Tilly finished her second egg. 'Well, Moll, I tried, I really did. But then one day Sissie went too far. She ruined my last pretty blouse on a night out with some farm boy. It came home as bruised and dirty as she was, and ripped. I asked Brad to have words with her but he wouldn't. I reminded him that I was his wife and he just said, "Wives aren't the same as family." So I decided to leave then, though I didn't tell him right away. Worked in a diner for a few weeks first, saving money for the Greyhound fare to New York.' Molly had no idea what Tilly could mean by this but let her continue. 'Then I just walked out one afternoon, caught the bus in town and worked for months in New York until I'd saved enough for my passage home.'

'Where did you stay?'

'The YWCA. Really cheap. I quite enjoyed that, actually.' Tilly smiled again, but not for long. 'Molly, do you think Miss Bea and Miss Evie would give me a job again? I don't

234

expect my old *vendeuse* position back. I don't care. I'll be happy to go back to the bee-hive. What shall I do?'

'Have a bath first. Miss Bea should be home at about five o'clock because she's been to some do at Clare's dancing school. Talk to her while I'm giving Clare and Ned their supper. He's home for half-term. You can have a lie down in my room until then. I'll see to your clothes. It'll be all right, Tilly, I know it.' Molly kissed the top of Tilly's head, thanking God as she did so that she herself had blessedly escaped marriage. 'This is my family. And it's yours too, sure.'

'Did you read about the Royal Wedding?' Evangeline closed the door behind her. Beatrice's office was close to reception where two clients were already waiting for their appointments. 'Shall we try again? What do you think?'

Beatrice looked up. 'Do you think we should bother? Aren't we blighted? We failed to get the last commission.'

'That was over ten years ago. No one will remember that. And look,' Evangeline spread out a fan of sketches that Cyril had sent from Paris, 'we're the first to see these, I think. Cyril had to photograph some early toiles of Mr Dior's new designs. The collection won't be launched for months and none of the magazines will have seen these.'

Beatrice adjusted her spectacles and looked through the pictures. The dresses were tightly waisted, their bodices with huge, flamboyant collars. The skirts – oh, the skirts! – were long and full. The models, clearly wearing glass nylons, posed with pointed toes on impossibly high and fragile heels. Hats with enormous brims threw sculptured shadows across their faces. 'These are marvellous, luxurious. But we don't want to copy, Evie. And the amount of cloth required for dresses like this — it's impossible.'

'Not now that some cloth is off the ration, surely? And not now that our suppliers can let us have quantities of the new synthetics as well as most of the traditional fabrics. Don't you read the papers?'

'As little as possible, these days, I'm afraid.' But Beatrice squinted again at the pictures, none the less. 'Lovely, isn't it, to see some swish and panache in clothes again? Tailoring is all very well but sometimes it was little more than an excuse to make the most of inferior cloth. Truthfully, Evie, I always thought our wartime designs flattered few of our clients.'

Evangeline could sense that Beatrice was weakening. 'And we wouldn't be copying. It would be madness not to make clothes that needed yards of material just because Mr Dior heard about the availability and acted upon it before us. Cyril said he's calling it the New Look — how's that for startling originality, anyway? We can steal a march here in London, thanks to Cyril. Think about it.'

'I will, Evie,' promised Beatrice as she hurried towards the door. 'And I'll think about the wedding dress, too. How long have we got?'

'To capitalize on our advantage,' said Evangeline, 'I'd say about two weeks.'

'Don't get too carried away, Evie. I'm warming to your ideas and I think we might have a stab at tendering for the Princess's wedding dress. But in a funny way I'm going to be the modern one now.' Beatrice peered over her rims. 'If we do that I think her dress should be as spare and plain as convention will allow. It can be beautiful, of course, but it can incorporate some of the new modern fabrics and techniques. And', Beatrice looked at Cyril's sketches, 'it should not be designed for a girl with an impossible, rangy mannequin's figure. The Princess is not built like that – she's bosomy and small. If we go ahead, our dress must be—'

'Fit for a Princess,' Evangeline finished.

A week later Cyril was in London with Jean-Luc. Beatrice and Evangeline had expected him to bring a beautiful, feckless boy and were surprised to meet a quiet, bespectacled Frenchman who might have looked at home in some seminar at the Sorbonne. It was Cyril who flirted and flounced, larded his conversations with *aperçus* and the latest Parisian idioms while Jean-Luc and Jack – to the gratified surprise of both men – engaged in easy yet intense conversation about cinema. 'Do you mind, Bea, if Jean-Luc and I retire? There are things that I need to show him in the study.' Beatrice smiled warmly at Cyril as Jack led their visitor out of the room, needing still to steady himself briefly against a bureau as he reached the door. Jean-Luc also turned towards Cyril.

'And there are writers in Paris at the moment whom I admire greatly. Jack and I may be able to find a way of approaching one or two of them and suggesting how their work can be adapted to cinema.' Jean-Luc smiled at Cyril. 'You will remember some of those whom we spoke to at that café near the cinema in the Seventh?'

'Of course. Heavenly in black, all of them.' Cyril raised his glass. 'Don't mind me. I'm just one of the girls today.' Jack and Jean-Luc took the Armagnac and a couple of balloon glasses. 'Do come back at tea-time,' implored Cyril as they left the room. He turned to Beatrice, completely serious now. 'Jack does seem much better, Bea. Or is it my imagination?'

'No, Cyril. Or I hope not. He is, little by little, recovering. This meeting with Jean-Luc is marvellously fortuitous. It's ages since I've seen him engaged like this. I'll bless you for ever if it means they really get on, work together. Jack's been floundering a bit recently, longing to get stuck into something but not quite knowing what or how. Perhaps that will change now.' She smiled. 'Have you seen Priscilla? I was hoping she'd be able to lunch with us today but she was, as she said, TTB. What does that one mean?'

'TTB? That's my Priss. Speaks like that all the time now – got it off you, Evie. Means Terribly Terribly Busy. Don't hold your breath, but I think she's lunching today with some American competitor of her old *Mode* people. She was pretty bullish about the possibility that they'd back her magazine project.' Cyril lit a cigarette. 'Even if they don't, Beatrice, you know as well as I do that Priscilla will not take no for an answer. Or rather, it won't matter how many times people say no, she'll get her way in the end. She'll blunder by and bluster past. She'll flatter her bank manager and terrify her creditors until she gets what she wants.'

He looked across the table at Evangeline. 'You've been very quiet, Evie. Are you all right?' She picked at her cheese. 'Not too terrible, Cyril. Awfully good of you to send those pictures over, some of them were quite inspiring. We're hoping to get the commission for the Princess's wedding dress, aren't we, Bea? Waiting to hear. It would be just the fillip the House needs. We certainly stole a bit of a march, anyway, thanks to little details of inspiration from Mr Dior.'

'No, Evie, that's not quite what I meant, although I'm

delighted if I was able to be helpful. I meant, how are you in yourself? You look wonderful as always, but you've been rather pensive, my dear, today.'

'I'm usually quiet these days, aren't I, Bea?' Evangeline looked at her sister for support. 'But nothing to complain about, really. Things have improved noticeably in the last year or so. People took ages to adjust to peace but it's happening, little by little. Order books are full as can be, especially since you helped us to open our eyes. Seems everyone wants a full skirt and stiff petticoats, they just didn't realize it. And some of our suppliers have been more than helpful about letting us have the pick of the better synthetics. We'll have to use those judiciously, of course.' She looked up and smiled. 'And Tilly's back with us. Almost like old times.'

Beatrice interjected, 'It's altogether quite a happy place, the workroom, Cyril. All those Beveridge report plans – you know, for better health, housing, education, welfare and so forth for everyone – have suddenly made people in London quite a bit more optimistic. We still have the shortages, but with this new government there's a feeling that, after all, the war might have been worth it. Jack's even been asked to make another film by the Ministry. He's dickering but I think he should do it. It's a new ministry, after all, not the old warmongers.' Cyril expressed intrigue.

'What is it? It's not really a secret but everything's still rather vague. Some festival or other. Something to celebrate peace and survival and renewal. It'll be based by the river and it'll be a sort of public park – a forum for industry and what people call "culture" and a place for ordinary people to have a pleasant day out. That's about all I know. It'll be in a few years yet, timed to commemorate the centenary of the Great Exhibition. Anyway, they want someone to film work in progress. I think Jack should do it, don't you? Leonard agrees with me. He's likely to be asked to become involved in the design of a whole series of permanent riverside buildings, you know, theatres, galleries, that sort of thing, on the South Bank.' Beatrice stopped, hearing herself gush. 'You agree with me, don't you, Cyril? Jack shouldn't pass up the opportunity?'

'I do indeed,' answered Cyril. 'But Evie still hasn't really answered my question.' He turned to her. 'I still want to know, Evie, how you are. You, not the business, not wedding dresses, or clients. Or how nice it is to be back in the mews again and be driving the Alvis. You. I want to know about you.'

'Oh, I get by,' answered Evangeline.

She looked outside. 'It's a lovely afternoon. I think I'll take the children to the park before tea. I wonder if Molly has any old bread for the ducks.'

CHAPTER EIGHTEEN

'Calm down, Elsie! Whatever is the matter? Do you want a glass of water? For God's sake, girl, control yourself.' Doris took Elsie's shoulders and was tempted to give her a sharp slap. 'For heaven's sake, what is it?'

Elsie breathed deeply. 'I had to take those trimmings upstairs, remember? And I heard Miss Evangeline talking to Mrs Palmer. I heard, I heard, I tell you! Tilly was there, she'll back me up.' She gulped. 'We're going to be making the Princess's wedding dress.' She clasped her hands. 'Imagine! She'll have to come here for fittings. We'll all get to meet her.'

Tilly stepped downstairs. 'Sorry, Elsie, but you won't. Miss Beatrice and Miss Evangeline will go to the Palace for that. The Princess won't be coming here, so you can forget all about meeting her.' Her face and voice softened. 'But it's us who'll make it, all right. It's a great honour and we should all be very proud. Miss Bea and Miss Evie will be down shortly to break the news official, like, and let me tell you that it's got to be a secret. You're none of you to breathe a word to anyone about the dress. No one. Miss Evie will show you the sketches so you'll all know you're part of it, even if some of you only have to do some stitching on a cuff or a trimming and she'll tell you what you have to do.' Tilly tried to keep her voice even but was unable to resist a great cry of joy. 'This is only the beginning, you know, everything's going to get better now.'

'Quite sure about this, Beatrice?' Penelope had returned from the kitchen and was wiping away the rissole grease from the frying pan with a scrunch of newspaper. 'Don't you both see it as a step back? A bit sentimental. Don't want to seem rude, Bea, dear, but the Royal Family is all about the past, isn't it? Thought you and Jack were more interested in the future.'

Beatrice smiled with ease and confidence. 'Of course, Pen. But I don't see any conflict here. The family is what we all fought and suffered for, the family is emblematic of regeneration. I don't think Jack disagrees, do you, darling?' He shook his head and smiled up at Beatrice. 'The Princess and her marriage embody the new order. New hope, new beauty, a new start. I'm not troubled by the commission. *Au contraire*, Evie and I, rather, are proud. We'll be contributing a little to the launch of a new age, and the dress will reflect that. It'll be as modern as can be while nodding towards the best traditions – those that we all wanted to save and preserve.'

Penelope forbore to argue. 'Lovely to see you sparkle again, Bea. Best of luck.' She remembered a package in the Gower Street kitchen. 'Be an angel, Leo. Can you fetch the fudge from the window-sill?' Anya and Ruth had brought it round earlier that day, she explained. 'And don't forget the Tokay and the little glasses.'

*

Evangeline slept. There was a scratching noise, and then a knocking. The postman was seldom so persistent but she could always call in at the post office later to see if there was a parcel for her. She turned over and slipped back into her warm doze. A shower of pellets hit her bedroom window. She woke fully, startled, but turned over again, still seeking sleep. There was another scatter of small stones and this time she looked down. Then the knocking began again, insistently. She put on a dressing gown and knotted it tightly, carefully stepping down the staircase. Evangeline felt irritated and sleepy still, was tousled and knew that last night's mascara must have smudged her cheeks. She opened the door by an inch. A figure leaned against it outside, the damp serge of the cloth of his coat steaming slightly in the low warmth of the early September sunlight. He almost fell into the room and into Evangeline's arms.

'Hugo.'

She did not know what to do first – to peel off his coat, to lead him to lie on the sofa, to find the last of her coffee, to hold him, kiss him, smell him. She guided him into the room and held him before she set him down. He was so thin, wrists fragile as a bird's and kneebones pressing hard as knuckles against her thigh as she led him in. His face was white and gaunt but his eyes huge and bright. His fingers were criss-crossing her face, long, pale and gnarled. She tore off his coat and flung it on the floor. The remains of scabs and scratches marked his face. Hugo's cheekbones, as they knocked into the softness of her own face, were sharp, his hands pushed through her hair. He sat down. The door was still open and she collected a small worn case from the step. Hugo took her face in his hands again and they both began to weep.

No words were spoken. After a little while Evangeline, reluctant though she was to leave him for even a minute, hating to take her hands and arms from him, ran upstairs and collected sheets and blankets. She did not think he was strong enough to negotiate the stairs. She made a makeshift bed for them on the floor downstairs, with plenty of pillows for Hugo. She undressed him and they lay down together. His bones cut into all her softest parts but she did not mind. She held him as tightly as any woman could.

Later, when Hugo had slipped into a brief, deep sleep she rested herself on an elbow and looked at his face, gently tracing her fingers along the lines which ran from his lower lids and met deeper ones around his mouth and jaw. The muscles in his neck were as well defined as ropes. She touched his chest and his shockingly emaciated limbs. There were sores on his back. She tipped her head across his shoulder and kissed the ones her lips could reach. Hugo stirred. With dry lips he began to kiss her. Evangeline was surprised by the strength in his arms as he held her. There, on the floor of her little Knightsbridge house, their life together began again.

Afterwards she helped him upstairs and brought him soup, bread and butter, a boiled egg, an orange and a piece of cheese. 'Not too much, Evie, darling. Stomach's still very shrunken. I'll have the cheese later, and some chocolate if you have any.' Evangeline crawled back into bed with him, smelling him. 'Do you mind if I sleep a bit more?' Hugo asked.

'You can sleep for ever. As long as I'm with you.'

'You always were,' he said as his eyelids flickered and then closed.

Over the next few days Evangeline dedicated all her time to Hugo. She explained to her sister that Hugo was back and

Beatrice did not demur when Evie said that she would stay at home. She coaxed him into eating properly and finally into talking. It would be years before he was able to give her the full picture, supply the worst details of life in the internment camp at Changi, but over the week or so after his return Evangeline learned enough.

Even his account of his journey back to England sickened her. Hugo was wise to spare Evangeline, for the time being, too many details of life in the camp.

'I was captured in 1941. They thought I was an engineer, knew from my papers that I was supposed to be helping with the railway. I refused to help build the railway for them: they wanted me to order teams of the other prisoners about, supposed to be some sort of foreman because I had skills and could have directed them in English. I was punished, of course. But no more so than other dissenters. They kept me alive because they needed my skills, I guess, and thought that I'd come round to their point of view, I spoke to you in my sleep. I know this because when I was in the cooler – that was a particularly nasty kind of solitary confinement, a stifling, airless cell without water – one of the guards kept asking me why I always called for Evie. "Do you want the night?" he'd say, as I stumbled to my feet at the point of his bayonet. They knew all about the torture of sleep deprivation. "You can have the night but you must wait." There was a horrible gleam in his eye. I wasn't treated any worse than the others. We were all starved and beaten and allowed to become so weak that we could barely work. The weakest died. Others were shot for the slightest perceived disobedience. Or for sport.'

'What saved you?' Evangeline pushed a square of chocolate between his lips.

'Don't really know. I had a terrible bout of malaria one time. That Crawley fellow was working as a medical orderly. That's a joke, for a start. Rather suggests that the camp was run under rules ordained by the Geneva Convention, doesn't it? No, I think he mainly administered shots to camp guards who had the clap. There are always people who pick up the cushy jobs. One day you'll know the whole story, Evie. All I can say now is that he'd got hold of some quinine and I pulled round. Maybe I'd been calling your name again while I was delirious and he remembered you. He always did have a soft spot, didn't he? I think he knew I knew you. How am I to know? Perhaps they still thought I might have second thoughts and help with the railway so it was worthwhile keeping me alive. But for them things were beyond saving by then. Suddenly it became chaotic. Next thing I knew was that the guards had gone and it was every man for themselves. Basically I walked across Burma and finally got a transport home. There are weeks, months, I don't remember yet. I suppose people must have looked after me, given me clothes, food, bandages for my feet.'

'God bless them,' whispered Evangeline.

Hugo lifted an arm and hugged Evangeline to him. 'Tell me again, my concentration is still so patchy. Tell me how you've been, Evie darling. I'm like a child who wants to hear the same bedtime story over and over. Tell me again and again and again why you didn't meet anyone else. I had your face in my head all this time, but I couldn't expect you to wait for me. I can hardly believe that it's true.'

'Believe it. It is true and there was no heroic self-denial about it. It was easy, there was nobody to want when I wanted so much to see you again. I'd have settled for that, only that, just the sight of you. Nothing else mattered. I'll

tell you everything eventually. We have lots of time now.'
She kissed his brow. 'Shall we walk across the park? Do you
feel strong enough? At the moment Bea and I are working
on rather an important wedding dress. You could come with
me to the workroom. Bea and Jack want to see you and I
really ought to put in an appearance.'

'So sorry, Evie. That wedding dress, of course. I'll never
make you neglect your work again.' Hugo's arm tightened
about her and his left hand stroked Evangeline's throat then
swept down in long slow movements towards her breast.
'Do you think the girls can cope with another one? Or shall
we just go to Caxton Hall? Special licence, I think you once
mentioned. Tomorrow?'

They dressed and walked slowly across the park. Late
afternoon, late summer sunshine beamed at them, glinting
on the brass plate by the door of the House of Eliott.